Numb

Yolanda Sfetsos

This is a work of fiction. Names, characters, places, and incidents either are the product of the author's imagination or are used fictitiously. Any resemblance to actual persons, living or dead, events, or locales is entirely coincidental.

Copyright © 2024 by Yolanda Sfetsos

All rights reserved. No part of this book may be reproduced or used in any manner without written permission of the copyright owner except for the use of quotations in a book review. For more information, address:

Tanuci69@gmail.com

First paperback edition 2024

Anuci Press edition 2024

www.anuci-press.com

Cover Design by Ruth Anna Evans

ruthannaevans.com (google.com)

ISBN 979-8-9905033-5-9 (paperback)

ISBN 979-8-9905033-6-6 (eBook)

This one's for all the girls who are trying to find themselves, while actively ignoring that pesky inner voice trying to stop them.

"There is a voice that doesn't use words. Listen."
—Rumi

ONE
NOW

Saturday, 3am
May 5, 2018

"You can see me, can't you?"

I don't answer, but of course I can see my shadow stretch unnaturally along the grimy wall in front of me. Watch helplessly as what's supposed to be a reflection of myself extends much taller than it should.

My heart races as a section separates from my left shoulder and skitters into the ceiling like a startled spider. How can my shadow stretch and split away like this?

Although I can usually rely on my eyesight to reveal the truth, my brain isn't as trustworthy. My mind likes to play tricks on me. And right now, I can't tell if this is a trick, a nightmare, or if it's really happening.

It's getting harder to separate what's real from what's not.

"I've finally got you where I want you," he whispers.

I open my mouth to respond but nothing comes out.

"Checkmate."

I'm paralyzed, useless. At his mercy.

"Be a good girl, Chester. Stay very still so I can show you what I can really do."

The sharpness of the voice always makes me wince, especially when he uses my name. For as long as I can remember, I've heard voices inside my head—whispers, as my mother calls them. Mum used to tell me that whispers aren't a problem because everyone comes equipped with their own personal internal voice. The inner narrative that takes over when I read and write or work through exam questions.

This is not *that* voice. This voice is harmful and awful, tries to defeat me whenever I feel positive enough to take control of my own thoughts and feelings. He feeds me lies and tries to weaken my resolve, makes me double guess my instincts.

"Keep very still and don't take your eyes off the wall."

I try to move my arms because I refuse to listen to him, but no matter how hard I try my limbs refuse to budge. I can barely wiggle my fingers and my feet are stuck to the dirt and hay-strewn ground.

"Don't fight me. You know this is what we've always wanted."

Maybe he wanted whatever *this* is, but I don't. I just want to live a normal life. I want to actually pay attention in school, and not have constant headaches knocking me out for hours at a time. I don't want to have a creepy voice telling me what to do whenever I forget to take my medication—sometimes on purpose. And I certainly don't want to surrender to whatever the hell this thing is.

No matter how many times the voice suggests I give up, I refuse.

"Watch closely."

I don't want to but find myself focusing on my shadow. I can see my arms are pinned at my sides and no matter how hard I push them to do something—anything—I can't. But my shadow raises both of my arms over my head.

This reflection is supposed to mimic my actions, but it's not me. So, how is he doing this? And who the hell is he? I still don't even know *that*.

"No." The whisper is barely a breath between my lips.

My shadowy hands bend the wrong way, the fingers twist at odd angles. Laughter echoes around my skull. I wince. Whenever this happens, I feel like the inside of my head is a barren corridor full of closed doors on either side, and whoever is doing this is hiding behind one of those. Waiting for me to finally open their door completely so he can take over.

"I like the way your body feels," he coos.

My shadow sways from side to side, in a disturbing full-body shimmy.

"I could definitely get used to wearing you."

"No."

"Do you know how to say anything else?" The laughter is loud and bounces inside what feels like an empty, cavernous skull.

That's when I notice *my* shoulders actually shift a little.

"Don't go getting any ideas, Chesty."

I hate it when he calls me this even more than when he uses my actual name, makes me so angry I want to punch myself. Because who else can I hit if not myself? This thing is inside me, and as much as I want him out, I don't know how to get rid of this pest. Only Mum knew how to keep him dormant and she's not here. My mother is gone, so she can't help me.

One day she disappeared, vanished. And no one knows where she is.

No matter how many times I will her to return, she doesn't. Elvi is still here and tries her hardest to help keep me in check, but she's not like my mother. Mum used to watch me like a hawk and could tell when I was feeling worse just by looking at me. She recognized all my tells and knew when I was cheating the pills.

"Get out of my head," I say.

"You know I can't do that. You know I will never do that."

"Why?" I scream, and it hurts my dry throat.

"Because you were promised to me. And no matter what, I will claim you."

Who promised me to him? This isn't the first time he's mentioned that I belong to him and therefore should allow him free access to my brain and body. But I never get straight answers from this smug voice and Mum refused to answer directly. All she told me was to concentrate and fight—keep the whispers at bay.

My shadow is bouncing on the spot, and I can feel the floor vibrate beneath me, stirring up enough dirt that it coats my tongue and fills my nasal passage.

Where am I?

I don't recognize this wooden wall, so I can't be at home. It's dark and shabby, the wood is rotten and splintered. It reminds me of those abandoned and supposedly haunted houses Darwin is always making me watch on YouTube.

"Jesus!" someone yells behind me. "What the fuck?"

I try to turn my head but can't because my neck is fixed in one position—forward.

"He's going to ruin everything. We'll have to take care of him—"

The awful voice is drowned out by a much louder one. "Seriously, Chess, you've got to stop doing this creepy shit."

I recognize this guy who calls me Chess with such familiarity, I feel like we know each other well. So, I zero in on *his* voice and suddenly remembered we were kids when he gave me the nickname. But I can't remember his name, and he sounds like he's talking through a crackly phone line.

"Block him out."

No! This guy, who calls me Chess, makes me feel safe. I can't remember his name yet, but I know he's... family. Someone I trust.

"Hey, can you hear me?"

I try to nod but my neck is still stuck.

Don't panic.

I focus on what my mum taught me about psychic attacks. *"The best way to fight them is by staying calm and focused,"* she always said, *"Visualization is one of the best weapons the human mind has at its disposal, so don't be afraid to use it."*

My fingers are tingling and I'm starting to get enough feeling back in my hands to open and close them. I imagine raising my fists and smashing the wall, to beat this impostor out of me.

"Leave me alone," I say and smack my right fist into the wood.

"Please, don't do that! You're going to hurt yourself." The other guy sounds like he's getting closer, and his concern makes a shiver race down my spine.

A hand presses down on my shoulder and I startle, jump.

My shadow remains stationary, both arms in the air.

"Don't slip away, we're so close."

Hitting the wall didn't work, but I know what will.

I struggle to take a breath and manage to lift my left hand to the side of my head. I see the punch reflected in front of me a second before my fist smacks into my temple. There's no pain but the shadow wavers and the other set of arms drops to my sides.

"Chess, don't do that."

I hit myself a second time.

The shadow deflates.

"Please!" The agony in whoever is trying to stop me tears at my heart and I'm not sure why.

I punch myself a third and fourth time but lose count when I keep slamming my fist into the side of my head. I don't stop until someone forcibly grabs me.

"Calm down, Chess," he says near my ear. "It's okay. You're sleep-walking."

I blink and calm my breathing long enough to spot a dormant shadow now standing in front of me, but it's blended with that of a taller person. We're standing in front of a familiar wooden wall. The panels run all the way across the room, and I know they hide a large wardrobe. Next to this is the yellow bookshelf he's packed with so many hardback books the shelves are buckling under the pressure.

"That's it, breathe."

I finally know where I am, remember who this is.

Darwin. His name is familiar and comfortable. He makes me feel safe.

"Are you back?" He's got one arm wrapped around the front of my midsection and the other is holding my fist. Our shadows blend and appear normal.

I managed a quick nod, but my neck still feels stiff. How long have I been standing in this rigid position? Was I in his room all along? So, why didn't the wall look or feel familiar before? I was definitely somewhere else. I was probably having a nightmare.

"I'm going to let you go now." Darwin slowly unwinds his arms and takes a step back before he spins me around until I'm facing him. He cups my face in his warm hands, forcing me to tilt my head back because he's taller. "Are you okay?" His gentle touch helps to keep me anchored. His brown eyes are wide and examining me too closely. "Do you know who I am?"

"Of course, I do," I whisper.

He doesn't say a word.

"Darwin."

"You remember me, that's a good sign." He's still staring into my eyes too intently and I feel like the bugs he used to catch outside when he would come home for the summer. "You need to focus on me. Come on. Chess?"

I try to push him away but I'm weak and pathetic, so the jolt makes no impact, and he leans closer. "I'm fine." The lie comes easily because his fingers feel good on my face, and I wish we could stand like this forever. In a cocoon of comfort and safety. For the first time since awakening from my latest disorienting nightmare, I feel self-conscious and inappropriate. Why did I come to his bedroom in the middle of the night? I see the light filtering through the outline of the blinds. It's daytime.

How long was I taken over this time?

I shrug him off as gently as I can, and he takes an awkward step back. I can't focus on anything for too long because I want to gobble up every familiar facet of his room. Wrap the details around myself like a blanket and forget about everything that came before he woke up and found me—an intruder.

My weird display has obviously disturbed him, it's written all over his face.

"Are you sure you're okay?"

I shrug. I feel so far removed from *okay.*

My heart sinks at the thought.

Why did my shadow stretch in front of me while I was stuck? How did a piece slip away? When did my shady reflection develop a mind of its own?

I peek over my shoulder and our shadows are completely gone because the sun is rising and streaming in through the twin windows above Darwin's bed.

Mum designed his room and Elvi built the series of levels. Mum was... *is* an interior decorator and furniture designer, while Elvi is a carpenter and artist, so she creates the pieces. Neither batted an eyelid when Darwin returned from boarding school when he was thirteen and announced he wanted a bed with steps and drawers underneath. Wardrobes masquerading as walls so he could avoid what he calls *distracting clutter* and keep all his belongings hidden. Even his desk is behind closed doors along the adjacent wall.

The boy doesn't like clutter, which is the complete opposite of me.

"What happened this time?"

His question rouses me from my musings. I've been spending way too much time inside my head lately and it's disturbing. *Maybe that's why the voice is inching its way inside.*

"Well?" He scratches the back of his neck and yawns, the action raises the hem of his *Looney Tunes* tee and reveals the tight line of his abdomen above the elastic of his pajama pants.

"Do you like what you see?"

What? The shock of hearing the voice asking such a question shocks me.

"If you like what you see, take it."

There's no way I'm ever going to do such a thing. It's not like that. Besides, he's my brother.

"Not really. Not by blood."

No matter what this horrid tormentor claims, Darwin *is* family.

"You're no fun. I can't wait to break you, Chess," the voice hissed.

I'll never let that happen. And why am I even responding?

A chuckle fills my mind and fades away.

"Chess, hello, I asked you what happened." Darwin says.

I look away, hoping he didn't notice me staring. "I don't know." And I really don't. The last thing I remember before finding myself facing the wall was going to the kitchen to get a glass of juice. "Oh, shit!"

"What? What's wrong?"

I race out of his bedroom and my bones creak with the effort, another reminder that I've been standing as stiff as a plank of wood for too long. At least I didn't give Darwin a heart attack when he found me acting like a possessed creep.

As I rush into the kitchen on socked feet, a groan escapes me.

The puddle of juice on the tiled floor is almost dry but glistens where the sun catches the spill. At least the cup is plastic and didn't shatter. Since I started randomly passing out all over the house and broke two glasses in the process—one which resulted in the scar on my jaw—we only keep plastic cups in the house. Mum and Elvi hid the glass.

Darwin charges in behind me but stops short. "Did you pass out in here?" He glances at me, and even though he tries to hide it, I spot the concern on his face.

"Maybe... I'm not sure." I can't see any sticky parts on my PJs or hands.

"Think, try and remember," he snaps.

The remark reminds me of the voice and I instinctively wince.

He notices. "I'm sorry. I didn't mean to sound so—"

"It's okay."

"No, it's never okay to sound like an asshole."

"You're not an asshole." How can he consider himself an asshole when he's saved me from myself so many times? He's my best friend, even closer than that because our mothers are married, and we've been in each other's lives forever. He puts up with my strange and odd behavior without hesitation. He knows whatever's happening to me isn't normal, but he's still always there. I depend on him way too much.

Yet, he never complains or hesitates to lend a helping or comforting hand.

"Sometimes I feel like one," he says. "I should stop asking questions."

"No, don't. You should ask more, so many more." I look at him and feel so much gratitude, I can't even begin to describe how lucky I am to have him in my life. If it wasn't for Darwin helping me find my way back from these delusional episodes, or him being my accomplice in hiding my latest accident, I might have given into that eerie voice years ago.

Where Mum tries to drum rules into me and pushes until all I want to do is ignore her, Darwin handles every situation with care and concern. My mother makes me feel like I need to be fixed, but he insists there's nothing wrong with me.

"Yeah, well, I think my timing's off," he says with a shrug. "Now's not the time for a hundred questions."

"It's okay." I offer him a weak smile and check the digital clock on the stove. "I have to clean this up before Elvi wakes up. I don't want to upset her."

He nods and doesn't contradict me because we both know how much my illness reminds her that Mum is still missing. That the cops haven't found a single trace of her, and that no matter how many times we drive around the suburb or ask around, she's nowhere.

I skirt around the sticky puddle and pick up the cup, which makes a slurping sound because it's stuck. I dump it in the sink and switch the hot water tap on. By the time I'm done wiping away the congealed juice, Darwin is already waiting with a mop and bucket full of foamy water.

"I'll take over before you ruin another pair of socks." He grins and grips the mop handle tightly. "I'm running out of socks."

"Oops." I self-consciously consider the blue and red lined pair I stole from him because they're so comfy and keep my feet warm when the weather changes. It's almost winter and my feet are always so cold.

"It's okay, just teasing," he says. "I know I've got great taste in clothes."

"Thanks." I can't help but grin because his eclectic outfits are often questionable.

"I've got this." He returns the smile. "You can get rid of that disgusting rag and I'll take care of this."

"You don't have to," I say. "It's my mess."

"I don't have to, but I'm still gonna."

I flashed him a thankful nod and head into the adjoining laundry room. When I dump the filthy rag in the garbage and notice it's almost filled to the top, I decide to take the bag to the wheelie bin in our backyard.

As soon as I've pushed my feet into a pair of shaggy boots Mum keeps by the door, I step outside. The cool morning air sweeps over me and I welcome the sensation. For most of my life I've been a little too warm, experienced too many fevers and hot flashes to actually enjoy summer, which kinda sucks when you live in Sydney. But lately, all the heat has been replaced with cold, so much cold.

And I don't think it's because of the seasonal change.

I make my way to the side of the house and feel a prickle along the back of my neck, but I ignore it. Instead, I lift the wheelie bin lid and am about to dump the knotted bag when I stop in mid-swing. A multitude of flies are buzzing inside and several take flight to separate themselves from the slithering maggots lying on the contents spilling out from a red garbage bag I don't recognize. I lean closer and swat at the flies trying to get into my eyes and nose.

We use biodegradable bags because, even though they make furniture out of so much wood, Mum and Elvi are all about our carbon footprint. We recycle, repurpose, and donate as much as we can. But now isn't the time to think about how we sort our rubbish.

The stench emerging from the bin is horrid, so I cover my nose with my other hand.

A soft moan makes my heart speed up.

Is there an animal trapped beneath all those disgusting maggots? Or are the maggots there *because* of a decomposing carcass? Oh god. Sometimes possums go through our rubbish, even ibises, and tear into the contents. Did one of them get stuck and die?

I gag and my fingers twitch. I should throw the bag in the bin, leave, and not look back. But the moan comes again and when the red bag squirms, I know I can't walk away from an injured animal.

So, I place the rubbish bag near my feet and dare to peek over the side of the green wheelie bin. The disgusting maggots are still writhing over each other as I swat the flies away from my face. The moaning sounds like a dog, not a possum or a bird. It's the sad whining my friend Su's terrier makes when he wants attention.

I hate that sound because it breaks my heart.

"Are you okay, doggie?" As soon as I say the words, I feel ridiculous. A dog isn't going to respond to my question. I'm not even sure this *is* a dog.

The moaning increases in pitch until it matches the drumming of my pulse.

"Shit." The daunting task makes my stomach lurch, but there's no other way to handle this. I take a quick breath through my clenched teeth. "Okay, you can do it. *I* can do this."

I lean into the wheelie bin and luckily, it's full enough that I don't need to reach in too far. As my fingertips push past the slithering maggots, they tickle my skin and I gag. I think of them as worms because worms help nurture gardens, right? But that doesn't help for long, so I dig my hand in deeper while ignoring the flies now buzzing in my ears, as well as the ticklish maggots, and think only about saving the poor trapped creature.

It takes a few tries, because this slippery bag feels more like some sort of gross membrane. I stretch a hole wide enough to dig my hands in and wrap my fingers around the furry scruff. A whimper reverberates against my skin, and I yank the animal up and out, trying not to gag when the half-eaten black puppy separates from the gunk inside the bag.

I'm so shocked, I nearly dropped it. But the one bright, amber-colored eye is open and staring. I can feel a heartbeat, and the tiny thumps echo my own. For several seconds, our pulses reach the same rhythm, and I feel a burst of strong emotion spread inside my chest.

"What's taking you so long?"

I jump, but somehow manage to hold onto the dog.

"You have to stop sneaking up on me like that," I say, though I certainly don't mean it. If Darwin didn't make a habit of being what others might consider a pest, I might never make it out of my head when the voice is at its strongest.

"Hey!" He peeks around me and his eyes widen. "What have you got there?"

"It's a puppy," I say. Now that I've found and rescued this little guy, I don't want to let go. "It's in pretty bad shape."

"He looks fine to me." Darwin reaches out and takes the dog from my grip, presses the bundle against his chest and starts making soothing noises. He's too relaxed around a half-eaten puppy.

I blink a few times, and that's when I realize the dog's face is now normal. I turn back to the bin and although there are several flies still hovering around, the maggots are gone. In fact, on closer inspection I notice they're actually noodles. Probably leftovers from the meal Elvi made and we hardly ate last night.

Having a missing person in the family plays havoc on appetites, as well as everything else. Where could my mum be? She didn't even leave a letter.

"I could've sworn there were maggots in the bin," I whisper.

"Maggots, really?" When Darwin spots the noodles, he raises a dark brow. "You've got to stop letting your imagination run wild."

That's the thing about Darwin. No matter what I tell him, he always makes it sound as if all my problems stem from an overactive imagination. My therapist agrees, and definitely thinks I focus too much on the worst-case scenario of every situation, which is why I imagine bad stuff. But Dr. Larunda still manages to make me sound like a neurotic, anxious mess. Whereas Darwin makes me feel like a kid with too much on her mind.

I prefer his diagnosis.

"Now, what are we going to do with this little guy?" The puppy in his arms is so black the fur shines in the same glossy way crow feathers do. And those pretty eyes—there are definitely two now—remind me of honey.

"Is it... okay?"

"Looks fine to me."

I glance in the bin again. "What do you think it was doing there?"

"I have no idea, but whoever dumped this precious bundle in our bin has secured themselves a special place in hell," he says, with a shake of his head. "How could anyone do something so callous?"

"I don't know, but it's disgusting." I sigh. "Do you think Elvi will let us keep it?"

"She'll probably make us take him to the vet and will give us a whole spool about this being our responsibility." He shrugs then starts scratching under the puppy's bristly chin. "Which is fine with me. What do you think?"

I pet the silky head and nod. Still can't believe my mind lied to me about how this pup really looked. "I'm willing if you are."

"Cool, let's give him a bath, then."

Darwin heads for the sliding door and I start to follow before I realize I still haven't dumped the rubbish bag in the bin. I throw the bag over the side and hear the squishy sound of maggots bearing the weight. *No, noodles.*

I start to follow but pause when my shadow catches my eye on the weatherboard siding. A section splits to the side before gliding back into place. After seeing a half-eaten pup when it was completely whole, I don't want to concentrate on anything else.

I'm about to step away when the shadowy shape leans forward even though I'm standing straight.

"This isn't over," the voice whispers in my head. *"Not by a longshot."*

Two
NOW

Saturday, 1pm
May 5, 2018

"And he's got all his shots now?" Elvi tucks a stray strand of auburn hair behind her ear as she watches the tiny bundle of fur with suspicion. I can't help but wonder if she thinks the puppy's going to attack her.

Unlike my mother, Elvi's always suspicious before trusting anything or anyone.

"*She* does now," Darwin says with a roll of his eyes. "Can you stop looking at her like she's going to kill you? Look how small she is."

It's true, Elvi looks petrified.

Nobody—a temporary name holder until we come up with something brilliant—is curled up on the dog bed Darwin insisted we buy at the pet store on the way home from the vet. The *bed* looks more like a cushion to me, but Nobody seems comfortable. And I don't know if it's my imagination or not, but she definitely looks bigger than she did this morning.

"Is she registered?"

"Not yet. Someone over eighteen has to do that," he replies.

"But our birthdays are next month, so we can get her microchipped and registered then," I add.

Elvi keeps staring and the pup yawns before rolling onto her back and exposing her adorable round belly. She's beautiful, nothing like the half-eaten mutt my brain tried to show me.

"So, we can keep her, right?" The smile on Darwin's face is the one he uses whenever he's trying to get his way.

She sighs. "I don't know... Has she got fleas or worms?"

"No," he says.

"Su's mum checked her for everything. She weighed her too," I say. "She told us Nobody is very healthy for someone who was dumped in the garbage."

"I don't like you calling her that." Elvi makes a pained face. "It's not a real name."

"Come on, Ma. We'll take good care of her." Darwin polishes off his mug of hot chocolate and eyes mine. He casually flings an arm over my shoulder. "Chess and I have opted for shared custody, and we'll come up with a proper name in no time. Right?" He waits for my support.

I nodded, trying to shake his arm off. He might not know, but he's getting stronger every day and his arm weighs a ton. I see the way girls check him out at school, and how Su holds his hand a little tighter when she spots their keen stares. Our Darwin is growing up into the kind of guy other girls check out constantly, and he doesn't even notice.

"I don't like the idea of a dog you found in the garbage living inside our house." She shakes her head. "What will Mena say when she comes back?"

My stomach somersaults. Elvi always speaks about Mum as if she's popped out for a walk to the corner shop to buy some milk. Even when she called the police or we routinely drive around the neighborhood, she makes it sound as if Mum's on a holiday she forgot to tell us about.

Darwin must feel my shoulders tense because he steps away and sits down. "Ma, when Mum comes back, she'll love Nobody. We all know how much she loves animals. She would totally want us to keep this pup."

"She *is* a bleeding heart," Elvi says with a rueful smile. "Remember the time we walked past that pet store downtown and she wanted to adopt the whole litter of kittens?"

"Yeah, she even assigned names based on the seven dwarves," he says.

I can't help but smile at the memory. The thought of having all those kitties excited me, but Elvi was quick to stop Mum from over-committing. Darwin is right about one thing, if my mother had trouble turning her back on animals behind glass, she would never refuse one dumped in our backyard.

Darwin laughs. "I was so upset when you told her we couldn't bring them home." He shakes his head. "Your fear of animals broke my five-year-old heart."

"Oh, stop it, you forgot about them as soon as Mena bought you a new Lego set."

"I still have that haunted house." It's clear to see how much Darwin loves my mother and has accepted her as his own. He's always called her Mum, while I can't bring myself to call Elvi, Ma, like he does. I've often been jealous because he finds it so easy to talk to my mother, while I mostly struggle to get along with her. Even though he spent a chunk of time away at boarding school, he still gets along better with her than I do. Or did.

All those years ago, when Mum helped Darwin build the haunted house, I focused on my invisible friend. I called her Shiny Pictures because she was covered in tattoos.

A shiver slides down my spine. I haven't thought about *her* for years, what made the memory resurface? The Lego haunted house, that's what!

Elvi stops laughing and stares at the sleeping puppy. "Okay, okay, you kids can keep the dog."

"Yes!" Darwin cheers. "We finally have a pet."

I almost tell him that he's had me all these years but bite my tongue because such a response is degrading and not really funny.

"It's the truth, though. You are his pet," the voice whispers. *"Or is he yours? It's hard to tell sometimes."*

I push the disturbing thought away and focus on Elvi.

"But I'm serious. You two are responsible for everything, including the small things." She glares at her son. "You'll make sure all her shots are up to date, that she's always clean." She starts counting things off on her slim fingers. "Plus, you'll have to take her for walks every day and I don't want to find a single turd in our backyard. And don't forget she still needs to be registered. Also, you must keep her clean. At all times."

"You said clean twice," Darwin points out with a big grin.

"How big does she get, anyway?"

"Not too big. Right Chess?"

I'd done some research but couldn't figure out her exact breed. The closest I found was the Staffordshire Bull Terrier, which aren't considered small dogs. "Um, yeah. She won't get too big."

"Good." Elvi stands and rinses her cup in the sink.

"Are you going to drink the rest of that?" Darwin whispers in my ear.

"No, you have it."

He drains the hot chocolate in seconds and dumps both mugs next to his mother's. She's still standing in front of the sink staring out at the backyard through the window, probably watching Mum's favorite chair. Elvi does that a lot, but it never makes my mother magically reappear.

That was the last place I saw her. I left her sitting on her chair in the backyard and by the time I'd reached the house, she was gone.

Darwin winds an arm around Elvi's waist and she rests her head on his shoulder.

"I miss her so much." She chokes with a sob. "I wish she would call or text—anything, to let me know she's okay."

He tightens his grip on her. "I miss her too."

I want to add my name because I miss her more than I ever thought I would, but whenever they share a mother and son moment like this, I observe from a distance. For as long as I can remember, Darwin and his mother have lived with us. Well, he was gone between the ages of six and thirteen, but he still popped back in during school holidays.

We've been a happy family for years, and although my closeness levels with Mum never measured up to theirs, we're still a tight unit.

Mum didn't talk much about her past, but Elvi likes to tell the tale of the two girls who fell in love and ran away with babies in their bellies.

Darwin and I are the same age, our birthdays are a day apart. A detail I used to obsess over and wanted to understand. As far as he's concerned, we're family because our mothers are legally married. I do wonder about our fathers, though. Why we never met them, and why they never bothered to look for us.

"I'm sorry." Elvi sniffs and wipes at her eyes. She untangles herself from Darwin and makes her way over to me. "I'm sorry for losing it, Chess."

"You don't need to be," I say, because I lose it all the time.

She leans over and gives me a quick hug. "I don't want to upset you."

"Ma," Darwin calls. "We need to speak to you about something else."

I want to shake my head, but with her still hugging me it would be awkward. Besides, I already told him I didn't want to talk to anyone about what happened earlier. I know him well enough to realize that's what he wants to talk to her about. He mentioned it enough times after the vet.

She squeezes me one last time and straightens. "What is it?"

He meets my gaze.

I shake my head, but he looks away.

"Well, what do you want to speak to me about?" She folds her arms and now looks suspicious. "Are you going to bombard me with more than a random puppy?"

"I don't think Chess is taking her medication," he says in a rush.

The traitor! He knows what it means when I pass out or sleepwalk more than usual, but he didn't bring it up earlier. And doesn't make a habit of telling me, so he must be really worried. Knowing he cares this much should make me happy about his concern, but it's hard to feel any gratitude with his mother glaring at me.

Elvi goes straight to the bottle of pills sitting near the sink. "Is that true?"

I shrug. "I might have forgotten a few times."

"Oh, honey, you can't do that." She uncaps the lid and pours two into her palm. "Dar, get Chess a glass of water."

He doesn't hesitate and in seconds I'm being force-fed and have two sets of matching eyes homed in on me. So, I swallowed the bitter pills and open my mouth to prove I swallowed them. Will I always have keepers?

"Not if you let me take over." The whisper sounds farther away than before.

"Happy now?"

Elvi places a hand on my shoulder. "Please, don't forget to take your medicine. It's important that you do."

"So, I can stay myself, right?" I cross my arms. "Whatever that means..."

She drops on the chair beside me. "Honey, I know how frustrating it can be if you don't understand what's going on, but you have to trust that Mena makes sure you take your medicine and go to therapy, for a good reason."

"Yeah, well, Mum ordered me to do a lot of things but didn't answer any of my questions."

She sighs. "What do you want to know?"

Funny how I never thought about what my answer to such a direct question would be. What *do* I want to know? I have a long list of questions: what's wrong with me? Why does my medicine taste like salt? Why do I have crystals on my windowsill? And why are there so many more around the house? Why did she insist I wear this bag of herbs around my neck even when I go to sleep?

But more importantly... Why did she leave me? No other question matters as much as this one.

Mum, where are you?

"That bitch is too far away to reach... I'm afraid."

I freeze. Why is the voice still talking to me? I took my meds and although he does sound a bit weaker, he shouldn't be here at all.

Laughter echoes through the unopened chambers inside my brain.

"Oh Chesty, you can't fix an ocean of neglect with a sprinkle of salt."

"Shut up."

"What did you say?"

I blink and Elvi's still sitting beside me. "I... I..."

She grabs my hands, forces me to look at her. "Did you tell me to shut up?"

"No."

"I heard what you said."

"I wasn't..." I shake my head, trying to convey I wasn't talking to her while attempting to silence the laughter. "I wasn't talking to you."

Her face pales. "Who were you talking to?"

I open my mouth to answer, but nothing comes out.

"Good girl," the voice whispers. *"If you tell anyone I'm here and that I'm stronger than ever, I'll make you hurt them."*

"No! I won't."

"Chester." Elvi's fingers tighten, hard enough to feel like she's crushing my bones.

"You're too easy." The laughter rattles through my head. *"They're going to think you're crazy."*

"They already do."

"Who are you talking about or talking to?"

"Ma, this is what I was trying to tell you." Darwin's words don't match the movements of his mouth. He's doing the worst lip sync ever. "She's been blacking out and talking to no one. I found her in my room this morning staring at the wall—"

"Shut up, Dar!" This time I'm talking to him.

He's standing behind Elvi's chair and looks upset at my outburst. "I'm trying to help." I hate to see the concern on his face because I want to be angry with him, not grateful. He worries too much about me.

"Yeah, well, maybe you shouldn't be so helpful."

"If something is happening to you, I need to know," Elvi says.

"Something is always happening to me." I pull my hands free from hers, stand and rush for the backdoor. Right now, I don't want to be around anyone. I don't want to be alone either, because my head is a very dangerous place. But I need to get out of the house and away from the people who care too much.

I push past the sliding door and hear Elvi tell Darwin, "Give her some space, son."

As I make my way across the yard, I realize a lobotomy would be a better option than space. My skin starts to itch, and I scratch under the sweater sleeve, not caring about the ugly red marks I leave behind. Without meaning to, I end up in front of Mum's favorite corner of the yard and stop.

The wooden chair is painted blue and has a black cushion-seat. I remember when Elvi made this for her. It was Mum's birthday years ago and Elvi let Darwin and I paint the legs. I was so proud of myself, and she loved the gift being a joint family effort. As soon as we gave it to her, she took the chair to the furthest corner and set it down. That's when Elvi surprised her with a matching side table, but this is painted brown. It didn't take long for Mum to convert the outdoor area into her personal reading and journaling corner.

Her woolen throw blanket is still draped over the backrest and three books are haphazardly stacked on the table. A pink cup with a saucer is next to them, and although the coffee has congealed on the bottom, none of us have dared to clear it away.

This is the last spot I saw her.

This is where she vanished.

Tears sting the back of my eyes as I absently continue to scratch my skin. I miss her so much and wish I didn't constantly dismiss her when she was with us. She probably left thinking I didn't care about her, and that's hard to deal with.

It's probably sacrilege but I grab the cream-colored blanket off the chair and sit down. I throw the fabric over my legs and lean back, close my eyes, and listen to the silence. We don't have any neighbors behind our house, so this is the perfect serene spot.

No wonder Mum loved it so much.

I half-expect the voice to respond with an assault, but my head is as quiet as the yard.

My skin no longer itches.

I'm as peaceful as can be and feel the comfort of knowing my mother is somehow watching over me. This is the closest I've felt to her in a long time.

I must have dozed off, because when I opened my eyes again the sun had completely disappeared, and someone switched on the porchlight. It barely provides visibility this far back, but it's enough to see where I'm going when I eventually decide to head inside.

I try to readjust the blanket, but instead toss most of the length over the side.

Shit.

When I yank back, one of the fringed bits gets stuck and takes a bit more elbow grease to loosen. Something comes loose from underneath.

Oh god. If I ruined the chair, I'll never forgive myself.

I lean over, search blindly for whatever has come loose and find the object amongst the fallen leaves. I wrap my fingers around the rectangular block and my heart skips a beat when I see what it is.

Even with minimal light, I recognize Mum's Dreaded Notebook. The one she paid more attention to than me. The one she constantly wrote in but was always careful to conceal. The grey fabric reminds me of suede and is sewn all the way around the front and back covers. Actually, the whole thing looks homemade. Even the symbols and pentagram appear to have been stamped outside of a factory. There's a ribbon bookmark poking out from between the pages. And the piece of black rope securing the contents is connected with a squiggly snake charm on each end.

My fingers itch to know what's inside. My mother's private thoughts are in here. Do I dare crack open this gateway into her life? Do I want to see what was so important she had to carry this around everywhere she went? I can't believe it's been hidden here all along. I honestly thought she took it everywhere with her.

Unless she put it there on purpose. But why?

"Hey."

For a moment I actually think the voice is back, but it's actually Darwin approaching. His ridiculous outfit is so bright he stands out in the semi-darkness. Unsurprisingly, no one at school laughs at him for wearing mis-matched colors. Instead, he gets high-fives and fist-bumps wherever he goes.

I look at him and as much as I don't want to, can't help but feel the sting of betrayal.

"Nobody was looking for you." He holds out the adorable puppy, as an obvious peace offering. "She's been scratching at the glass door since you walked out, but I wasn't sure if you wanted to see her…"

I do want to hold the pup, especially when those tender amber eyes are looking at me that way. But I don't want to put the notebook down. So, I flash it in front of me.

His eyes widen. "Is that what I think it is?"

I nod.

"Where did you find it?"

I almost don't tell him, but we tell each other everything. Well, almost everything.

"Under the chair."

"Ah, that makes sense." He glances at the book and his Adam's apple bobs. "Did you read it?"

"No."

"Why not?"

"A big oaf interrupted me."

He laughs. "Suppose I deserve that."

"You deserve worse." I place the notebook on the coffee table and hold out my arms. "Give me the puppy."

Darwin slips her into my open arms, and I settle the furry bundle onto my lap. She yawns a few times, enjoys the pats, and promptly falls asleep. I find comfort in her soft fur and unquestionable trust.

"I think this dog might be a cat," I say.

"She's a puppy, they sleep a lot."

"Yeah." Looking at her now makes me wonder why the hell I found her in the bin in the first place. Who could have put her there?

Darwin crouches down in front of me and places both hands on my knees. "Look, I'm sorry about before, okay?"

"Is that your idea of an apology?"

"You know it is."

"I didn't want Elvi to know how much I've been struggling," I say, with a sigh. "She's got enough to worry about with Mum being... you know."

"She already knows." He squeezes my knees. "It's also our job to look out for you, and she deserves to know if you're not okay. Plus, you need to open up about what you're going through because we want to help."

"I know you do, and I appreciate it but that's my mother's job." My chest constricts. "She's the one who watched me like an annoying boss and half-answered my questions." I sigh. "I don't want to be a burden, or for you to feel like I'm your responsibility."

"Chess, we both know that's not what Mum did. She looked out for you. Sure, there were things she left out, but there has to be a reason." He shakes his head. "And I could never look at you as a burden, you know that."

"It feels like that's exactly what I am. To all of you."

"Well, you're not." His dark eyes are bright and shiny in the dim evening light and his jaw is clenched. "You're not a burden to anyone, especially not to me."

"Thanks Dar." He always knows what to say and how to say it. I sometimes wonder how I got so lucky to end up with such a wonderful boy as my stepbrother.

"So, do you accept my apology?"

"Are you going to make a habit out of dobbing me in?"

"Hey, I didn't mention the punching or the juice spill, so cut me some slack."

I would prefer to have him stew for a few hours—possibly overnight—but one look at his pleading eyes breaks my resolve. "Ah, okay. Yes! Why can't I stay mad at you?"

"No one can stay mad at me for long."

I make a gagging sound, although it's true. Even when Su gets annoyed with him, the next time I see them together, they're holding hands and whispering to each other again. Sometimes I wonder about what they say, but never ask.

"Why do you think Nobody was in our wheelie bin?" Best to focus on things that are real to me. Understanding relationships isn't one of my strongest points.

"Maybe someone wanted us to find her."

I bite my tongue before adding that at first, she was a half-decomposing body. I pat the side of her head I was convinced was melting away when I found her, and she trembles in her sleep. "I'm glad we did."

"Yeah, so am I." He stands up and stretches. "You're a bloody hero, Chester Warden."

"So are you Mr. Balloon-pants, uh, I mean Darwin Warden."

He laughs and it echoes around us. "We should get inside. It's getting a bit nippy out here."

"We probably should." I glance at the notebook.

"Are you taking it with you?"

"Do you think I should?" I ask, uncertain.

"I don't know about taking it inside because if Ma spots it, you won't even get a chance to crack it open," he says. "But I definitely think you should read it."

I mull over his words. "Is it supposed to rain tonight?" I tip my head back and consider the cloudless sky. Stars are already twinkling up there and the moon is bright.

"How the hell would I know?" He shakes his head. "Besides, I suspect that the notebook has survived a great many storms."

"You're right." I nod, knowing what I should do. "Can you take Nobody for a sec?"

When the pup is safely back in his arms, I tuck the notebook into the cranny beneath. I never noticed, but the space is a small open drawer added specifically for Mum's Dreaded Notebook. I tuck it back inside, place the blanket the way it was and join Darwin.

Nobody looks comfy snuggled into his chest, so I snake an arm around his waist and we head back into the house. As we pass the kitchen and spot Elvi, I flash a smile, and she nods in response.

"Don't stay up too late," she says as she stands. "I'm going to the workroom and will probably be working most of the night."

Darwin sighs. "Don't push yourself, okay?"

"I won't." She shakes her head. "Oh, and you two better come up with a real name soon!"

"Picking the perfect name takes time." He rolls his eyes at me.

"Not naming a living creature ASAP is risky."

"What do you mean?" I ask.

She's quiet for a second. "If an animal or child isn't named quickly, they're at greater risk of being hunted by the demonic."

"Uh, yeah, okay, Ma. That makes perfect sense." Darwin scoffs. "Thanks for another creepy comment no one wanted to hear."

"Why?"

"Chess, don't encourage her."

Elvi purses her lips. "It's an old superstition, don't worry about it."

I nod but feel a chill race down my spine. The way she's still looking at me as if she's biting her tongue, and her convenient answer, makes me uneasy. There's more to this name thing and I suddenly feel as if it relates back to me.

Three
Before
Nine months ago, August 2017

"Are you hearing any whispers at the moment?"

"Do you mean right now?" I asked, hoping the expression on my face spelled out innocence and not guilt.

"Not right *this* instant." Mum stopped flicking through her notebook long enough to stare at me. Her brow furrowed as she considered me too closely. "You know exactly what I mean, Chester. Please don't play games with me, this is serious."

So much for my portrayal of innocence. "No, I'm not." Unless she counted my snarky inner voice, which was working overtime *right now*. "And do you have to refer to your notebook all the time about everything?"

"I need to mark all of your achievements and weaknesses, the triumphs and problems—"

"Yeah, okay, I get it."

"Are you feeling itchy for no reason?" She was back to flicking through the countless pages filling her mysterious book. The cloth-bound grey book was etched with black symbols and a pentagram and had a black ribbon bookmark sticking out. I'd never been able to sneak a peek inside because she was very defensive about its contents.

"No. I'm not." I sighed, because now that she'd mentioned it, I was starting to feel totally itchy. But that was probably because she was staring at me so closely. I scratched my palm.

Mum cocked a perfectly plucked eyebrow. "Did you take your medication yet?"

I grabbed the two white pills sitting next to my empty cereal bowl and popped one into my mouth, washed it down with a big gulp of water and did the same with the other. Taking medication every day should have made taking these easier, but it hadn't. And the salty residue always lingered inside my mouth for way too long. These tablets tasted like a mouthful of the sea. At least she wasn't making me drink them with a glass of salt water anymore.

"Show me."

I opened my mouth wide, and she clutched my jaw, took a good look to make sure I wasn't hiding the two pills under my tongue. I supposed this was my fault. Several days last month, when I couldn't be bothered taking these silly things because I had a sore throat, I'd hidden both under my tongue and flushed them away. When the voice inside got louder and I started passing out around the house, she figured out exactly what I was doing.

"Good girl." She let go of my face and kissed the top of my head. "I know you hate taking them, but they're a better option than what all the other doctors wanted to prescribe you. Those drugs are much too strong and will numb your brain, which in your case would only make things worse."

"Does Dr. Larunda want me to take these other medications too?"

"No, that's why I like her."

Dr. Larunda—I still wasn't sure if that was her first name or surname—was another constant in my life. She was the latest in a long string of doctors Mum had forced me to see since I was old enough to understand something wasn't right with me. My mother was always force-feeding me pills to make sure I *"stayed myself,"* but never elaborated on exactly what she meant by that. I attended a therapist every week, and she'd never actually told me what my condition was either. Sometimes I thought they treated me like a five-year-old child who couldn't possibly handle the truth. Instead of a curious seventeen-year-old who wanted to know what the hell was wrong with her.

"What did they want me to take?"

"Janax, Xanax... something like that." She waved it away with her pen as if the names weren't important, before adding a note. "But they're not necessary. You've been taking the same pills for years and they work wonders."

"So why do I need to go and see a doctor, then?" If she was going to feed me whatever she wanted, why make me go to speak to a shrink at all? It was annoying and took up too much of my time. Time I could be spending with Su and Darwin.

"We've been through this before," she said, avoiding my eyes. "Dr. Larunda is an expert in her field—"

"Oh, right. She's the expert, but you're the one bossing her around." It didn't make any sense from where I was sitting. Mum was leaving out so many important details about my condition, but no matter what I said or how many times I asked, I couldn't make her tell me the truth.

"I don't boss her around." She was still jotting something inside her precious book, but somehow continued to hold a conversation. "We simply discuss what's going on and she suggests ways of helping you. If I don't agree, we look for other alternatives."

"Mum, you're a furniture designer, what do you know about medicine?" How did she even get away with this? Why would a psychologist listen to her alternative medicine and New Age remedies?

She placed her pen on the open page and even from here, I could see the thick ink blot. "You don't seem to know anything about me, Chester."

"That's because you keep me at arm's length! You're always too busy to answer my questions and clam up whenever I want to know things that concern me." I stood, pushed the chair back, and ignored the screech. "You never give me a straight answer about anything, or you're always too busy to explain."

"That's not true." She shook her head, her eyes blazing. "You're the one constant in my life, the only thing I think about day and night. Everything I've done and will ever do is because of you—for you."

I snorted. "The only *thing*? Maybe that's what the problem is, *Mother*. I'm not a thing." She had a knack for making me feel like her personal science experiment. "If you took a few minutes to actually listen to me, you might realize that I'm a person."

Mum shut her notebook, placed it on the kitchen counter and sighed. "Chester, you have no idea what you're saying."

"I think I know exactly what I'm saying!"

"Are the herbs in your spirit bag fresh?"

"See, Mum, you're not listening to me." My hand instinctively went to the necklace under my shirt, the one I hadn't bothered to check for weeks. I hated it when she turned our conversations away from the real issues of why I needed a therapist, to some stupid herb and crystal baggie she made me wear every day.

"I listen to everything you say, that's why I ask you things."

I opened my mouth to respond when Darwin stormed into the kitchen like an oblivious, colorful Jack-o-Lantern. Only he could get away with wearing a bright orange tee, black baggy sweatpants, and green sneakers for mufti-day. My usual sweater/hoodie over leggings/jeans outfits encouraged more teasing than his outrageous display.

"Good morning, ladies." He didn't even pause or noticed we were in the middle of an argument as he grabbed his lunch out of the fridge while chomping on a red apple. "Are you ready to walk to school, Chess?"

"Yes," I said.

"Do you have your gold coin?"

"Of course." All our mufti-days at school were for charity.

"No, you're not ready," Mum said. "This conversation isn't over."

"Actually, it is." I dumped my empty bowl in the sink and shouldered my schoolbag, which was already packed. "Let's go, Dar."

"Chester!"

"Bye, Mum." I pushed Darwin into the corridor, ignoring my mother's persistent calls.

He stopped in the hallway, shrugging my pushy hands off his back. "Are you sure you should leave like this?"

"Yes." I encouraged him to move before she caught up with us. "Come on, let's go."

"Okay, okay." He made his way down the hallway and opened the front door but paused in mid-motion when his phone dinged. He pulled it out and stared at the screen for several seconds with a goofy smile on his face.

I sighed. "What is it?"

"Huh?"

"Chester, come back here!"

I ignored her, curious about what would make Darwin smile like a goofball. "Who did you get a text from?"

"Oh, uh, one of the guys sent a joke." He pocketed his phone. "Let's go."

His long legs were suddenly in motion, and we walked outside in the nick of time. I could already hear Mum's heels clacking down the hallway.

I slammed the front door behind us, shutting her out.

Four
NOW

Sunday, 3am
May 6, 2018

I can't sleep. The sheets are sticking to me, my pillow is hurting my neck, I can't find a comfy position, and the whirlwind inside my head refuses to stop. At least Nobody seems comfortable in slumber at the end of the bed. I still can't help but wonder about where she came from and why she was dumped, but at least Su's mother confirmed the puppy is healthy. Even if she couldn't verify an exact age or breed.

No matter how many times I try the breathing exercises the countless doctors have suggested through the years, my heart is still beating too fast. And my thoughts are spiraling. If I'm not careful, I might invite the voice back in.

Luckily, after Elvi's insistence that I take the pills hours ago, I haven't heard my tormentor.

Maybe I should've thanked Darwin instead of sulking and getting upset with him. Why and how did he always manage to do the right thing? The kindest and most empathic options came easily to him. But I don't want to think about him either.

I groan because I can't force myself back to sleep and get out of bed. Careful not to wake the pup, I tiptoe through the quiet house with my phone in hand. I pause outside Darwin's half-open door and can hear his even breathing.

I'm surprised Nobody stayed with me instead of him. Girls usually fall in love with him very easily because of his easy-going manner.

I slip out the backdoor and slide it shut as carefully as I can. My eyes dart to the workroom at the end of the yard and there's still a light burning inside. Elvi must still be in there. Since my mother disappeared, she spends most of her time hidden away in the shed. I guess it helps keep her mind occupied. I almost head that way but decide to give her the privacy she obviously needs.

There's nothing I can say to Elvi to make her feel better.

My breath hitches and I swallow down the sob trying to escape me. She bugged the hell out of me, and her pushy ways drove me crazy, but I miss Mum so much.

Come back, please.

I catch a quick movement from the corner of my eye and turn my head in time to see a skittering shape on the grass. I'm suddenly frozen to the spot because I think the voice is back to manipulate me, but that's not my shadow. It's someone else's.

A chill runs down my spine. I shut my eyes to clear my vision and when I snap them open, it's gone.

I take a shallow breath and exhale before tilting my head back. The moon is high in the night sky, and so shiny I don't need to access the flashlight feature while making my way down the rest of the path. It's cool but the air is still, and my ugly hooded woolly cardigan is enough to keep out the cold, so I don't get sick.

Mum's chair is exactly how I left it.

I study the spot for several quiet moments and flashes of the many times I've seen her sitting here race through my mind. It's such a visceral sensation that I imagine she's actually there before she vanishes all over again. This time I don't drape her blanket over me, and instead fold it into a square so I can place it on my lap and use it to prop up the notebook.

My hand knows exactly where to go this time, and I have Mum's Dreaded Notebook on my lap in no time. I run my fingertips along the tight stitching on the sides and over the slight bump the stamped pentagram design has left behind.

She didn't like to talk about her interest in the old pagan ways, the occult, or whatever else this pentagram meant to her, but she always said it was important to protect yourself against psychic attacks. She claimed negative energy could cause serious harm and did everything she could to help me combat the constant threat inside me.

Why didn't I pay more attention or actually listen? I absently reach for the spirit bag I'm supposed to wear all the time and can't even remember where it is. Wasn't I wearing it before?

I unhook the metal snake clip on the notebook, opened the cover and find a large-sized sticky note on the front page. The black ink makes the letters stark, but the moon doesn't provide enough light.

After checking to make sure I'm still alone, I hit the flashlight icon on my phone and point the beam over the note.

Chester, if you're reading this, then I'm probably already gone.

Tears sting my eyes, blur the words. I wipe them away with the back of my hand because I don't want to smudge the print and send a blast of light all over the yard. I quickly put my hand down and try to concentrate. If I give myself away, I won't get the chance to read anything else. And this note is heartbreaking enough.

I exhale and point the light over the page.

Make sure you stay strong, keep taking your pills and whatever you do—never give into that disgusting voice. Because now that I'm gone, he'll try everything to get to you. But you must stay strong and fight. Now's the time to fight, my brave girl.

As the words sink in, I feel a new resolve flow through me and decide that when the voice tries to say something again, I'll shut my mind off by slamming all the doors. I must do whatever I can to make sure he doesn't slip out of whatever room he's trapped inside.

The voice is a haunting pest, but he's not free yet.

I hope Purson sent you a protector.

"Purson?" I whisper into the night. Who or what is Purson? I don't remember ever meeting someone with this name... Yet, something about it sounds familiar.

It's also time for you to finally read this book of revelations and do what I couldn't—defeat the evil threatening to consume you. I'm so very sorry. I love you so much, Mum.

I can't believe it took Mum disappearing for her to tell me some truths. Is it too late now? She called me brave, but I can't remember a single day of my life where I felt strong enough to apply that word to myself.

With shaky fingers I turn the page, point the light and her name is written in beautiful calligraphy.

Philomena Marie Warren.

I've got a framed version of my own name done in the same design hanging on my bedroom wall. *Chester Rose Warden*, which is the surname Elvi and Mum both took and gave us after they were finally legally married. It's a combination of their maiden names—Warren and Arden.

The next page is stained with dirty fingerprints. I don't know if it's dirt or blood, but I lean closer and reposition the open book because these smudges actually spell something out. It's one word: *Earth*.

So, the smudging must be dirt. I run my fingers over the gritty surface and swear I can feel the rough texture stir.

I flick ahead and the paper flies up, straining against the binding to send a cool breeze into my face. The word *Air* appears once the page settles back into place.

The following page is shouldered along the edges and feels hot to the touch before an actual flame pops up. The word *Fire* materializes before my eyes.

I know what's coming next even before I trace the wrinkly edges and my fingertip dips into a pool of liquid in the middle. The letters stir around the ripples and form *Water*.

Is my mind playing tricks on me again?

I probably shouldn't, but I turn back and check every page again. The same thing happens as each of the four elements reveal themselves. She somehow captured them *inside*. And I don't understand how or why.

Following all of this is a handwritten phrase in her familiar scrawl: *To conjure, one must first command the elements.* But the next two pages are nothing more than columns of tiny text with dates listed next to each element, and a cross or tick placed at the end. It's not until the fifth page that all the rows become ticks and a smiley face is drawn at the bottom.

I recognize Elvi's smiley because she always draws it on the fridge whiteboard and our calendars. I'm about to move forward, when something rubs up against my ankle and I start. Switch off the flashlight and stay frozen for a second.

"Oh my god, it's you." The pup is rubbing her head against my leg and when I catch her gaze, she whines. "How did you get outside?" A dog can't open a sliding door. Besides, I can see it's still closed. I hope she didn't wake Darwin because I'm tired of interrupting his sleep.

Nobody—I hate calling her that—won't stop crying, so I tuck the journal back into its hiding spot, pocket my phone and place her on my lap. "You couldn't sleep either, huh?" I press my face into the back of her scruff, and she smells nice. "Did I wake you when I left? I'm sorry."

A cold wind blows through the yard and pushes the hood off my head. I tilt my face to the sky and find it's now completely covered with clouds. When did that happen?

I take a quick peek over my shoulder and find the workroom lights are still blazing.

"Let's get inside before it starts to rain," I say to the pup.

The first drop hits my head when we're halfway through the yard, and by the time I'm sliding the backdoor closed, it's pelting outside. Did I make a mistake by leaving the journal out there? No, a book with elements trapped within can surely survive a little rain. Even Darwin said the same earlier because Mum's Dreaded Notebook has been through many storms.

Nobody shakes in my arms and when I look down, I realize I've wrapped her up in Mum's blanket. She's still asleep and looks comfy snuggled into the fringed wool as we head into the corridor.

The darkness is absolute, and my heart skips a beat when a silhouette skitters across the ceiling. I check but there's nothing there. Yet, I'm sure I saw something. I tighten my grip around the puppy, and she moans. It sounds heartbreaking and I don't know what to do.

"It's okay," I whisper near her soft, floppy ear. "Let's go back to my room." Maybe after all of this, I'll be able to get some actual sleep.

Her body rumbles one last time, and she settles down.

I stare at the ceiling for several seconds before ducking back into my room but don't notice any murky movements this time. Between Mum's note, the strangeness trapped within her journal and the sudden rain, I've probably freaked myself out.

"Now's the time to fight, my brave girl."

My body chills as I head back to bed because I could've sworn that was her voice inside my head.

Five
BEFORE
Ten months ago, July 2017

Her office was big but too dark, and nothing about the space felt remotely soothing. The murky corners to my left made the room feel like there were only three tangible walls and the fourth extended into a void.

The other offices I'd sat in were usually painted in bright colors to make young minds comfortable and encourage them to be chatty, or had large windows to let in natural light, and revealed cityscapes or manicured gardens. Others were painted in serene tones to fool patients into a docile state of false relaxation. Some contained toy baskets for younger kids or an eclectic selection of scuffed books. I'd even been in one with a great selection of handheld consoles. This particular doctor used to have a pinball machine that he'd let me use at the end of our sessions. He'd been my favorite, but my mother didn't agree with his laidback attitude.

Different people had different ways of ensuring the patient felt some level of comfort and trust. Opened up willingly and made progress.

This doctor, one my mother couldn't stop praising, seemed to be a different breed altogether. One I hadn't encountered yet. Her office was painted a charcoal shade dark enough to pass for black and was set up like a minimalist commune. Two tall lamps stood in each corner of the room like guards. A big, chunky desk sat in front of the only window, and a matching chair resembling a throne was placed behind it. Even the red velvet curtains tied to the sides gave the illusion of royalty.

The only thing on her desk was an ink blotter, a pot of ink and an actual quill. No files or papers. Not even a desktop or laptop. She did have a row of tall cherry-wood filing cabinets along the wall adjacent to the window.

Maybe she's a neat freak like Darwin.

"So, how old are you, Chester?" Her voice was raspy, seeming to echo around this empty place. "Do you prefer to be called Chess, or is Chester okay?"

"Chester's fine," I said. "Only my friends call me Chess."

"I see." Her eyes seemed to see right through me. "So, how old are you?"

We'd been sitting in silence for a while, and this was her first question? My age would definitely be a detail my mother had already provided. I gazed out the window and couldn't help but think about how creepy this building was. A red brick square monstrosity with a huge white cross stuck to the front. Mum told me this used to be a hospital of some sort but was now a medical Centre. Even with the curtains drawn and the blue sky outside, the light didn't seem to penetrate into the office—hence the lamps.

"I asked you a question." Her staccato tone was unsettling.

"I'm seventeen."

"You look younger." Her large, unnerving eyes seemed too big for her slim face. She wasn't exactly pretty, but there was an alien beauty about her. Almost made me think of her as a caricature of a person.

"Yeah, I've heard that before." I squirmed in my seat. "Too many times to care," I uttered under my breath.

"Does it bother you?"

I shrugged. "Maybe I'll look really young when I'm old too." I met her gaze, determined not to let her outstare me. "So, no, it doesn't bother me."

She nodded slowly, silently considering my words even though she didn't write anything down. "What do you do for fun?"

"I like to read and watch movies. And hang out with my friends."

The way her pale hands sat perfectly folded on her lap made her shoulders appear too rigid. Her body posture was as intimidating as her stare. From the way she'd crossed one long leg over the other, to the incredibly tall heels and the perfect fit of her white blouse and skirt.

She didn't break eye contact, but I constantly did. Yet, as soon as I looked at her again, I found her watching me like a hawk. Dr. Larunda's nose was long and slightly resembled a beak. She carried herself in a very controlled manner and everything about her, except for the single blonde streak on the left side of her red hair, was symmetrical. The way she sat so rigid made me think of her as a bird of prey, with folded wings waiting to swoop in on her victim.

Right now, I'm her victim.

"When you say friends, are you talking about your brother Darwin?"

Ouch! Her knowing so much about me already made me squirm in my uncomfortable seat. Mum had obviously filled her in on all the sad and important bits about my life. She probably knew about the voices in my head too, that I hardly went out because my best friend happened to live in the same house, and that I didn't seem romantically interested in guys or girls.

A small smile curved her thin mouth. "Do you argue with yourself often?"

I wanted to wipe the smirk off her face. "I don't know what you mean."

She inclined her head and the muscles along the side of her neck bulged. "I can see how much thought my question incited in you."

"Are you psychic?"

"I don't need to be psychic to see how much a simple question affected you." She tilted her head slightly, as if she were listening to someone else in the room. "Your stepsibling is also your best friend." It wasn't a question, more of a statement, but she waited for a response.

"Yes, he is." How could he not be? I'd known him my whole life, we'd grown up together. Darwin was the one who used to pick me up whenever I fell off my bike because he had no trouble staying on his. He'd been the one who played board games with me and let me win. He taught me how to play chess. Helped me with my homework while he was in boarding school and didn't mind that I constantly emailed him a barrage of questions. And even with the distance between us, he'd still noticed how much I struggled to remember my line of thought, or when I complained about too much noise inside my head.

Darwin is the only person who keeps me centered.

"Do you have a lot in common?"

"Yeah," I said. "But I also have another best friend. Her name is Su and we've known each other since primary school."

"But you all *hang out* together," she stated. Again, not a question but a dead-panned statement.

"Yes." Where was she going with this? I tried to collect my thoughts because every possible answer collided inside my mind like a hot mess. Most doctors had the same effect on me, but this one seemed particularly skilled at scrambling my brain. "Su was my friend while Darwin was away, still is." Why did I feel like I had to justify this?

"I see." She lowered her head and made me wonder if she was listening to me at all. "Does that make you angry?"

"Does what make me angry?"

"That Su was only yours before and now you share her?"

I scoffed at the weird suggestion. "Su is a person. She's my friend but she was never *mine* and certainly doesn't belong to Dar. She belongs to herself."

"So, you believe in modern ideals."

"I believe people aren't owned," I said. "So, yeah, I suppose I do."

The burgundy armchair seemed perfectly tailored to her sleek frame. While the identical one I occupied made me feel like a kid too small to fit on a huge couch. The toes of my sneakers barely touched the carpeted floor.

"You don't believe in people being promised to others?"

"Like an arranged marriage?" I laughed, seriously had no idea where she was going with this line of thought.

"Not necessarily." Her eyes strayed to a point over my shoulder but when I took a quick peek, I found nothing there. "Souls can be promised or offered to another in many ways. The rituals vary but amount to the same thing—ownership."

"You've lost me." I disliked the way she sat so still, making her look more like a statue than a person.

"The reason why you're here is because sometimes you feel as if your mind is slipping away from you, am I right?"

"Yeah, but—"

"There are too many voices crowded inside your head, and at times it can get really hard to distinguish which one to listen to. Or which one is yours." The doctor didn't continue until I nodded. Her eyes were gleaming. "Is that an accurate account of how you feel?"

I sighed, but managed a nod.

"This phenomenon often arises when someone has been promised to another."

If I didn't take my pills every day and the voice got strong enough, this was *exactly* what he claimed.

"Hearing voices is often interpreted as madness, but don't we all hear a particular whisper in our heads *all the time*?" She watched me closely. "Even as I speak to you right now, there are inner whispers agreeing or denying with what I'm saying. We all have a conscience we're told to pay attention to, and aren't we encouraged to trust our instincts? We have strange ways of personifying and labelling so much about ourselves, yet as soon as someone hears more than one voice, we're told there's something wrong with our brains."

"But that's right, isn't it?" I licked my lips, and suddenly felt the questions pop into my head. "Hearing a voice that sounds nothing like you isn't normal. And when this voice tells you to do bad things or threatens you by saying he'll take over... surely that's crazy."

"Is that what yours tells you?"

"Yes. My voice is cruel and sounds like a man. No, it sounds like some sort of beast who wants to consume me."

Her eyes widened slightly, and she glanced over my shoulder again. "Do you hear this voice all the time?"

"Not if I take my medicine."

"The pills your mother gives you every morning?"

"Yeah."

"And what happens if you don't take these pills?"

"The voice gets really loud, and I pass out, then wake up and don't remember how I got there." I shook my head because I hated remembering this bit. The disorientation was something I'd never get used to.

"So, you lose time?"

I nodded.

"You must keep taking your pills." She pressed her thin lips together so hard they formed a white line. "She's right, without those pills we'll lose you to this voice and might never get you back."

"What does that mean? And where would I go?" If someone else managed to take over my mind, where would I end up? And that made me wonder, what was I really? If some random voice could take over, what kind of weak excuse for a person was I?

"Are you okay?" Her eyebrows were knotted together but the concern in her words didn't reach her eyes.

"Asking weird questions always makes me anxious."

"You suffer from anxiety as well?"

"A bit," I say, though my mother denied this every time I'd mentioned it.

"Are you taking any medication for this?"

I shook my head.

"I'll speak to Mena because you definitely shouldn't get worked up and risk a panic attack in your condition."

"I wouldn't bother. Mum won't let me take any other drugs but those two pills in the morning and the odd herbal tea."

She cocked an eyebrow. "Is that so?"

"Yeah, she says they would interfere with my real medication."

"Not if taken as prescribed." Dr. Larunda glanced at her hands and sat so still, I wondered if she was wearing an earpiece and listening to someone else's instructions.

The timer on her desk chimed.

This woman was so old school, she didn't set her phone alarm and instead had some sort of weird contraption on top of the filing cabinets.

"That concludes our first session." Her porcelain features didn't reveal any emotion when she looked up. "I'd like to see you once a week. Does Monday afternoons work for you?"

"I guess."

Dr. Larunda stood and she reminded me of a stick insect unpacking itself. She headed for her desk, opened a drawer, and pulled out an ornate rectangular chest. She rummaged inside until she found a small cardboard box. "These are anxiety meds," she said. "I know you said your mother won't let you take them, but I'm your doctor and I believe you need them." She held the box out but kept it steady. "If you ever feel overwhelmed, I want you to take a quarter of a pill. Half if you feel like you might pass out from hyperventilating, okay?"

I hesitated, avoiding her intense scrutiny.

"I'm putting my trust in you, Chester. Will you trust me too?"

"Are you sure I should be taking that?"

She cocked an eyebrow. "If you take them only when you need them, yes."

"Uh, I'm not sure..."

"If you don't take them like M&Ms, your mother will never find out, and you'll have another coping mechanism at your fingertips."

"I'm a minor. Why are you giving me anything without my guardian's permission?"

"Because you're my patient and after my assessment, I've decided you need these to help calm you down sometimes. You're right, I have an obligation to your mother because you're a minor, but my biggest concern is you. My loyalty is with you and something like this is protected by the patient-doctor confidentiality clause. I'm concerned about your wellbeing." She held the box out. "Do we understand each other?"

"We do." I took the medication and shoved the box into my back pocket, where Mum wouldn't think to look. As weird as this woman appeared, I felt a certain kinship toward her because she happened to be the first doctor who'd told me to keep a secret from my mother.

"Good," she said. "Now, if you don't mind, please wait outside while I have a quick chat with Mena."

"Okay."

"Tell her to come in, will you?"

I nodded and left the office without a backward glance.

"How did you go?" Mum jumped to her feet as soon as I entered the lavish reception area. How could we even afford this doctor?

"She wants to talk to you."

"Was there a problem?"

I shook my head and hoped she didn't read any suspicion on me.

"If you need me, tell Purson and he'll call through to Larunda."

"Who?"

"The receptionist." Mum kissed the top of my head and wandered into the office. Before she closed the door, Dr. Larunda said, "She's exactly as you described her."

I turned away from the closed door and considered the squat man sitting behind the reception desk. A bushy beard concealed most of his round face and when he stood, he was bursting out of his blue shirt.

He flashed me a smile when he caught me staring and pointed at the opposite corner of the room, where an array of cups, sugar, a water fountain and even a mini fridge were positioned. "Feel free to grab refreshments while you wait."

I nodded but sat down instead, careful not to squash the box in my back pocket.

All I wanted to do was replay the strangest counselling session I'd ever experienced over and over in my mind. Maybe even share the experience with Darwin to see what he thought about all this.

This doctor was different. She seemed to ask the weirdest questions and made the strangest comments, but at least she'd offered me a level of respect I'd never encountered from an adult before.

Six
NOW

Tuesday, 3pm
May 8, 2018

"What're you going to write your essay about?" Su asks as she loops her arm through mine, and we continue down the street.

"I don't know yet." Writing a two-page essay about a depressing poem that doesn't make sense is not something I want to focus on while walking home from school. I'm back in that awkward place where I don't like going to school and can't wait until the next break because concentrating is starting to hurt my brain. Besides, I'm over everyone and everything, can't be bothered listening to my teachers ramble on about how important our last year of school is. I'm tired of all the useless and overdone analysis about things that were written hundreds of years ago. But this is our life and it's only right that I at least pretend to make an effort for my friend. "What about you?"

"I don't know yet either."

We both giggle. I miss her being my partner in hating school.

Darwin runs ahead, spins, and stops in front of us. "I'm going to write about how beautiful you are, my fair lady." He takes Su's other hand and kisses the back before bowing like a doofus.

"Aww, Dar, you can't write about me," she says.

"We're discussing poetry, and your beauty is going to be my inspiration." He straightens but is still holding onto her hand.

I roll my eyes. "The poem is about a crazy person who strangles a woman because he's a demented jerk." He knows exactly what this poem is about. Besides, he took all the comradery I was feeling with Su and replaced it with his ridiculous romantic notions. I suddenly want to get home. All I can think about is Mum's Dreaded Notebook. I want to read more.

"I know what it's about, but I'm not going to focus on the tragic violence. I want to concentrate on the beauty." He smiles at Su and she's positively beaming.

"Well, I'm going to concentrate on the insanity." I unhook my arm from hers, giving her the freedom to go to him. I know it's what she really wants to do.

"Are you sure that's a good idea?" he asks.

I put a hand on my hip. "What's that supposed to mean?"

"It doesn't mean anything." He tucks Su against his side and even in my sour mood I can't help but notice how cute they are together. The tall, lanky guy with a mop of dark hair and the dress sense of a clown is perfectly complemented by the petite and totally adorable girl with the great fashion sense. Su even makes our school uniform look good.

"Sure, it doesn't," I say, and the anger is swelling up inside.

"That's it," the voice whispers, *"don't hold back your rage. Who does he think he is, anyway? He thinks he knows you better than anyone, but he's wrong."*

"You don't think a crazy person should be concentrating on the craziness of someone else, right?"

"Hey, that's not what I'm saying at all!" Darwin's eyes are wide and when he lets go of Su to stand in front of me, I can tell I've upset him for nothing. He's playing around and as usual, I'm going off the deep end.

My dark mood pops like a balloon.

"No, you silly girl, give into anger. It will make you stronger."

I shake my head because the voice is wrong. Whenever anger washes over me, I feel weaker, and he gets louder.

"That's right! I get louder to make you stronger."

"I don't need you," I whisper.

"Chess, look at me," Darwin says. "Stop talking gibberish."

I meet his gaze and strength flows into me. "What?"

He shrugs. "Whenever you get angry, you start talking gibberish."

"You sound like something out of a horror movie," Su adds.

"Thanks a lot."

She winces. "I'm sorry."

"She didn't mean anything by—"

"I know, Dar. I'm just not feeling like myself lately." Whatever that is. "Since Mum…"

"I understand."

His sympathy is as strong as his determination to keep me on track. Although the three of us know I've had issues for years, I guess it's easier to blame my mother's disappearance for my deterioration. But it's more than that. I'm twitchier than usual and slept in this morning, so I didn't have time to take my pills. I barely had enough time to get dressed, brush my teeth and chase Darwin out the door.

I feel bad, I really do. I promised I'd take my medication as instructed and I didn't. Now, the voice is already slipping through.

Darwin's still talking but I can't hear a word he's saying. His lips enunciate in slow motion and when I try to ask what he's saying, nothing comes out. All I can see is smoky curlicues shredding the corners of my vision.

The street is suddenly drained of pigment. A world of black and white replaces the familiar, everyday colors.

My pulse speeds up and my mouth feels dry.

Darwin reminds me of a choppy drawing with shadings on his face that highlight his cheekbones. Su is nothing but an outline behind him. A few weeks ago, I told the doctor my two friends were starting to blend into each other and now, they really are.

Beyond them, the street is empty. The buildings are charcoal streaks, and one stands out in particular. It's not a tall structure, and I'm not sure if it's an apartment block or a store. At the moment, it's a series of uneven lines with a vaguely humanoid figure looming on top.

A lonely horned silhouette with a mane of long hair stands on the roof. A tail swings to the side and although the creature is completely colored black and faceless, I'm sure they're staring right at me.

Who is that?

They take a step, closer to the edge of the roof, and the movements are so familiar I can't help but feel like I know who this is. For a split second, I think it's Mum, but it can't be. She wouldn't watch from a distance, and she certainly doesn't have horns or a tail. But there *is* someone from my past who looks like this.

My invisible friend, Shiny Pictures.

But I haven't seen her in ages, and she was always so colorful.

I blink and some of the blurriness fades, but they're—no, *she*, because Shiny Pictures was definitely a girl who reminded me of a pony—is still there.

"*Chester.*" My name drags out from somewhere, but for once it's not from inside my head because it's her. There might be distance between us, but she's talking to me.

"Chess, can you hear me?"

I can hear you. I can hear both of you.

I know my answer wasn't spoken out loud, but I don't care.

The horned figure stares at me, and I can't look away.

"Chester, look at me."

I am looking at you.

I'm hearing someone else's questions but responding to Shiny Pictures.

"For fuck's sake, come back to us!"

"You're going to hurt her," someone else says.

"I'm here if you need me." She dissolves into smoke and the residue takes all the black and white from my vision. The choppiness slips away so that when I blink again, I'm staring into Darwin's brown eyes and my brain feels like its rattling inside my skull.

"Can you hear me?"

"Yes, I can hear you!" I practically shout. "Stop shaking me, I'm going to get whiplash."

He stops abruptly and leans down to stare into my eyes. "You can see me now?"

"Of course, I can see you. Why wouldn't I be able to see you?" Such a silly question when everything but the horned and tailed figure from my past faded away only moments ago.

He hugs me so hard I can barely breathe. "Thank god you're okay," he whispers into my hair. "I thought you'd left me for good."

"I'm not that easy to get rid of," I say, trying to lighten the mood and catch my breath. And when I see the horrified way Su is looking at me, I fear I might have finally traumatized two of the people I care the most about. "What happened?"

When Darwin lets go, Su takes over. She enfolds me in a tight hug, and my arms hang at my sides awkwardly. "I was so worried," she whispers into my ear. "I was going to call an ambulance."

"Why?" I draw back and glance from one to the other.

"You went so pale and still," she says. "And this time you didn't speak."

"You totally spaced out on us. I've never seen you like that before." Darwin is dragging his hands through his hair, making the ends stick out.

"Okay, but why are you both so freaked out?"

He shakes his head. "I don't know how to explain it."

"You don't know how to explain what?" I ask, confused.

"Your eyes didn't gloss over," Su says, biting on her thumb nail. "They turned white."

I scoff. "Yeah, right!"

"I'm serious, they did." Su spits out the bit of nail she bit off.

I hate to be the one responsible for this nasty habit making a comeback.

"Chess, I saw it too. I saw your irises disappear. No." He presses both hands against the sides of his head. "It was like a white shutter was covering your eyes."

It's not a cold day and there's no breeze, but Su is shaking.

"That doesn't make any sense."

"Something really strange is going on and we need to work out what it is." He considers me for a moment and seems to want to say more.

"Dar, I really need to get home." Su gives me an apologetic shrug. "I'm sorry, but my parents are waiting for me."

He seems indecisive for a moment. "Why don't we make sure Su gets home safe and then try to figure this out?"

I nod numbly.

Darwin goes to Su and whispers something in her ear.

I feel a tap on my right shoulder and spin around but there's no one there. Only a wisp of smoke in the air that fills my nose, but it's not entirely unpleasant. Familiar is the way I would describe the smell.

"Don't be afraid of me," the female voice whispers in my ear.

Goose bumps race over my skin and I shiver because I'm positive she's still here with me.

"Come on, let's go." Su takes my left hand and Darwin takes my right.

"Are you sure you're okay?" he asks.

I manage a nod because the lump lodged inside my throat won't let me speak.

"Good, let's go home."

The three of us walk down the street together. Even though I'm shielded by my two friends, I still catch constant movements from the corners of my eyes. I don't know if it's shadows or smoke, but something is definitely following me. Or might now be attached to me, I'm not sure.

Eyes are watching from every direction, making my skin crawl. It takes every bit of willpower I have to pretend I'm fine. That I'm not losing my mind to this paranoia. The comfort of their hands is the only thing keeping me grounded to reality, because I suddenly feel as light as a feather. As if I'm about to float away and only Darwin and Su can keep me anchored to the real world.

A crow caws overhead and when I tip my head back to catch a glimpse, the bird crumbles to ash in the sky.

MUM'S (DREADED) NOTEBOOK
February 1st, 1999

It feels strange to write anything other than results for the endless experiments He wants me to do before I prove myself worthy. Or rather, until He finally realizes how big of an asset I am if he'd just give me the chance.

Anyway, adding actual notes inside the notebook I made was His idea. He told me it's time I start to record real information—including thoughts, observations, and goals. Not only the burned and crinkly pages I've filled so far. Or the lists of my (many) failures and (impressive) accomplishments. I need to add *real* details. He says not to use this like the diary of an adolescent girl, but like a journal—my personal grimoire—to record random bits of important experiences and information, as well as my personal accounts of invoking. He also wants me to draw pictures. That last one is going to be a struggle because I can barely draw a straight line, let alone some of the things I've encountered in the last three months.

But I'll give it a try.

I'm nothing if not persistent, and now that I've caught His attention, I plan to keep it focused solely on me. We all want to catch his attention and do whatever we have to in order to do so. I let my ambition and skill shine enough to single me out from the long line of devotees, but I'm not alone. He has chosen two of us. The other girl is prettier than me, has a much nicer body. Where I'm curvy and small, she's slim and oh-so leggy. I hated her from the moment we met. Or at least, I wanted to hate her. But since we're both his chosen ones—gosh that sounds so wanky, but it's true—and we have to spend so much time together, I'm getting to know her better. And she's so much more than I expected.

She's funny and smart, and so nice to talk to. We never run out of things to chat about and talk late into the night about our hopes and dreams. But we can't tell Him that we're becoming friends, so we compete whenever He wants us to. Allow Him to bait us against each other—whatever it takes. We both know what's at stake and there's no way either one of us is going to back down, but if what the rumors say about the last challenge are true… I'm not sure I can go through with this.

I wonder if she will. She says she wouldn't—couldn't possibly—but who really knows anyone at the worst of times? Because what we're doing here, it's all about beating out the competition and proving your worth.

I really hope these are the kinds of things He wants me to mention in my journal. I also hope that he keeps his word. He promised he would never read anything I write, claims that a practitioner's grimoire is sacred and must never be shared. One's knowledge is supposed to remain with them and them alone. At least, that's what *He* says. I don't know if I agree yet.

The other girl said she can teach me a spell to mask what I don't want him to read, but I said no because we're not supposed to use any kind of magic without Him overseeing. The last thing I want to do is to get thrown out for breaking the rules. Besides, I've found the best hiding spot.

What else? Oh yeah, last night I invoked my first one. While that's not as impressive as it sounds because this thing is the equivalent of vermin, it's still progress and I'm going to take it as a win. If I start small and work myself up the food chain, who knows what I'll be able to invoke next? Of course, He doesn't want us to call on anyone without Him around and would certainly not allow us to reap any of its rewards.

I'm not even going to try to draw this thing, but I will say, I'm super excited about my achievement and will continue to aim higher. I know it's probably blasphemous to say, but I'm no longer doing this just for Him. I'll always worship the ground He walks on and want to impress him until he sees I'm the only one He wants and needs, but the power is addictive.

I want to feel that much control flow through me again, and soon. But now, I have to go because I can hear him tiptoeing into my chamber. He's breaking His own rules by sneaking in. But, as long as my roommate fakes being asleep, like I do when he slips into her bed, we'll be okay.

Seven
NOW

Thursday, 4pm
May 10, 2018

The knock on the door startles me.

Not because I was asleep, but because Mum's words echo inside my head. As if I need another voice to haunt me, I've now welcomed the very confusing inner thoughts of a much younger version of my mother. A person who sounds nothing like the woman I know. This one reminds me of an obsessive, over-the-top damsel who wants to please some mysterious douche. And she couldn't even draw! I've seen Mum's sketches, and she can design flawless pieces of furniture and even entire rooms—houses if she has to—at total ease.

"Chess?" Darwin's voice is soft as he peeks around the open door, letting in the light from the hallway.

"Yeah." My arms feel shaky and at this stage I don't know if it's because of what I read or because of what happened the other day. Why did Mum sound like she was taking part in the *Hunger Games*, or some other equally strange dystopian trial? Not to mention that creepy dude sneaking into her room. Ugh. What was going on there?

The best I can hope is that this is some sort of English composition challenge, and she was making it all up.

"I didn't wake you, did I?" He stands there, unmoving. I can't even see the expression of his face because of the glaring glow behind him.

"No." I tuck the notebook under my pillow. I'm not ready to share the contents of this with anyone yet. Not until I read more and hopefully figure out where this strange story is going. I want to get some sort of clue about what might have happened to my mother by reading the damn journal she carried everywhere. But now I'm not sure I can handle whatever mysteries are hidden inside. Then again, she did leave a sticky note telling me she wants me to read it.

"Did you take a nap?"

"Nope." Truth is, I did lie down and even closed my eyes. I let my mind wander but when my skin got itchy and all I could think about was the wisp of smoke I'd seen on the street and imagined she was inside my room, I gave up. So, I snuck out to the backyard and brought the notebook into my room to read.

I don't know what Darwin was doing at the time. He was probably texting Su.

"Are you sure you shouldn't get more rest?"

"I'm good."

He steps into the room but leaves the door half open. I've closed the blinds so even though there's a rim of daylight along the sides of the window, it's still gloomy.

"Listen, whatever happened to you the other day wasn't good." I've heard this tone before, the one time I apparently slapped him across the room.

"Thanks for stating the obvious, Sherlock." I shake my head. "But I've already told you, I don't want to talk about it."

He sighs and it's loud enough to echo around the room. He makes his way inside and sits on the end of my bed. "I know what you said, but—"

"Where's Nobody?" I didn't notice her slip out of the room.

"Running around the backyard," he answers. "I took her for a walk to do her business and now she's playing with the flowers. It doesn't take much to distract her."

"That's true." I smile because that dog certainly makes me happy. There's something about her that I can't explain, like we're connected on a subconscious level. "Sorry I'm not the best puppy parent."

"It's fine, you still spend plenty of time with her."

The truth is, Nobody is the one who goes out of her way to spend time with me because I'm usually distracted. But I don't say this out loud.

"So... are you seriously going to avoid having this conversation?" He sighs. "I don't know what's going on, but I feel like you're keeping things from me. Like you're avoiding me."

"I'm not avoiding you, Dar." I close my eyes for a second, trying to wash away the pesky guilt because he's right. I'm keeping more things than usual from him.

"Okay, what happened when we were walking home the other day?" Even in the dim light I can see how shiny his eyes are.

This time, I sigh and throw my head back against the pillow in the most dramatic way possible. "I don't know, okay?"

"Was it the voice?"

"No, yes, maybe..."

"You have to pick one. It can't be all of them."

"Fine, I heard *a* voice."

His face falls and I quickly sit up, wrapping my arms around my legs.

"You're hearing new voices now?"

"No, it's not like that." She wasn't exactly new. "This one isn't threatening. God, I sound like such a nutjob!"

"No, you don't, keep going." He taps the top of my head.

"This one was softer," I say. "She was trying to communicate with me."

"Jesus, it really freaks me out when you say shit like that."

"So, you don't want me to tell you? You can't have it both ways."

"I do, it's just…" He glances at the closed window, at my messy desk and the bedside table with three books and their separate bookmarks. All unfinished because I can never read one book at a time. Sometimes I wonder if I'm reading a different story for each different voice. But that sounds demented. At least I keep returning to *Alice in Wonderland* because that's one story I can't get enough of.

"It's just what, Dar?" I have my chin propped on my knees and stare at him, trying to read his mind, but he's not an easy person to figure out. If we weren't close and didn't talk to each other all the time, I would never be able to guess what was on his mind.

"You scared the crap out of me, okay?"

"I know. I scare the crap out of myself sometimes." A scratching sensation starts in the back of my throat, pushes a raspy cough out of me.

"What's wrong?" Darwin slaps my back twice.

I think the feeling is gone, but it comes back with a vengeance. "I don't…"

"Do you need some water?"

Nausea sweeps a hot wave up my esophagus, and I rush to my feet. The world spins, seems too crooked to be real. Every step I take feels like I'm walking on the wall instead of the floor and I try to stay upright, but I don't know if I am. I have no idea how I make it to the bathroom, but I do. Gooey vomit gushes out of my mouth, but the discomfort isn't gone.

I gag and the action burns my throat.

What did I eat to make me feel this sick?

"It's okay, take your time." Darwin holds my hair away from my face.

He must be the reason I made it to the toilet on time.

My entire body convulses as something long and black slips out of my mouth in excruciating slowness. I feel every scrape before whatever I'm throwing up slips into the toilet bowl. The sense of urgency and sickness fades instantly, but my throat is raw and my mouth tastes awful. What's worse is staring at what I threw up.

My head swirls for a whole different reason.

Darwin rubs my back with his other hand. "Is that all of it?"

I cough and manage a quick nod. I want to say so much more—thank you for making sure I got here on time, thank you for holding my hair, thank you for not being grossed out—but can't manage a single word. It takes me a few attempts to get the hang of swallowing.

"What's going on?" Elvi steps into the bathroom and pauses, covering her nose with a hand. "Oh, my goddess, are you okay, honey?" She rushes to my side but stops when she glances into the toilet. "What in heaven's name is that?"

"What?" Darwin keeps rubbing my back and takes a peek. "Is that a feather?"

I don't bother with an answer because of course it is. I threw up a long, glossy black feather that stinks like rotten egg. The crow exploding into nothing on the street replays inside my mind.

"This is a bad omen," Elvi says.

I wonder what she means, but don't ask because I can't speak yet.

"Ma, what do you mean?" Darwin asks for me.

She looks divided, as if she wants to answer but isn't sure she should. Instead, she directs her attention back to me. "Clean up and come into the kitchen when you're ready. You need a chamomile tea to help calm your stomach."

I nod.

When she's gone, Darwin helps me up and sticks close as I rinse my mouth out with water. Nothing about this is right, but getting the feather out strangely feels cathartic because it was wedged inside, and I had to purge the awful thing for a reason.

"One sec," he says when we reach the door. He heads back to flush the toilet. "I can't believe you threw up a feather."

"Are you going to… tell Elvi about… what happened the other day?"

"Do you think I shouldn't?" It's a weird way to put it, but makes sense.

"I think you should do… what you think is… right." It hurts to speak, but this is a conversation we need to have.

Darwin stops in the corridor and forces me to face him by grabbing both of my forearms. He leans closer, making sure our eyes are level. "This isn't about wrong or right, and you know it. When I found you standing in my room facing the wall the other day and I told Ma, you flipped out. I don't want to make you feel like you can't trust me."

"I trust you, Dar."

"Then what do you want me to do?"

I suddenly think of something—or rather, someone who might be able to shed some light on this absurdity. "How about I speak to Dr. Larunda first? My next appointment is only a few days away."

"Didn't you say she scrambles your brain?"

"She does, but she's getting a bit better at not being so creepy."

Darwin smiles. "Yeah, says the girl who spewed out a bird feather." He thinks for a moment. "What bird was that from?"

"A crow."

"Not a magpie or raven, or even some generic breed—you know it's a crow for sure?"

I nod.

"So, you speak to your doctor about all this, and then what?"

Hopefully, I'll have read enough of Mum's notebook to have *some* answers. Or at least, that's what I hope happens. But it's not what I tell him. "We'll go to Elvi and tell her all about the strange stuff. She might be able to help us sort through it."

"She'll bring it up now."

"I know, but I'll just skirt around the real issue. It won't be hard to pretend I'm confused, since I have no idea what's going on. But I do know one thing for sure," I say. "I'm not getting any better."

Tears blur his face and I feel silly for wanting to cry. But how can I not? My mother's missing, the whispers are multiplying, I'm seeing an invisible friend, and I threw up a damn feather.

"Are you scared?"

"No."

"You don't have to lie because I'm definitely scared." I've never seen him so worried, and I've put him through a lot.

"Okay, maybe a little." I lean into him and press my cheek against his chest, concentrate on his heartbeat. "I don't want to lose myself to this."

"Can I ask you a question?" He rests his chin on top of my head and his voice reverberates in my ear.

"Sure."

"Do you think Mum's disappearance has anything to do with all of this?"

"What makes you say that?"

"I don't know." He sighs and it echoes against my face. "It seems to get more aggressive when she's not around. Do you remember that time she went on a business trip for a few days, and you almost knocked me out?"

My heart stammers. How could I forget?

"She's been missing for weeks now, and I feel like whatever's happening with you keeps getting worse in her absence."

"We have to find her," I say.

"Right, we'll do what the cops can't."

"Maybe," I say. Because I'm starting to think the reason why the police can't find her is because they're not looking in the right places. I don't know where that is exactly, but Darwin has shaken something loose inside my head. Mum was almost obsessive about watching me, and she had a good motive. Maybe her Dreaded Notebook will tell me exactly why.

"Kids!" Elvi calls from the kitchen.

"Come on, let's go and get some witchy brew into you," he says, stepping out of the hug.

"You haven't called Elvi's tea a witchy brew for a while."

"Suddenly, everything feels a little stranger."

I laugh and it tastes like someone died inside my mouth. "You go ahead. I need to use the toilet for a sec."

"Do you want me to wait out here?"

"No, I don't need you to wait. I can manage to go to the toilet on my own, thank you." Somehow, the admission sounds stupid when I clearly had plenty of trouble the last time I was actually in the bathroom.

"Okay, okay." He raises his hands in surrender and glances at my feet. "I'm glad we managed to save my socks."

"Oops, sorry," I say, checking out the red and green pair I'm wearing.

Darwin grins and walks away.

I wait for him to leave the corridor before wandering back into the bathroom to rinse my mouth out several times, with warm water this time. When I'm satisfied, I wipe my chin on the towel. The open toilet bowl catches my eye.

The black feather is still floating at the bottom even though Darwin flushed it away.

I flush a second time and rush out of the bathroom, hurry towards the kitchen.

As I step inside, Elvi's phone rings. She answers, listens for several seconds, and drops onto the closest chair. My heart thumps against my chest and I barely make it to a seat myself.

Darwin and I watch her until she disconnects.

"What's wrong?" he asks, breaking the silence.

Elvi wipes a hand over her face and dumps her mobile on the table. "They've found someone that fits…"

My heart skips a beat and I feel cold all over.

Darwin stands and goes over to pat her back. Between his mother and me, the poor guy's going to be so over erratic emotion one of these days.

"What did they find?" he asks, gently.

She looks at me when she answers. "The police found a woman matching Mena's description."

My heart sinks and I feel numb. "It can't be her," I say.

"They're hoping to ID her and will get back to me as soon as they know for sure." She swallows. "They'll probably need me to come in and verify—"

"I'm telling you, *it's not her.*" If I keep saying this, I'll make it come true.

"Of course, it's not." She stands and heads over to grab the two steaming mugs she's already prepared. "Now, let's get some tea into you, and maybe you can eat a little something as well."

I nod but doubt I can eat a single bite.

EIGHT
BEFORE

Three months ago, February 2018

"Chester, come over here!"

"Why?" I stopped halfway to the backdoor and cursed myself for not going around the front. I was trying to sneak into the house via the kitchen to avoid Mum, but she'd caught me in the act.

"I hardly see you anymore." She waved me over with the hand clutching her phone. The other was—of course—holding the Dreaded Notebook.

I groaned. The last thing I wanted was to chit-chat about the usual crap she loved to hound me about. *Not today.* Not when I'd failed my mathematics test, and barely got a passing grade for the English essay I was positive I'd aced.

"I've got homework to do," I lied.

"Oh, come on, this won't take long," she called. "I want to show you something funny."

I rolled my eyes and reluctantly made my way along the path until I reached her favorite chair, dragging my sneakered feet the whole way. "I wanted to at least change out of my uniform." The bulky checkered skirt and flimsy white shirt felt like a burden all day, so I couldn't wait to strip them off. Now, it was another convenient excuse to stall.

"It's okay," she said with a smile. "It's Friday, anyway."

Today was a nice day so she wasn't draped in her blanket like an old lady. Mum was wearing faded jeans with holes at the knees and a black tank top. She was barefoot with her dark hair swept up in a messy ponytail. Even without makeup she looked pretty. There was something youthful about her this afternoon.

"Having a good day, are you?" I teased, because there should be rules against mothers being this chipper while their daughters suffered through a miserable day at school.

"Yes, I am." Between the glint in her eyes, the coy glances she gave the shed she shared with Elvi and the cheeky grin on her face, I suddenly had a good idea why she might be in such a great mood.

"Oh! Ew." I make a face. "Will you two ever stop being so into each other?"

"Not if I can help it." She poked her tongue out in a very childish gesture. "How about you—found anyone special lately?"

I shook my head. "You make it sound like I find a new *special* someone every other week."

"Maybe I'm hoping you find at least one some week." She lowered her voice, as if making an offhand comment, but I still heard her. "You're too fussy."

"Maybe you're too nosy." I'd never heard other parents acting this way. Su always complained about hers constantly telling her not to get distracted by boys so she could concentrate on her studies. *My* mother encouraged me to find someone on a daily basis, even though I didn't want anyone, and had already told her plenty of times.

"So, no one tickles your fancy?" She cocked an eyebrow. "No one at all?"

"Nope."

She raised a hand to shade her eyes from the sun. "I'm getting worried about you."

"I thought you were going to show me something funny." This was the opposite of funny. It was yet another one of her interrogations and after such a crappy day, I wasn't in the mood. Not only were classes bad, but I hadn't been able to find Su or Darwin during lunch and had to eat alone.

"I was. *I am!* But I also want to have a chat about what's going on with you, that's all." She placed the trusty notebook on her lap and patted the coffee table. "Sit with me and tell me what's new. How's Year Twelve going?"

"Nothing's new and school still sucks," I said. "And before you ask, I'm taking my meds regularly and I'm not hearing any homicidal whispers. Plus, therapy's as good as can be expected—but you already know that." Being a smartass probably wasn't a good idea, or even the nicest way to respond to her interest, but I hated when she acted all innocent and coy. She already knew everything about me, and controlled most of what I did outside of school. Didn't I deserve a little privacy? The only thing she didn't know was the few times I'd snuck in a small fraction of my anxiety meds.

I eyed the journal sitting on her lap. For someone who was so secretive, I didn't understand her constant invasion into my life.

Mum was quiet for several seconds. When she spoke, her eyes were focused on the house. "I suppose I deserved that, but I'm not your enemy." She glanced in my direction but didn't look directly at me. "In spite of what you might think, I'm actually interested in your life beyond all of the complicated stuff. I want you to meet new people, to venture out into the world and experience new things. And I want you to find someone who makes your heart race."

"But why are you being so pushy about it?"

She sighed, finally meeting my gaze. "I only want you to be happy."

"I'm already happy," I said.

"Well, you're good at pretending to be."

I rolled my eyes at her comment because no one did passive aggressive like my mother. "Okay, let's follow your train of thought. You don't believe I'm happy, but think that by getting involved romantically with someone, I'll be happier?"

"I'm not saying you need someone in your life in order to feel complete," she said. "But falling in love is an experience most teenagers chase, or accidentally find themselves in. Yet, you don't seem to be interested."

"I'm not like most teenagers."

"You'd be surprised how much you really are like so many of your peers."

They don't have male whispers in their ears, or female voices counteracting in the most mysterious ways.

I bit the response back before it slipped out. No point in circling back *there*.

"What if I'm not interested in falling in love?" I'd never brought this up before, and often wondered if I should. But now seemed like a good time to ponder the subject.

Her dark eyes widened, and she sat up, placing the phone on top of the journal already on her lap. "What do you mean?"

"I know you think my mental illness will be cured if I fall in love, but it won't."

"That's not what I'm saying. Actually, I've never said that."

"You didn't have to." I dumped my backpack on the grass and sat on the edge of the coffee table, which was holding a single thick hardback. I licked my lips a few times, almost stopped myself from explaining further. "What if I *am* different to other kids in that regard? What if not wanting to get involved with anyone is a conscious decision?"

"Is it because no one catches your eye at school?"

"Mum, people catch my eye all the time. There are a lot of pretty people around, but I don't want to get involved with any of them. Not just at school, I mean anywhere." I'd checked guys out at the shops and when we went to the movies. I had no trouble pointing out a cute guy and even fantasized about holding hands with the one who'd served us a few times at the grocery store. But when I thought about actually doing anything more with him, I lost interest because it meant opening up, completely. And I couldn't do that, wasn't ready. How could I get to know someone when I hardly knew myself?

"You're still young and the world is a big place with endless possibilities," she said. "There's bound to be someone out there that'll catch your attention someday."

"But what if there isn't?"

"Don't think like that, Chester."

"That's not what I mean. You're not getting it." I sighed, tried again. "What if there'll never be a perfect partner for me because I don't want to involve anyone in my shit-show of a life?"

A shocked expression crossed her face, but she wiped it away almost instantly. "Why would you say that?"

I didn't think she was listening. Not really. And if she was, my message wasn't getting through.

"I think I know what's going on," she said.

"You do?"

She squeezed my hand. "And I don't want you mooning over a boy you shouldn't."

"Um... what do you mean?" Confusion clouded my thoughts.

"Do you have inappropriate feelings for Dar?"

I sputtered a laugh, but the expression on her face fizzled out my humor. "Oh! That's a serious question?"

She patted the back of my hand. "I know how easy it is to get confused—"

"That's so messed-up, Mum. Why would you even think such a thing?"

She seemed to consider her words. "You two share a very special bond."

I rolled my eyes. "I don't know what's gotten into you today, but you're *way* off."

"I'm sorry... I'm only trying to understand you."

"Uh, okay." I shook my head, trying to figure out why she'd even bother to broach such a screwed-up concept.

She examined my face for a long time. "I worry about you, that's all."

"That doesn't give you the right to fabricate something so... wrong."

"I know and I'm sorry."

I sighed. "I love Dar like a brother, consider him to be my best friend in the whole world, and will always want to be around him. You've probably seen me looking at him with wonder because I think he's amazing. I always have and always will. I consider myself lucky to have someone like him in my life. After all the things I've put him through and everything he's seen, he still wants to be around me. So yeah, I'm going to worship him a little."

She cringed at the word, and I didn't understand why.

"Okay, okay, I get it," she said. "I still want you to find—"

I leaned closer and took her hand. "And maybe I will, someday, but at this moment in time, I have no interest in falling in love. I need to get to know myself before I can let anyone else in. Does that make sense?"

Tears shimmered in her eyes. "More than you'll ever know."

"I'm sorry if this upsets you."

"No, that's not why I'm crying." She wiped the tears away from her face. "It's because you've finally confided in me."

I nodded because I didn't know what else to say.

"I'm so happy you finally told me something real." Mum leaned forward and threw her arms around me.

I hugged her back and closed my eyes. I couldn't remember the last time we'd exchanged a real moment. I would never forget this uncomfortable conversation and hoped it would be a pivotal point in our relationship.

When we pulled apart, she wiped the last of her tears and said, "Please, don't ever feel like you have to keep secrets from me."

I nodded but couldn't promise that I wouldn't.

"Are you ready to watch that video?"

"After all this build-up, it better be funny!"

A few minutes later we were both laughing at the cat and dog in the cutest, most hilarious clip I'd seen on YouTube for a while.

"I don't understand why we don't have a pet if you love animals so much," I said.

"It's better if I don't."

"What's so funny?" Elvi waltzed over with a huge beaming smile on her face. She never walked anywhere or entered a room; she swept in with her long flowing hippie dresses and messy bun. Her feet were as bare as Mum's. "I could hear you laughing all the way from the workroom."

"We're checking out a funny dog and cat video," I said.

"How are you, honey?" Elvi pressed a hand on my shoulder and tilted her head as she considered me. "Did you have a good day at school?"

"It was okay." No point in worrying them about how shitty the school year was shaping up was when my conversation with Mum had changed something between us.

She glanced at the house. "Is Darwin inside?"

I shook my head. "He said he had to do something." Something so mysterious he couldn't tell me what it was.

"So, are you going to show me this video, or what?" Elvi plopped herself onto Mum's lap. Luckily, she'd made a sturdy chair otherwise we'd all be laughing for a very different reason.

After watching the video several times for maximum hilarity, Darwin and Su arrived. Both were still wearing their school uniforms. I tried not to stare or wonder about their timing. As they approached with smiles on their faces talking about something I couldn't quite catch, I thought they might be standing a little too close.

"What's everyone doing, and why wasn't I invited to this party?" Darwin called.

"We're watching funny videos," I said, since I'd become the spokesperson for the event. "Where did you guys go after school?" I was fishing, trying to figure out if they'd gone somewhere together.

"I was coming home and found Su at the front door," he said, too quickly.

She didn't say anything, but I caught the flush on her cheeks.

Yeah, these two were definitely hiding something. But I didn't care right now because I was finally in a good mood and didn't want anything to ruin it.

"Is anyone hungry?" Elvi asked.

Darwin said yes and so did Mum, but Su shrugged.

"Why don't we order pizza?" I suggested.

"Sounds good to me," Elvi said.

I stood. "I'll go and order!"

"We can order from here," Darwin said, pulling out his phone.

"We have a menu in the house."

"It's also online," he said.

"It's okay." I was halfway across the yard when Mum caught up with me and wound an arm around my waist. "I can do it on my own, you know."

"I know you can," she said with a smile. "But I thought it might be fun if we order all the stuff Elv and Dar don't like."

"We'll make sure to add anchovies to at least one pizza," I said. "That'll get Su, too."

"And pineapple."

We laughed as we entered the house, and I'd never been happier in my mother's company.

Nine
NOW

Monday, 4pm
May 14, 2018

I drag my sleeves down, trying to hide the bruises around my wrists and forearms. I'm thankful for autumn because wearing baggy sweaters and hoodies helps me fit in, while hiding my injuries. I've been getting random bruises all over my body lately, and it's not from passing out or smacking into things.

Sometimes I think someone is trying to push their way out from beneath my skin.

These appeared this morning after I woke up from an awful and vivid nightmare. About a phantom monster chasing me inside an abandoned building—thanks to Darwin making me watch another one of those creepy videos last night. When the creature gripped my arms and I tried to pull away, I woke up. But the marks were still there.

I don't want to focus on what this means, but it certainly freaks me out almost as much as this office. It's freezing in here and I swear bugs, rats, or something else are crawling along the walls. There are too many places where the light fails to penetrate this vast room and it's making me twitchier than usual. Is that a breeze coming from the darkest wall on my left?

"Are you cold?" Dr. Larunda notices my compulsive actions instantly.

I've been trying hard to act casual, but of course she spots my neurotic sleeve pulling and squirmy manner. "No." It's a half-lie because it's not only her office. Lately, I can't seem to warm up. A deep-rooted chill continually pierces from the inside out. No amount of tea, coffee or soup helps.

"Are you sure?"

I nod, and the jerky action makes my neck creak. That's another thing, I wake up every morning feeling tired. Yesterday, my feet were filthy, and I can't explain why. All I know is that I woke up with a start because Nobody was barking at the bedpost, and I was standing on the bed facing the wall.

"I can raise the temperature on the thermostat if it will make you more comfortable."

"I'm fine." I haven't been *fine* for a long time. At least I took my two pills this morning. *Ah, that's another lie!* Darwin was on my case all weekend about taking my meds. Who could blame him after my paranoid episode in the street, and spewing up a feather a few days later? He watches me too closely, and his intensity is starting to remind me of Mum.

And this is very bad because I miss her more every day.

"Are you sleeping?"

"Yes."

"Having bad dreams?"

"Yeah."

A crease forms between her light eyebrows. "What are you dreaming about?"

"Getting chased."

"Who's chasing you?"

I shrug. "I never see him, but I know there's a monster breathing down my neck."

"Is the dream always the same?"

"Pretty much. I'm inside an abandoned building, or a farmhouse. Maybe it's a barn, I'm not sure. The walls are made of rotting wood and there's dirt and hay on the ground."

"How did it make you feel when you thought the authorities had found your mother?"

Her question takes me by surprise because it's got nothing to do with my answer or the dreams I mentioned. But she doesn't even bat and eyelid. Her face is perfectly contoured and I'm not sure if it's because she's good at putting on makeup, or if the lighting in her office makes her look this way.

The two corner lamps are on and standing guard, their illumination is making creepier shapes than usual. The shadows in here feel heavier than anywhere else, and they're continually shifting. I can see the movement from the corner of my eye and it's unsettling, but I don't say anything.

So much of my time during these sessions feels like a test.

"Chester, stop getting distracted and answer my question." She's got her legs crossed and is as unmoving as ever. "How did it make you feel when the police thought they might have found your mother?"

Her words make me cringe. I know she's not trying to be unkind. She truly wants to know how it made me feel. It's her job. "I knew it wasn't her."

And I had because, deep down inside, I somehow knew. Or hoped so much and so hard that holding onto the thought was a lot easier than accepting she might be the poor woman found dumped in bushland on the outskirts of our suburb. I hope that woman doesn't have a child waiting for her, because I can't even begin to imagine what being told your mother is dead feels like.

My mother used to annoy me, but now all I want is for her to come back.

"That's not what I asked," she says, considering me with those cool eyes. "How did it make you feel when, even for a split second, you actually imagined she was found?"

"I felt like I was getting dragged into darkness." This is an answer I hadn't expected or even thought about, and it chills me to the bone. A shiver creeps down my spine. Did one of the whispers answer for me?

"You're answering the wrong question," the doctor says. "You're voicing how you felt when you thought she might be dead, but that's not what I'm asking."

"What are you asking, then?"

Her eyes narrow slightly and her head tilts ever so slightly. "I want you to tell me how it felt when you thought they'd finally found her. That she would be coming home."

She likes to play hardball, this one. "I felt happy, because if the police found her... she would finally come back to me."

"You never once considered her to be dead?"

"No."

"And the thought of finding her alive makes you... *happy?*"

Coming from her, this revelation sounds like an unbelievable concept, but no matter how many mixed-up feelings or weird memories I have of Mum, I miss her. I love her and wish for her safe and unharmed return all the time.

"Yeah," I say, wondering where this is going.

"Then you have to start getting proactive about finding her."

"You think I should go to the police and demand—"

"No, that's not what I'm saying at all." A breath escapes her, so slowly the action seems drawn out. "They won't be able to give you any real answers."

I meet her composed gaze. "I don't understand."

"Let's not play games, Chester." Her eyes are shiny and so focused, all I want to do is look away, but I can't. "I know you're reading her grimoire."

"I'm reading her what?" My pulse quickens. I'm familiar with that term because Mum mentioned it in her notes, but how can *she* possibly know that?

"You're reading your mother's grimoire. Her journal, diary, notes—whatever you want to call it."

"What makes you think I'm reading her *grimoire?*" I can't say Dreaded Notebook because she might read too much into that.

"Are you saying you're not?"

I sigh. "I am, but *how* could you know?"

"I know a lot of things."

"So, you *are* psychic?"

She shakes her head, and a glint of a smile curves her mouth. "I've already told you many times, I don't need to be psychic to read you. You're like an open book to me."

"Why bother asking questions, then? Why not just read me like you say you can?"

"I can't help if you don't understand what's going on," she says. "Besides, where would the fun be in that?"

I cross my arms and sit back in the chair, wishing it would swallow me.

Silence fills the room for several minutes. Long enough to make my skin itch and for the swirling on the ceiling to make me nervous.

"A grimoire is a very personal journal, where one records thoughts and findings, experiments and discoveries." Dr. Larunda finally breaks the silence and her left eye twitches. "Everyone who partakes on any level of demonology keeps one."

I shake my head and want to laugh, but none of this is funny. "My mother doesn't know anything about demonology." Who the hell cares about demonology outside of movies and books? I've read enough paranormal and horror novels to know exactly what she's talking about. The word is self-explanatory.

"I don't think you know anything about Philomena."

It's like a slap in the face. That day in the kitchen, last year, when I had a fight with Mum and left her hanging on the conversation she wanted to finish, she said something along those lines. But I brushed her off because she made me feel bad about my attitude. Not because she hid a life full of supernatural experiences.

I stop as soon as the thought slides through my head.

Mum never spoke about her past and her diary makes her sound like a completely different person, someone I don't know. Not to mention those four elements she captured inside a book. I know I felt the dirt, air, fire, and water. If I crack open those pages again, I'm sure they'll still be trapped within.

I glare at my therapist, and she doesn't break eye contact, but the slight twitch is still there. She's never shown this much emotion before.

"And you know my mother?"

She shrugs one bony shoulder. "I only know what she's shared with me, but I've heard about her before. Her name pops up in certain… circles. She's well known for her work. Anyone able to outsmart the powerful usually is."

"You're talking about her interior design business, right?"

Dr. Larunda shakes her head and not a single strand of hair slips free. "I'm familiar with her *other* work."

"You've seen the furniture she designs?" This is like pulling teeth.

"No." One of her high heels swings ever so slightly. "How much of her grimoire have you read?"

"I just started."

"Even from the beginning, her notes should seem a little odd, no?"

She's fishing, I can tell. Although Mum has obviously concealed strange things, I find a ferocious need to protect her honor. "Maybe."

A smile quirks the corners of her thin lips, almost like someone else is raising them for her. There's nothing natural about this woman. "Don't ever share her secrets. A practitioner's grimoire is very personal. The fact *you're* reading the book might be considered a violation. If so many of the contents weren't directly related to you, maybe I would be tempted to inform the correct channels." She pauses, takes a breath. "But I won't because whatever you find will probably benefit your condition."

My heart thumps too fast and loud. "I know Mum's still alive."

"How?" Her eyes are practically glowing.

Shadows scurry down the corners of the room and I'm sure there's a face somewhere in all that murky darkness.

"I just do," I say. "And I agree, the cops aren't going to find her."

"Why?"

"They're not looking in the right places."

Dr. Larunda shifts in her seat, something she's never done before. Then shocks me by pressing both bony elbows against her knees to lean forward. "You're a clever child, and it's no wonder you're vastly pursued." She looks me in the eye, so intensely I think she might be reading my mind before she sits back again. But this time, when she does, I see a bald almost translucent creature glowing beside her. It has a cerulean body and cups a hand over its mouth while whispering into her ear.

When I blink, it's gone.

Is my mind playing tricks on me or is *something* attached to my therapist? My skin starts to itch and uncertainty races through me in a torrent of fear.

"I..." I don't understand what's going on.

"I think you do," she says with a smile. Although most people's faces lighten up when they smile, hers doesn't. She seems alien, like an insect hiding beneath human skin. "The dreams you're having aren't nightmares, they're really happening." Her eyes drop to the sleeves I'm still tugging down. "You're being pursued from the inside."

"No, they're bad dreams." The dirty feet, barking puppy, exhaustion and bruises all point to so much more—something too freaky to consider. Now that she's thrown the word *demonology* out there, I guess she thinks she can suggest anything. No matter how outrageous it sounds.

"The abandoned building is your mind, and he's trying to shut you in." She keeps my stare. "If he succeeds, he'll roam free, and you'll finally be his to control."

"Who is he?" My pulse speeds up because she has to be talking about the voice.

"If you refuse to listen to what I'm trying to tell you and insist on asking irrelevant questions, you're going to face a life of soul imprisonment."

I suddenly want to leave because I feel like a pinned butterfly everyone is trying to keep in place. "Are you going to have me committed?"

"Forget about human constructs and laws." She shakes her head, and her eyes are shimmering. "I'm trying to keep you from being locked away inside your own mind. None of us wants that, especially not your mother. She's devoted her life to making sure that doesn't happen."

My head is already throbbing.

"I think it's time you stop taking the pills." Her tone is stern and sharp.

"What?"

"The two pills you sometimes remember to take, and other times don't, you need to stop taking them completely." She tilts her head. "It's time to face your demons."

I shake my head. "But all I've ever heard my mother and Elvi say is that I *have* to take them no matter what. You've said the same thing."

"It was essential before, but now it's time for you to stop."

"But when I do, bad things happen."

"What kinds of bad things?"

I lick my lips. Now's the time to bring up everything I told Darwin I'd discuss with my doctor before letting Elvi in. "The other day, I didn't have enough time to take them and as I was walking down the street, I spotted a horned demon on top of a building who disappeared in a cloud of smoke."

"Did you recognize them?"

"No," I lie.

"Remember what I said before, I can read you like a book and know when you're lying."

I sigh, turn my attention to the window. "Okay, I did recognize her."

"How?"

"She was my invisible friend when I was little," I answer. "But I hadn't seen her in ages, and she spooked the hell out of me."

"Did she try to hurt you?"

"No, but then I saw a crow dissolve into ash and fall from the sky," I say. "And I feel like someone's constantly standing behind me. Plus, I threw up a black feather. And that day I *did* take my meds." I lick my lips. "His voice seems to sneak through no matter what."

"I see." Her fingers tightened in her lap. "I believe it's *definitely* time for you to stop taking these pills because the salt is no longer strong enough to protect you."

"The salt, what salt?"

"The pills are salt tablets."

"No, that's not true." I struggle to grasp the right words. "They're my medication—"

"Chester, since the moment we met, have I lied to you or betrayed your trust?"

"No."

"Then why are you questioning what I'm telling you?"

"Because it sounds insane." I sit forward and tap my foot against the plush carpet. "You're talking about demonology and salt and grimoires, as if it's the most normal thing in the world, but I've never even heard those words outside of fiction." I'm panting now, can feel myself getting so worked up I'm almost out of breath. "And you're telling me my mother is at the center of all of this. Of course, I'm going to be a bit skeptical."

I blink and Dr. Larunda is suddenly crouching in front of me. She takes my hands in hers, and a soothing sensation washes away the prickly vibrations.

"I usually keep you calm with my voice, but you're too worked up today." Her eyes are huge orbs of blue spinning stars and I feel a bit woozy. "I understand how strange this all sounds, unbelievable even. But I've never lied to you and refuse to start now. You need to stop taking salt pills, and you need to learn everything you can from Mena's grimoire. It's time to end this torture." She squeezes my fingers. "You deserve to be free from all of this."

"But I told you, bad things happen when I stop taking my meds." I lick my lips, repeating the obvious like a mantra. I'm no longer nervous or worried, only confused. "The voice gets sharper and takes over. And now, I'm dealing with a second one and am seeing weird stuff everywhere."

"Let me put it this way, what you're seeing is normal." Her hands are soft and warm. I was wrong about nothing being able to clear away the cold within.

"In what world is any of this *normal?*" I'm shocked and sit forward, nearly fall off the damn seat and into her lap.

"Chester, haven't you figured this out already? What you're suffering from isn't mental illness," she whispers. "The voice you hear and what he wants, should have clued you in enough by now. Since Mena's gone missing, it's become very obvious. This is all part of the cycle. The next phase, if you will."

"I don't understand what you mean."

"The voice you've heard for most of your life is a harmful one. All he wants is to take over and destroy you, and that's why you're having dreams about being chased. If he's able to manifest into your dreams, he's getting a tighter grip than I realized. It was vital for us to keep quiet for as long as we could, and the salt tablets plus the sacrifices she made were enough." She sighs. "Or at least, for as long as it took for the second voice to finally get through and gain your attention."

"You're wrong." I shake my head, and at least the throbbing pain is gone too. "The second voice belongs to Shiny Pictures and didn't appear out of nowhere. She's come in and out of my life, and—"

"I know she has, but she wasn't strong enough to get through entirely. And now that she has, it means you're finally strong enough to face the challenge."

"What challenge?" I glance at our joined hands and notice they're glowing. No, we're not glowing. Delicate blue hands are engulfing ours with their brilliance. We're not alone, there are three of us in this office.

"Do you want to find Mena?" she asks, which has nothing to do with my question.

"Of course." Mum's written words slip into my mind—*Now's the time to fight, my brave girl*—that's what she wrote in the Dreaded Notebook. Strong, brave, challenges... these aren't tasks I'm ready for.

"Then you have to stop taking the pills."

"But the voice—"

"Will only take over if you let him," she says.

"But he has before, and I've done..." Darwin cowering at my feet, and countless of shattered objects around the house are only a few reminders.

"You're stronger than you think. And although there'll be times when the voice may overpower your mind and you'll feel helpless, and don't understand how you got wherever you end up, there are many other times when you can withstand the influence. You have to put up a fight." She pauses and suddenly seems out of breath. "You can win this battle. It's the only way to get her back."

Now's the time to fight, my brave girl.

When I read those words, I made a conscious decision to fight against the voice. And now Dr. Larunda is asking me to do the same.

"I want to be strong, but I don't think I can." I fought these inner demons all my life and although I resented Mum for constantly bugging me, I also depended on her to keep me sane. How can I believe in anything without her pushing me?

The chime goes off.

She releases my hands and the cold rushes back into my fingers. Dr. Larunda is already sitting on her chair, gaze stuck on me, as if she hasn't moved at all.

"You think she's still alive too, don't you?"

She nods. "I know she is."

"Are you sure about the pills?"

"I'm positive."

"What about the anxiety meds?"

"If they help, keep dosing but don't overdo it. We need you to be as sharp as a tack." She pauses, stares into the space between us. "Philomena was right about most of the pills other doctors are so eager to prescribe. Those medications are helpful for others, but not you. They would have altered your brain chemicals and made you more vulnerable to possession."

"Are we now talking about the voice like it's not a figment of my imagination?"

"It never was, Chester," she whispers. "It never was."

"*What* is he?"

"I can't give you that answer, because it's something *you* need to work out for yourself." She sighs. "But you must continue to read the grimoire until you get the answers you've always wanted. And the instructions to help you get through this trying time."

"Okay." What else could I say? Everything about this woman always struck me as odd, so this conversation shouldn't shock me. It should validate that even though I often think of myself as crazy, I'm really not.

"I'm sorry our time is up, but we'll talk again next week." Her eyes are losing their luster, almost seems like all the color is leaching out. "And if you ever need to contact me outside of business hours, my assistant will give you my personal number."

I nod and stand, head for the door even though I feel like the dark ceiling above my head is full of sentient shadows with razor-sharp teeth waiting to tear into my flesh.

She calls my name and I look over my shoulder. The translucent being is there again, the top of its body disappears into the nook and crannies of the doctor's left side. It's practically a humanoid torso with a tail at the end, one that disperses droplets of glowing ink onto the carpet.

"Did you get the familiar?"

"The what?"

She listens to the whispers for a second. "The guardian... did you get the dog?"

"Nobody? Yeah, I got her out of the garbage bin," I say. "That was another shock to add to the collection—the half-dead puppy who miraculously came to life when I pulled her out."

She frowns. "You called her Nobody?"

"We haven't come up with a name yet."

"You better come up with one soon. If she doesn't have a proper name, she won't be able to protect you."

Elvi warned me about this, yet I still can't think of a perfect name.

"Stop taking the pills, keep reading the grimoire and for fuck's sake," she snaps loud enough to make me finch. "Give your dog a name."

I close the office door and think I hear the doctor say, "Come to me," followed by a multitude of scampering feet and a moan. I'm tempted to take a peek, but her assistant is calling out to me, trying to get my attention.

"Miss Chester, this is the doctor's emergency number." As the receptionist makes his way around the counter, he suddenly becomes a lion riding a bear. But is back to being a stout bearded man between blinks.

I take the slip of paper, trying not stare at the transforming man. "Thanks."

"You take care now," he says with a bearded smile.

"Yeah," I say, giving the assistant a wave. "You, too."

"Chess, are you ready?"

I almost jump because I'd forgotten Darwin drove me to my appointment. He insisted, wanted to know what the doctor had to say about my weird experiences, and will probably grill me all the way home.

"Is everything okay?" Darwin whispers when he sidles up beside me.

"Yeah," I say.

But as we leave the office and wait for the elevator, I have to admit to myself that I'm really *not* okay. I'm not ready to deal with everything I heard and saw in Dr. Larunda's office, or to find out the truth about my mother. I also don't know what name to give our dog, and I sure as hell am not ready to be *strong* or *brave* against a voice that's kicked my ass so many times already.

Ten
Before
Two months ago, March 2018

As soon as I stepped through the sliding door, the smell of salt tickled my nose and I almost sneezed. I'd been taking these pills long enough to know what it meant whenever I got home, and the kitchen smelled like salt water. It reminded me of the beach, which we used to visit a lot when Darwin and I were kids but hardly went anymore.

"Hey Mum, what're you doing?" I swung my backpack onto one of the chairs and headed for the counter.

Her hand was cupped over an open plastic bottle, and she was filling it with white pills. "You're home late," she said with a smile.

"No, I'm not."

"Darwin got home a while ago." She glanced at the stove clock. "And Su was with him."

"Really?" I didn't know why he'd left school early but did know they'd both ditched last period without telling me. I concentrated on her because thinking about my two closest friends keeping secrets made me sad and twitchy. "So, what are you doing with the pills?"

"I picked up a new prescription this morning," she said. "You know I like to make sure they're all in there."

I nodded but noticed the white specks all over the countertop and the load of dishes in the sink. Until now, I'd thought we might have finally closed the gulf between us, but she was still acting secretive and clearly wasn't telling the truth. I knew she was lying because she didn't pick up any prescriptions, she made these pills. I wasn't sure why she felt the need to lie about something so obvious.

Since our very honest conversation in the backyard last month, we'd been getting along well.

"Are you okay?" A worry crease formed between her eyes.

"Yeah, I'm cool." But I wasn't exactly cool. I'd started having strange dreams about getting stuck in a darkroom and talking to someone I couldn't see. I knew it was a *she* and that she was always there watching me, but after I woke up our conversations faded. No matter how hard I tried, I couldn't remember what she'd said. There was something familiar about her too. Almost as if I'd known her for a long time and we'd already had these conversations, but I didn't know why.

"Are you sure? You look distracted."

"I'm always distracted."

Her gaze fell on my hand. "Are you feeling itchy again?"

"No, but every time you ask, I start feeling like insects are crawling all over my skin," I said. "So maybe don't ask me so much."

"Getting any headaches?"

I shrugged. "When I get my period, or if I've got too much homework." Also, if I didn't get enough sleep because I kept waking up from nightmares and didn't want to risk going back to sleep. That kind of thing happened a few times, but worse than that was the time I'd woken up and found myself sleeping on the ceiling. That happened a few years ago too and I had to get Darwin to help me get down. I never did figure out why or how something so freaky happened, but I didn't tell Mum because she'd flip out.

"Are you feeling colder than usual?"

"It still feels like summer, so I'm not feeling cold at all." But even that was a bit of a lie because I knew exactly what she meant. Sometimes I got a chill deep inside and no matter how many layers I put on, or how many hot beverages I consumed, I couldn't shake it. The feeling would eventually go away on its own. Usually.

"Good." Her eyes scanned my face and bare forearms. "You're not hearing any whispers trying to convince you to do things, right?"

"None whatsoever," I said with a nod. *At least that's true.* "Are you done with the interrogation, or do you want to know more?"

A grin curved her lips as she wiped the bench clean.

"So, were they all there?" It was time to ask *her* some questions.

"Were *what* all there?" She was busy searching for something under the kitchen sink.

"Were all the pills there?"

"Yes, of course." When she stood, she was holding a familiar wooden box in her hands. "I like to make sure you don't miss taking a single pill."

"How could I forget with you breathing down my neck?" I tried to sound as annoyed as possible, but if taking these stupid pills helped keep me grounded, I would. Or *should,* until I started feeling restless or simply forgot all about them.

"Take a seat, I'm going to teach you how to make your own spirit bag." She placed the box on the counter and lifted the lid.

"But I want to go and see what Dar's doing."

"Darwin will be there when we're done." Her hands were moving fast, grabbing one piece after another, and laying everything out between us. "It's time you learn some of these skills for yourself."

I glanced at the spirit bag I was wearing under my school shirt. "But you make them for me, why do I have to learn?"

She sighed, dropping a tangle of yarn. "I'm not going to be around forever, you know? Besides, it'll be good for you to learn how to start making something this cool. They make great presents and I know Su is always eyeing yours."

I nodded because Su was oddly fascinated with a lot of our family rituals. She loved the slight twang of salt in the air and always commented about the incense we used. Mostly, I didn't know how to answer her questions and avoided talking about the weird stuff as much as I could, but she never stopped asking.

Until Su started asking questions and commenting when she'd first come over years ago, I hadn't thought any of our customs—blessing every room in spring, sweeping the floors at the end of the week to clear away negative energy, placing crystals on windowsills, using salt to purify—were abnormal. I thought everyone's parents had these kinds of rituals in place to keep harmony in their house and ensure psychic levels were kept on the positive side of the scale. But apparently, they didn't. Su called it New Age mumbo-jumbo, but Darwin and I had lived with these customs all our lives, so I didn't think it odd or even interesting.

Mostly, I let Mum and Elvi do their thing.

She pulled out several scraps of colorful fabric and laid them out in front of me. I liked that she used her fancy sawtooth-bladed scissors to cut the squares.

"The first thing you need to do is choose your fabric and ribbon."

I considered the pieces and grabbed a black square with a silver horseshoe print and yellow ribbon.

"Nice choices," she said. "Horseshoes are lucky charms and yellow makes everything brighter."

"Why do you always suggest I pick something with horses?" It was worth asking again, to see if she bothered answering this time. I wasn't Sagittarius and wasn't born in the year of the horse.

Mum paused for a moment and smiled. "The horse is your sign."

"But it's not."

"I'm not talking about astrology," she said with a sigh. "I'm talking about custodian signs."

"What are those?"

"The only ones that matter."

I didn't bother with a follow up question because she wouldn't answer, and even if she did, the response would be so vague I still wouldn't get it. Instead, I pointed at my choices. "What's next?"

She dug her hand into a plastic container, grabbed a handful of crystals and held them out. "These are your filling." She slipped the combination of small rocks and crystals into my palm. I recognized the rose quartz and the black onyx but didn't know the pretty blue one. "What's this?"

"The Lapis Lazuli relieves stress, also encourages peace and harmony," she said. "It's good for your wellbeing."

I nodded because this sounded good to me. She didn't usually let me pick my own crystals, always chose those for me. She also picked the herbs, which she added to the combination. I could smell the lavender mixed in with all the other ingredients.

"Now that you have all of your ingredients, let your energy flow through them."

I pressed the mixture together in the palm of my hand and closed my eyes. I never felt anything flow in or out, but put on an act for her benefit. I opened my eyes and carefully let the contents slip from my hand. I made sure the herbs made a nice nest for the crystals.

She nodded approvingly. "Now close it up."

I folded the corners and pinched the fabric together, made a little baggie, before twisting the top to make sure nothing slipped out. Mum helped me wrap the length of yellow ribbon around enough times to make it tight and I tied a knot, followed by another. The length of ribbon was still long, and I knotted the ends together to finish off the necklace.

When I offered it to her so she could bless the bundle, she shook her head.

"Pick it up and repeat these words after me."

This was the first time I was actually doing this myself. She usually cupped the completed spirit bag and whispered the fancy words to herself.

"Are you ready?"

I cupped the fabric baggie the same way I'd seen her do a hundred times. "Yep."

"These crystals and herbs are blended with care," she said.

I repeated the words.

"When I wear this token of protection, nothing dark will ever take me."

Saying *those* words made my skin crawl and I could have sworn something shifted beneath my skin. A strange sensation rippled inside my very core.

"Now you can put it on."

"What about the old one?" I asked, hesitating.

"I'll take care of it."

I handed her the limp baggie, which didn't smell like anything. Mum always told me *this* was when the necklace needed to be replaced, so I wasn't sure if she'd noticed or if she'd decided to do this at the spur of the moment. Either way, I popped the new one over my head and couldn't stop feeling a sense of accomplishment. The scent of lavender filled my nostrils and made me feel safe.

"Why is it so important to have these protections renewed?" I asked, not sure whether she would answer or not. My mother was a strange creature sometimes. She wanted to know how I was feeling 24-7 but whenever I asked her questions, she rarely answered. And eager as she seemed to teach me stuff, it was usually a distraction. So, what was she trying to distract me from now?

She stared at the spirit bag I'd given her. "Negative energy can destroy lives and tunnel into our heads. I want to make sure you're surrounded by safety and comfort. It'll help with your condition." She met my gaze. "Haven't you noticed that when everything is renewed, the whispers quieten for longer and the anxiety fades for a while?"

I nodded.

"Are you still practicing the mind exercises I taught you?"

"Sometimes," I answered.

"Good, keep practicing. It's like anything—muscle memory is a powerful thing. If you keep doing the exercises, it'll pay off in the long run."

"Okay."

"Anyway, I've held you up long enough. Why don't you go and get changed and take it easy for a while before getting stuck into your homework?"

"Sounds good," I said. "And Mum, thanks for this."

"Now that you know how to make one yourself, you can lead the way next time." She met my eyes and they shone with a sad gleam. "I'll supervise a few times, but after that you're on your own. Maybe you can teach Dar, too."

"Yeah, right." He was worse than me and would probably hound her with a thousand questions and theories... which might be why she wanted me to show him. "Hey! You don't want to teach him yourself, do you?"

"That boy is impossible to tutor." She patted my hand and grinned. "I think he'll listen to you, though."

"You have too much faith in me," I said. "I can't control him."

"Oh, no one controls that boy, he's a wild spirit." Her smile widened. "You both share that quality. You're different in so many ways, yet very alike."

"Think I'll leave now," I said with a laugh. After her bizarre accusation about my feelings towards Darwin, I didn't want to get into this.

I wandered into the gloomy corridor and a chill wound its way around my body.

Whether I regularly took my meds or not, the darkest corners around the house always played tricks on me. I often spotted swirls out of the corner of my eye and when I turned, there would be nothing there. I quickened my step and headed straight for Darwin's room.

That he'd left school without me again was starting to annoy me. I enjoyed walking home with him and Su, but she was also mysteriously MIA lately. I was starting to suspect they were avoiding me on purpose. But why?

I was about to barge in but stopped. The door was mostly closed, but he clearly wasn't alone. I stepped closer, carefully pushed the door wide enough to peek inside. It took my eyes several seconds to figure out what was going on.

Darwin was lying on top of Su, and they were kissing. She looked comfortable with him on top of her. They kissed like it was natural... like they'd done if before. A feeling of betrayal flooded through me, making my body feel hot and stuffy.

Her fingers were lost in his thick hair. One of his arms kept him propped up, while the other hand was under her shirt.

"Is this okay?" he asked.

Su kissed him. "Yes, it's definitely okay."

They smiled at each other and something inside me cracked. For some reason, I couldn't move. I wasn't entirely interested in what they were doing but was captivated by the way they were doing it. They seemed to fit together perfectly. Su had her legs spread on either side of his slim waist and even though there was a significant height difference, he fit snuggly between them.

Their kissing quickened, and their breaths grew erratic.

The longer I stood watching, the farther away I felt. Almost as if an invisible hand was physically pushing me away, into a never-ending corridor. I felt like I didn't belong with these two people I cared so much about. They now shared a special bond. One I could never compete with. Strange that I'd never considered Darwin would fall in love or in lust with someone one day, let alone my friend.

I'm supposed to be the one who keeps us together.

Now I would become the outsider, the third wheel.

The crack inside me grew because I was losing them.

I blinked, and they were so far away. I wasn't jealous about what they were doing, I was upset because neither had trusted me enough to tell me they were together.

"They didn't tell you because they like to keep secrets from you."

I tried to raise my leg but remained frozen to the spot.

My hands went to the spirit bag around my neck as I waited for more awful words to tumble into my brain, but none came. Had the voice spoken at all, or were those my own muddled thoughts? Sometimes it was hard to tell.

I wanted to walk away from this situation and go to my room to mope, but I still couldn't move. I took a few shallow breaths and repeated the chant I'd said over my spirit bag.

Wish I'd never seen this.

I was trying to regain some level of control and not call any attention to myself, but the odds of that happening seemed pretty slim when I was standing at his door like a creeper.

Luckily, the couple on the bed were too wrapped up in each other to notice. Su was trying to pull Darwin's T-shirt over his head, and he was nibbling on her jaw while she giggled.

I closed my eyes and focused on breathing, not on their intimacy. By the time I opened my eyes, I was inside my bedroom facing the wall and wondering how I got there.

Mum's (Dreaded) Notebook

December 23, 1999

Boiled holy water

Table salt

A sprinkle of rock salt

Two drops of lavender

Newborn tears

Elderly tears of happiness

Tears of sadness from the mourning

Blend all ingredients together into a glue-like substance and shape each individual pill.

Leave in the sun for 12 hours and store in plastic containers.

*

These are the forbidden ingredients and instructions for making fortified salt pills with the strongest psychic protective qualities. I stole the recipe from Him while He was busy ordering someone around and left me alone in his office. He has all sorts of spells and recipes for a variety of things, and I intend to take several with me before I leave.

He's stupid to trust me, but I haven't given him any reason not to. Not yet.

The salt pills are a fiddly thing to make but have very strong magical properties. By taking one or two each day, the negative psychic energy of the demonic can be kept at bay. And that's especially important for someone like me, someone who's invoked the demonic on several occasions and doesn't want to risk possession. Not to mention if a foe wanted to send a demonic entity my way, by taking these pills I could combat them. As long as the intake is regular, because forgetting a single dose can only result in cracks in our psyche. Slippery ways for the demonic to worm their way in, because that's something they're very good at.

The echelon minion I invoked came very close to getting inside my head, and they're an annoying gluey thing to dispel. These types don't care about taking over your mind or spirit, they'll simply toy with your internal organs until something bursts. This is why He revealed this option to me. Told me to take two pills before trying to invoke anything and of course, He was right. The next time I tried, the minions and imps got nowhere near me.

Hold on, I'm done glorifying Him… I despise him. I wish him all the ill will in the world. And I refuse to refer to him like he's some sort of false god.

I can't believe it's come to this. But if we're going to survive, we have to leave this place and never look back. Plus, we'll need to arm ourselves with an arsenal strong enough to keep us hidden and help us find a way to provide financially for ourselves—instant money and skills. That's what we need.

We have to protect ourselves from what will inevitably happen next.

I can't believe I trusted him, gave my total devotion to his cause because everything he told us was a lie. I feel like such a fool, an idiot. But how can I blame myself when he was so charming and convincing? Yeah, screw using uppercase for a sham of a man. He's someone who preys on people looking for something arcane to believe in, for a cause worthy enough of total immersion. Well, he conned me. I fell for his looks and words, gave him everything I had until I couldn't imagine a single moment without having his influence in my life.

That's all gone now. The love I thought I felt for him was nothing compared to how I feel about *her*. She's the real love of my life and now that we might find ourselves in the same predicament, we need to get as far away from here as we can. It's not safe for us, or for…

But first, we need to be sure. Neither of us is going to tell him what we suspect and will have to make sure we hide the more obvious effects as best as we can. At least we have each other and that's something. We can cover for one another and make sure he doesn't find out what's really going on or figure out our plans. If he does, he'll get rid of us and start all over again with new girls. He's told me this himself. As much as he keeps secrets from everyone, his strongest asset is his image and the fear he commands. All his disciples need to believe in *Him* wholly. They can never doubt a word *He* speaks. Or none of the ritualistic ceremonies will work. And he loves to exploit everyone as much as he can—can command most of us at will.

The upcoming ceremony is vital. This was going to put him at the top of the demonology trade he's coveted for so long. Yet, without our full cooperation, he'll have nothing. We're going to destroy him—his reputation, ambition, a lifetime worth of work.

I want to be responsible for destroying everything he thinks he has.

The ceremony was supposed to show everyone that although we weren't legally married, we're still his two child brides and will willingly receive his seed. He said we would be taken care of, would be his virgin wives until the night he laid us out side by side and filled one of us with a child. And I believed him, I believed in everything. Even when he started sneaking into our beds and told us a bath would restore our virginal status. I trusted his word. I actually felt honored to be one of his two chosen mates and welcomed him every time he wanted to take me.

And because of his lies, we're both waiting for the results.

We weren't supposed to be with child until after the ceremony. We were to be taken by *Him* for the first time in front of witnesses, under the crescent moon, and by the next full moon one of us was supposed to have his child growing inside. The one who is positive is supposed to kill the one who isn't. The thing is, I also checked his texts and found a detail he forgot to mention: the pregnant woman is merely a vessel to deliver the baby. Once she does, he himself will kill her too.

His virtuous plans include killing both of us.

I won't let him. Not now that I suspect we're both pregnant.

His insatiable appetite for slipping into our beds has shattered all my belief in him. But I can't be angry about everything he's introduced me to. Because of him, I've found true and honest love. Because of his need to play sexual games and force us to do things in the bedroom I never would've imagined doing with another girl, I realized what she meant to me.

We're in love, but he doesn't know that either.

As soon as we get the blood test results, we're leaving. I might not believe in his teachings anymore, but I have faith in our joined ability to learn. I'm sure we can make it out of here together, alive and with enough knowledge to do what he will never truly allow us to do—raise the demons we desire.

We can do this. *I can do this.*

After he slapped her because she turned him away one night, I promised myself I would do whatever it takes to ruin him. Even as he left her alone, crying and cradling her face because unlike me, she can't bear to keep the charade any longer, and he lay on top of me instead—I promised I would destroy everything he's created with the blood and sacrifice of others.

Death isn't enough for him. Destroying everything he's built, that's what's going to ruin him.

We're walking away from his blinding influence. We're leaving behind his self-proclaimed demonic religion. We're taking the one thing he wanted the most—an offering.

Eleven
NOW

Thursday, 3am
May 17, 2018

There's a dog barking somewhere. In the distance, I think.

I can't tell because my ears are clogged and my eyes are so focused on the splintered and rotting wall in front of me, that my vision blurs. A sudden chill sweeps up around me, ruffling the white nightdress I'm wearing so that it tickles the back of my calves. This is an outfit I would never choose for myself, but nightmares have a way of warping reality until it's unrecognizable.

I don't remember how I got here. I don't know where *here* is. But I was running away from someone when this wall appeared in front of me. Now there's nowhere else to go. My bare feet are stuck to the dirty floor. I can see tiles hiding under the dirt and hay, puddles of water lapping at my heels and toes. But that's not why I'm stuck.

Maybe Dr. Larunda was right, and I'm trapped in this dream for a reason. Or I'm losing my mind and can't tell the difference between a nightmare and reality.

After throwing up a feather, I can't trust anything. And seeing a horned creature in the middle of a crowded street isn't normal either.

But when was I ever normal? What is normal, anyway? My normal has always been a pendulum swinging between fragile as a porcelain cup and as invincible as an anvil. Some days I feel like my head is going to tear me apart from the inside out. Other days I feel like I can defeat anything and anyone without a second thought.

Mostly I feel the former, but who's keeping count?

I suddenly miss Mum so much it manifests as a pain in my sternum. Thinking about her might help me stay focused.

"Mum... are you here?" My voice sounds brittle.

She doesn't answer.

No one answers.

The pain in my chest intensifies, feels like a block of ice is wedged inside.

My shadow stretches. My arms are pinned to my sides, but she's got her hands up in the air as if she's playing some childish game or reaching for something.

"Stop it," I say.

I'm sure I hear the words out loud but can't be sure anymore. So much of my life seems to play out inside my head that I'm not sure what's really happening in front of me and what's not. But my therapist said this is real—all of it.

The thought makes my stomach twist.

My shadow's arms are longer than they should be as they reach up and come back down holding something small. That's when I realize this isn't my shadow because she's standing behind me, but we're not connected.

"What're you doing?" I ask.

Shadow doesn't answer and I almost jump out of my skin when her ebony hands push out of the wall, and she shakes whatever she's holding in front of me.

"You must stop taking the pills," she whispers in my ear.

"Mum?" Shadows don't speak, but this definitely sounds like her.

"Don't be frightened, he's not here at the moment."

The back of my hair ruffles because someone is definitely standing too close, causing my fingertips to flicker. But I can't move, I'm too freaked out.

"I didn't take them this morning." I still can't tell if I'm speaking out loud or not, but I'm sure she can hear me.

The shadow is shaking whatever she's holding out between us and when I focus hard enough, I'm surprised to see there's a dirty toilet here. Although she's clearly pouring something into the bowl, I can't see what it is.

The constant barking gets louder, accompanied by a low growl.

"Mum, is that you?"

The wooden slat walls bleed red and at first, I don't know what's happening. Not until I realize it's not actual blood, but the crimson hue of a familiar darkroom. My eyes adjust enough to spot the trays and photos everywhere. But these aren't pictures, they're my memories. There's a photo of Darwin and me sitting at the beach on a cloudless day as we make a sandcastle together. I remember that day because we'd never made a castle so perfect. But we built it too close to the waves and when the tide came in, our creation was destroyed.

My heart stutters because if the voice finds this place…

A gentle pressure against my shoulders makes me jump, but of course I don't dare move because I'm terrified.

"Mum?"

"No, but don't be afraid," she says, and her voice is soft and melodic. "This had to be done."

"It's you… Shiny Pictures."

The woman sighs and the sound of hooves hit the floor. "Yes."

The barking is so loud I feel the echo inside my brain.

"I know you," I say.

"You've always known me. But you've never been strong enough to remember completely. I think that's about to change."

"Are you here to help me?"

"I will be soon."

When my eyes snap open, I'm standing in our bathroom. She's gone, and so is Mum. I'm in front of the toilet and I'm wearing my own PJs.

"No, don't!" someone yells.

I flush on instinct and it's not until I see the familiar white pills swirling away that I realize what I've done. I'm still holding the small bottle used for housing my meds—my salt tablets. But that's not all. There are opened and discarded plastic bottles all over the sink and on the floor.

"Shit, you actually flushed them!"

I spin around, grateful to have mobility again. I clench and unclench my fists, wiggle my toes against the clean tiles and look around. The overhead light is on and I'm not alone. Darwin is holding Nobody back by the collar and it suddenly dawns on me how big she's getting. Is she growing unnaturally fast, or is this normal growth? I have no idea.

"Chess, why did you flush the pills?" His eyes are so wide I've never seen this much white around his irises.

"I... I don't know how I got here." I dump the empty bottle in the sink along with the others and lower my gaze because the shock and confusion are too much. I don't know how to deal with any of this, and the sound of hooves is still ringing in my ears.

I can remember what little she said to me. She told me I wasn't strong enough to remember her before but that's going to change.

Everyone keeps mentioning the same thing, but I still feel weak and lost. And was the other, taller shadow my mother? But why would she get rid of the pills? Or did she make *me* get rid of them? I don't know what's happening and my head feels like it's going to explode.

"Hey." Darwin takes my hand. "You must've been sleepwalking again." He glances at the sink. "Only this time, you were busier than usual."

I stare at the discarded pill bottles and hear Dr. Larunda telling me to stop taking them. Maybe I was supposed to do this, and someone gave me a nudge.

"I guess…" I blink fast.

"You *were* sleepwalking, right? It's how you ended up in here." He's trying to find an explanation and I can't help.

I can't even remember getting out of bed. Yet, I somehow found Mum's hidden stash of pills and got rid of every single one.

Darwin's fingers touch my face. "Chess?"

I jump at his touch, and he drops his hand.

"Sorry."

"No, it's okay." It's hard to shake the cobwebs, but I need to focus. "You're probably right, I was sleepwalking."

"My socks are filthy, where did you go?"

"I don't know." I probably went outside to wherever Mum kept the stash.

"Your hair is wet and it's raining," he says, holding the dog tighter. "Have you been outside?" He points at the sink. "And where did you find all these, anyway?"

"Um…"

"Come on, talk to me." He sighs and his hair flops into his eyes. "I'm trying to figure out what's going on."

"I don't know, okay?" I hate to get angry with him, but I'm not in the mood for a hundred questions. I'm trying to figure everything out and he's making it harder.

Darwin has never done that before. He's always made things better, clearer. Yet now he's breaking up my thought pattern, confusing me further. I can't answer his questions because I don't know the answers, and his constant barrage is making me cagey.

He's silent for a moment, and his eyes sadden. "I want to help but I don't know how."

"I don't think you can." I shake my head. "Whatever's happening to me is something that needs to play out and I'm not sure where it's going to lead."

"Wherever it leads," he says, squeezing my hand. "I'll be there every step of the way."

I manage a quick nod, even if I don't think he can be there.

He glances over his shoulder. "We better get this cleaned up before we wake Ma, and she starts asking even harder questions than me."

I nod and when he lets go of Nobody, she heads for me. Her tail is wagging uncontrollably, so I pat the fur along her back. I feel bad for not giving her a proper name yet. Apart from Darwin, no one else has been able to penetrate the walls between *lost me* and *found me* like she does.

Nobody was barking earlier because she was trying to get me back. I'm sure of it.

"Thank you," I whisper and hug her tight until our hearts beat as one. As I pull away, I can read the understanding in her pretty eyes. "We should come up with a real name for you soon."

"We can always call her Sally or Diana."

"We're not naming her after your fantasy girls." I roll my eyes. "Besides, when a freaky therapist tells you about the importance of giving your dog a name, I think she means it has to be an appropriate one. It has to feel right."

"And Diana, Princess of the Amazons doesn't fit?"

I pat her one last time before adding a handful of white plastic bottles into the bag he's taken from the wastebasket in the corner. "No, it doesn't."

"And Sally the living ragdoll who helps save the Pumpkin King isn't worthy either?" He dumps more bottles into the bag and shakes his head. "They're both strong and kind heroines, what's not appropriate about naming a dog after them?"

For a moment I'm not sure what to say because he's right. But I get the feeling there's going to be a lot riding on the right name for this particular dog. "I just think she needs something different... original." I meet her lovely eyes. "She needs the *perfect* name."

He stops to stare at her for a few seconds. "What do you think she meant by Nobody protecting you anyway?"

I'm glad we spoke about my latest therapy session on the way home the other day, because so much of what happened doesn't seem real anymore. But having shared the details with him means there's someone else who knows. "Not sure, but it's yet another freaky thing to add to the growing list."

"I looked up what a familiar is."

"What did you find?" With the amount of research my mother used to do, one would think I would've done the search myself. But I didn't for the same reason as always—I'm scared about what I'll find.

"They're supposed to be demons able to take animal form so they can accompany, attend to and obey witches," he says. "There are a bunch of other meanings, but I found this one more interesting than the others."

"You and your demon talk." I roll my eyes. "Where are you looking this up, on an occult message board from hell?" Wish I could laugh, but Dr. Larunda also mentioned demonology.

"Don't blame me if that's what the search found. It's not limited to witches, by the way. Demons are supposed to be able to gift familiars to those who summon them." He shakes his head. "I know how it sounds, but after all that demonology talk…"

"I know." We've gone too far, seen too much, and heard even more for me to deny there's not something demonic going on in our lives. My own mother filled the pages of her *grimoire* with these types of entries. She was so casual about invoking and rituals and ceremonies that I can't call him out on this. My mother was into some weird shit and because of her, I got caught up in it too. Dr. Larunda practically spelled that out for me.

And who is Purson? According to Mum, that's who sent Nobody to me.

"Do you remember when I asked you about using a Ouija board and you lost your shit?"

I nod, dumping the last of the bottles in with the ones he already collected.

"It doesn't seem so silly now that your therapist mentioned demonology, right?" The hopeful gleam in his eyes confuses me. I'm not sure if he wants me to admit he's right, or if he's keen on trying out his theory.

"Still sounds dangerous, though."

He raises a hand, palm up. "I didn't say we should try it. I'm just trying to make a point."

"Okay. Point made."

"I've been thinking about all the stuff she said to you." Darwin is gripping the bag tightly. "It's why I heard Nobody barking and you doing whatever the hell you were doing. I couldn't sleep, everything's going around my head and I'm trying to figure out what all the clues mean."

"Did you come up with anything?"

"Not really, but I know one thing for sure, whatever Mum's into, it's the reason why all of this is happening to you."

I bite my tongue before protesting or coming to my mother's defense. He's not wrong in his assumption because the doctor claimed as much, and Mum's Dreaded Notebook confirmed even more.

"Maybe we should grab her journal and see if we can find something—"

"No." Not after the last entry I read. So much of what she revealed is too personal to share with anyone—even him. At least, not yet.

"Why not?" He squints at me, looks as if he's going to push but sweeps his gaze around the bathroom to make sure we haven't missed anything. He ties the bag and adds, "You didn't have to flush them all, you know?"

"I didn't..." Should I tell him the shadow did it, or made me do it?

"Chess, I saw you—"

"That's not what I mean."

"O-kay," he says, flashing me a pained glance. "I'm going to dump this in the bin. You go and wait in my room."

"Yes, sir," I salute.

He brushes past me on his way out.

I stand in the middle of the bathroom for a few seconds trying to find the other shadow, but she's nowhere to be found. I sigh and Nobody follows me out. As we make our way down the darkened hallway, she presses against my leg and keeps scanning the ceiling. I can't see anything up there, but I can certainly feel the activity.

I don't dare look, though.

"I'm getting closer now, Chesty."

I shut my eyes and wince.

"Don't worry," he whispers. *"It won't hurt... much."*

Nobody's growl comes from deep inside her throat, but I can't bear to open my eyes and instead clutch my head with both hands. The laughter rings so loudly I swear I'm going to go deaf.

"What's wrong?" Gentle hands pluck away the grip on my temples, encouraging me to open my eyes. "Hey, it's okay. You're okay." Darwin cups my face and stares into my eyes. "Focus on me, there's no one here but us."

It takes a few seconds to get my breathing back under control and to not feel as if my brain is going to implode. When I feel better, I wrap my arms around his midsection. The feel of his hard body and his even breaths help me get some sense of normalcy back.

"He's so loud," I say. "I think he's getting closer."

"I won't let him take you, okay?"

"Okay."

He pulls back and the concern darkens his face. "Why don't we go to my room for a bit?" He snaps at Nobody, "And you need to keep it down or I'm taking you outside."

She whines and follows us into his bedroom with her tail low to the ground.

Darwin closes the door, and Nobody heads straight for his bed. She jumps on and curls herself into a furry ball at the end, her eyes closing almost instantly. What did she see out there that made her so angry? And now that I've flushed away all those pills, is the voice going to finally kill me?

"What happened?" He wraps an arm around my shoulders and leads me to the small couch he keeps against one wall.

We sit close together, and his gentle grip doesn't falter.

"The voice was really loud and physically hurt."

"But Nobody can't read your mind, so why was she barking?"

"I think she can see things living in the shadows."

He looks up, searching.

"Not in your room," I say. "Out in the hallway and the bathroom."

"Oh." He sighs. "And can you see them?"

"Sometimes I see things shifting out of the corner of my eye, but when I look there's nothing there."

He doesn't seem convinced. "We've all done that before."

"That's happened to you too?"

He nods. "Lots of times."

"I thought it was only people with signs of madness—"

"Well, we're all a little mad, aren't we?" His smile is wide because he's made this reference on purpose, but he can't hide the concern in his dark eyes. "I hope your doctor's right, and that not taking the pills will help this settle down. But I don't understand why you had to get rid of all of them."

To make sure I don't take a single one. "Me too," I say.

He inches even closer until our thighs are touching. "You have to promise me that you'll at least take her advice about fighting the voice."

"I will."

"Let's see if we can get some sleep, okay?"

I nod and lean my head against his shoulder. "Thank you, Dar."

"You're always welcome and…" His words fade away.

The next time I open my eyes, I'm kneeling in my bedroom and the large rug underneath my bed is ripped and tossed aside. My fingernails are torn and bloodied. A pentagram is scorched under my bed, *into* the floorboards. I'm holding a pair of scissors and have already scratched off a large chunk of the circle.

"That's a good girl."

My hands shake. How did I get here? What did I do?

"You severed the protection."

"Chester, no!"

I peek over my shoulder and find Elvi standing in the doorway. She looks terrified and confused. A guttural moan escapes me. The weight of the scissors is intense, and I refuse to give up the strength they provide.

"She deserves to die," the voice whispers. *"For her part in what they did to me."*

His words sound sincere and true, but I know the woman standing in the doorway, and love her. I don't want to hurt her.

"Do it."

No.

"Do it now!"

"I don't want to."

"Chester, put those scissors down!"

The compulsion to shut her up is strong. Why is she nagging me all the time? She's not my mother. And that's another thing. Why isn't she the one who disappeared? It's not fair that I have to suffer so much, and Darwin gets a free ride. Maybe it's time he knows what it feels like to have his world turned upside down.

"Darwin needs to know what real pain feels like." His thought sweeps through me and my mind glitches.

No, I don't want to hurt Darwin. He's done so much to keep me grounded and safe.

The control slides out of my brain, and I tumble into the abandoned room with its rotting walls and cold air. I'm inside a splintery cage, all alone. Even my shadow has left me.

I smack the walls with my fists, trying to beat past the surface until the planks crumble in front of me and I'm back inside my body. But I can't control my limbs and rise like a marionette on strings. When my feet lift and I'm floating a few inches above the floor, I feel invincible. I know what I have to do.

With a tight grip on the scissors, I raise the weapon above my head and leap off the floor with an inhuman growl.

TWELVE
BEFORE
Two months ago, March 2018

"Where are you going?" I asked as Darwin strolled past my open bedroom door. I'd been waiting for him to leave his room after I heard him whispering on his phone earlier.

"I'm ducking out to the shops for a bit." He threw his *Hello Kitty* keychain into the air and caught it once, twice, three times. He was trying to avoid my eyes.

"Can I come with?"

"Oh, I won't be long," he said. "I'm only going to the grocery store to get something for Ma. You know, boring stuff." He leaned against the doorframe and smiled.

"I don't mind." I rocked my chair from side to side, trying to unnerve him.

"Uh..."

No point in playing this very tedious game of waiting for him to confess. He was a hard egg to crack and wouldn't spill until I pushed him. "I know where you're really going."

"What?" He tried to look oh-so innocent. "To the shops—"

"You're going to meet up with Su."

"No, I'm not." The slight flush on his cheeks gave him away.

"I saw you together."

"So? We all hang out together." He pushed off the frame and stepped into my room.

"No, I saw you *together*. You were making out with Su in your bedroom."

"What?"

"Stop pretending to be shocked," I said, crossing my arms. "You were on your bed kissing. Do you need me to tell you more of what I saw? Because I can tell you what your hand was doing if you want." I was playing dirty but didn't feel as guilty as I probably should. Not when I was purposely left out of this loop. I didn't need to know nitty-gritty details but telling me they were together was something they could have shared.

Darwin sputtered. "Were you spying on me? On us?"

"No, I went to your room last week to see if you wanted to hang out and found you all hot and heavy with *my* friend."

"She's my friend too."

"I know." Yet that hadn't stopped me from throwing the statement out there like some sort of weapon. The weirdest thing about all of this was trying to figure out why they didn't tell me they were together. I had no idea why Darwin would keep this a secret, but even stranger that Su chose to stay quiet when she'd already mentioned having a huge crush on him plenty of times.

"Then why did you say it like she was only your friend?"

"Maybe I'm trying to make you feel bad, so you know what it's like to be left out."

"Chess, I..." His phone beeped and he reached for it but stopped himself.

"Don't ignore her on my account," I said, crossing my arms.

"Don't be like that!"

"Don't be like what? Upset that my best friends got together and decided to keep it a secret from me?" Was I acting juvenile? I wasn't sure. Maybe I should have talked to Mum about this first, rather than flinging accusations. But I was angry and hurt and confused.

He sighed and ran a hand through his hair. "I'm sorry, okay?"

I swiveled my chair to face my desk. Now that we'd started this conversation, I wasn't sure I wanted to keep going.

"Hey, don't give me the cold shoulder."

I ignored him to focus on my closed laptop.

He swiveled the chair around so that we were facing each other. He propped his hands on either side of the armrests, pinning me in. Now that Darwin was in my face, I couldn't avoid him or the issue. I was the one who'd brought it up, after all. If I hadn't wanted a confrontation, I shouldn't have said anything.

"Don't be angry," he said. "We were going to tell you. Really, we were. I just didn't want you to…"

"You didn't want me to be jealous? Is that it?" I shook my head, never losing eye contact. "If that's what you were worried about, I'm not."

"That's not what I was worried about."

"What could possibly make you think it was okay to keep me out of the loop?"

"You have enough things to worry about, okay?" He pushed off the chair and started pacing, running both hands through his hair until he messed it up. That seemed to be his tell, the one thing he couldn't help doing whenever he was stressed or trying to drive a point home.

"Ah, yes, don't upset the crazy girl." It wasn't a nice or fair response, but I was in a shitty mood and obviously didn't care how bad I made him feel.

"For fuck's sake, that's not what I mean!" He stopped pacing. "You've been through so much—go through a constant battle every single day—and I didn't want you to feel left out." I caught the shine of unshed tears in his eyes. "Su and I are your best friends, and I didn't want you to think that because we were together, we would forget about you."

"Yeah, well, a sure way to make sure I don't get *that* message is to start dating behind my back and keep lying about where you're going and who you're with." I rolled my eyes because I wanted him to know how annoyed I was with both of them. My anger was already cooling. His reaction confirmed how much this was affecting him.

"I'm sorry," he said. He crouched in front of the chair so that we were level. "I know it's stupid, trying to protect you and instead ending up hurting you…"

"I thought that maybe, you seeing what I go through with Mum would've given you clue enough about that." No one—not even Su—knew the extent my mother went to in order to *protect* me from everything she deemed harmful. And a lot of the time, her protections were what was guaranteed to hurt me.

He hung his head. "I know and I'm sorry."

"Don't be, I'm cool with this." I sighed. "Well, now that you've finally fessed up I am. Although, I might want to make Su stew for a bit. Torture her with guilt for a while longer. It's only fair."

He chuckled. "She's going to kill me if I don't tell her—"

"You had no problem keeping a secret from me."

"Actually, it was agonizing. I could barely look at you because I felt like I was stabbing you in the back. The guilt was eating me up."

"Yeah, it certainly looked that way when you had your tongue down Su's throat."

"I never said it was hurting my libido, gee."

I smacked his arm and he pulled away, faked being hurt.

"I promise I'll never keep secrets from you again," he said, raising a hand in the air as if taking an oath. "Aren't you going to do the same?"

I shrugged. "Think I might be owed at least one secret."

"All right, all right, that sounds fair." He smiled.

I sat back in the chair. "So, you and Su are an item now, huh?"

"It certainly feels that way," he said with a wink.

"She's had a crush on you for a while now... who made the first move?"

"She did."

"I guess she took my advice."

"You told her to ask me out?"

"I told her that if she had the hots for you, there was no point in adoring you from a distance." This relationship thing seemed messy and complicated, but why beat around the bush? Why not take the plunge? "Besides, there were way too many girls already plotting to get your attention. She had to hurry the hell up before someone beat her to it."

"Ah, you flatter me." Darwin had the audacity to actually blush.

"I'm actually glad you two got together. I just can't believe you thought I would be anything but happy."

"I told you. I didn't want you to feel left out." He took my hand and laced his fingers with mine. "Even though I have a girlfriend now, it won't stop me from being around. I'll never leave you, Chess. I'm still going to honor that pinkie promise."

"Good, because I would never rescind that promise either," I said with a smile.

He kissed the top of my head before getting to his feet and heading for the door. "So, uh, how much did you see when you were spying on us?"

"I wasn't spying," I said, offended. "And I only saw you two kissing." A little white lie never hurt anyone.

"Okay." He knocked on the doorframe. "Hey, now that you know, do you want to come along?"

"And become the third wheel? No thanks."

"That's not what will happen," he said with a sigh. "I didn't lie about the shops. Su wants to buy you something. You know, to soften you up for the big news. But now that you know, I guess *you* can surprise *her*."

"Oh, I like the sounds of that." I thought it over. "Will there be ice cream involved in this transaction?"

"Quite possibly."

"Sold," I said, throwing a hand into the air. "I just need to get my shoes on."

He waited for me in the hallway and as we left my room, I was glad we'd finally had this discussion. No matter what, I couldn't stay angry with Darwin.

Thirteen
NOW

Friday, 4am
May 18, 2018

"No, stop!"

The scissors slam into the wall above Elvi's shoulder and my mind clears. I retract my fingers from the handles and my heavy arms fall to my sides. I take a step back and find the sharp tip stays embedded in the wall. I struck so hard the scissors were stuck halfway *into* the wall.

"Chester..." Her voice is low, but firm.

My breath is coming too fast as I back away. I glare at my hands, hoping to get an answer about why I attacked her with a pair of scissors. What was I even doing with them in the first place?

"You can fight this." Elvi's hazel eyes are bright and wide, she holds her left hand palm-up as if she's trying to calm a wild animal. "Don't give into him."

"I'm... I'm sorry." Tears spill from my eyes, blurring my vision and making my breath unsteady. My chest feels like it's sticking, as if my lungs are full of glue.

"I know, but you have to regain some sense of control." Her hand shakes, slightly. "If you don't, he'll get a grip on you again."

I feel like there's an internal war raging inside my head. I want so desperately to throw my arms around Elvi and let her hug away all the painful thoughts and feelings, like Mum used to do. But the violence and vitriol I felt towards her is still washing over me. Making me feel dirty and wrong.

What's happening to me? Is this what getting rid of the salt pills means?

I glance over my shoulder and stare at the rug underneath my bed—the one Mum joked kept the monsters away. It's torn to shreds and Nobody is pawing at the section of pentagram I've scratched off.

"I did that." Those three little words make my throat ache. The scratches are jagged, have torn the floorboards into splinters. I'm not sure if Nobody is trying to play with the damage or put it back together.

"Yes, you did." Elvi's tone has a harsh edge I've never heard before.

"Why was it there?" I don't need to ask her what it is. My mother taught me all about the pentagram and I have a keyring of one hanging from my schoolbag. When a circle is drawn around each point of the star, it's supposed to provide magical protection around the area. What I don't understand is why there's one under my bed.

Elvi sighs. "It was there for your protection."

I turn to face her. "Who put it there?"

"It's to keep him out of your dreams."

"That doesn't answer my question."

She sighs, but still doesn't say anything.

"Did Mum put it there?"

She nods. "We both did."

"And neither of you told me?" I'd been sleeping on top of a pentagram for all this time and had no idea.

"Mena didn't want you to know."

It's almost as if saying her name gives her the strength she lacks. I can't wrap my mind around putting so much of your self-worth in the hands of another person. Now that I've seen this woman transform from a happy, bare foot hippie with a permanent smile into a sad, distracted woman who cries when she thinks no one can hear her... I know firsthand what loving someone can do. It destroys you, cuts you into as many shreds as the ripped rug under my bed.

Even after all the crap my mother wrote down in that dreaded book of hers, and the horrible things Mum and Elvi went through, she still imagined a real life ahead of them. Now she's missing and her partner has become a vacant version of herself.

"Why didn't she want me to know?" I say, and it's a bit too loud. "Did she think it was better to keep me in the dark and make me think I was crazy, rather than know the demonic truth?"

"You don't know anything about the truth."

Tears are now spilling down my face, but a chuckle escapes me. "I know a lot more than either of you think."

"I'm going to cut you some slack because of what happened, and because I know how much not having Mena around is affecting you, but you should think about showing more respect to the people trying to keep you safe." She lowers her arms, and they hang limp at her sides. She's wearing an old terrycloth robe and slippers.

I remember Darwin and me giving her the slippers last Christmas.

"Shouldn't I show the same level of respect that's given to me?"

"That's not fair," she says, and shakes her head. "Everything Mena did was to keep you away from his clutches..." She looks away and presses her lips together, as if realizing she's said too much.

"You don't keep a child safe by surrounding her with secrets!"

I've read enough of my mother's journal to understand I'm the daughter of an arrogant individual corrupted by power and ego.

"It was the only way to keep you safe."

"But I'm not safe, am I?" I step closer. "I've had voices inside my head for as long as I can remember. I've passed out and done things without having a single memory of doing them." My eyes stray to the scissors. "I don't think that qualifies as *safe*, do you?"

"We sacrificed everything for you." Her shoulders are actually shaking, and her twitch. I've never seen Elvi angry—didn't think she was capable of such an emotion. She didn't even protest about sending her own son away to boarding school for years.

Of course, as we got older and I started understanding the dynamics of their relationship, I realized Elvi wasn't a passive wallflower. Elvi and Mum adore each other and are deeply in love, but they're equals. After reading all about the turbulent way they met—maybe her name wasn't mentioned, but I knew who Mum was referring to—a lot of their fevered intimacy makes more sense.

"I didn't ask anyone to sacrifice anything," I spit.

She looks away, stares at the bed I pushed across the room. "I know you didn't, honey."

"Does Darwin know about any of this?"

She shakes her head.

"So, you've been lying to us our whole lives," I say, a little louder than I intended.

"You just came at me with a pair of scissors." Her eyes flash with anger. "Don't you dare throw accusations around when I'm finding it hard to keep things together without Mena."

"Can't you do anything without her? Does she have to hold your hand to do everything?"

I don't see the slap until her open palm hits my cheek.

The sound echoes around the room and I recoil.

She gasps and looks apologetic, instantly.

Nobody appears out of nowhere, positioning herself between us. She's barking so loudly the windows rattle.

"How dare you?" My cheek throbs. The anger boils over, makes me feel like I've got acid bubbling inside my stomach and it's brewing up a storm.

"I... I didn't mean to do that." She holds her hands to her chest. "You're being so unreasonable, and I'm trying the best I can." A sob escapes her. "I wanted you to stop saying such cruel things. I don't know where you begin, and the darker part takes over."

Nausea sweeps over me, and I lean forward, throwing up on the floor between us. Barely missing my faithful guardian, who is still growling at Elvi.

My throat feels raw and my body weak, but when it's over I'm relieved. The nest of black feathers is as upsetting as the rotten egg stink. Even Nobody backs away.

"What's happening to you?" Elvi actually has the nerve to appear both sympathetic and appalled. As if she doesn't know how to deal with me, and she really doesn't.

Darwin rushes into the room and stops abruptly. "What's going on?"

Neither of us replies, so his gaze roams around the room—at the scissors, the puddle of spewed-up feathers, the growling pup, the splintered floor—and settles on the bed.

"What in the fuck happened?" He's wearing pink *Hello Kitty* PJ bottoms and an oversized white T-shirt. His hair is pointing everywhere, but the expression on his face doesn't match such a fun outfit.

"Watch your language," Elvi snaps.

"No offence, Ma, but I think my language is the least of our concerns." He circles around the puddle and makes his way toward me.

He takes my hands gently away from my cheek and frowns. "Are you okay? What happened to your face?"

"Why don't you ask *your mother?*"

He quickly glances at her, obviously confused. "Ma, you look like you've seen a ghost. What's happening?"

"This doesn't concern you, Darwin." She lifts her chin. "Go back to bed and we'll talk about this in the morning."

"This doesn't concern me? Get back to bed?" He echoes her words but in a stunned and outraged tone. He seems torn between us, uncertain. "You woke me up with your screaming!"

"I'm sorry," I whisper.

"It's okay." He squeezes my hands. "But why are my scissors stuck in the wall?"

Elvi shakes her head, looks away but I spot the tears.

"Can someone fucking tell me what happened?" I can feel his impatience growing, but none of it seems to be aimed at me.

"You have to stop being so overprotective of her," Elvi finally says. "If you let her manipulate you anymore than she already does, you'll lose yourself too."

"Okay, I have no idea what any of that means, so why don't you unpack it for me?"

"She destroyed another safeguard and came at me with scissors." Elvi is shaking, but he stays with me. By *my* side. "She wasn't herself. I think it's getting harder to remember who she is." She glares at the pile of feathers, unable to hide the disgust and fear. "We need help."

"Don't talk about me as if I'm not even here." After our exchange she's going to pretend I'm not in the room? There's an awful taste in my mouth, but at least the nausea has left my system.

"She's right," Darwin says. "You shouldn't say such awful things."

Elvi laughs. "Oh, I haven't even started saying anything awful."

"What's going on with you?" He steps between us, as if he's afraid she might lunge at any minute.

"You have no idea how many times I wish you'd been the one to disappear instead of her." Her words are clear and vicious, and there's no denying who she's talking to.

"*Ma!*" Darwin blocks me completely.

"She's an abomination!"

"You need to stop now," he says. "I don't know what's going on, but you need to stop before you say something you'll regret."

Elvi opens her mouth to reply, but instead starts to cry.

I take the chance to slip out of the room as her son finally decides to offer the comfort she deserves and wraps his arms around her. I should be surprised about her reaction towards me, but how can I be when I attacked her? Sure, it wasn't actually me and I fought against hurting her, but she doesn't know that. She's known me my whole life. She knows the truth about my conception and about the struggle, but why does she blame me entirely when Darwin is also a part of this?

Nobody sidles up beside me as I step outside. The air is cold but feels soothing on my overheated face. I can't believe Elvi slapped me. Neither of our mothers has ever come close to striking either of us before, but I suppose things are different now.

We're too far gone. Or maybe it's just me.

I'm wondering about what to do next when I feel a weight thump against my chest as I jog into the middle of the yard. I reach up and am surprised to find my phone is tucked into my breast pocket. I might not remember putting it there, but I've been carrying the thing around with me lately, in case I wake up somewhere other than home.

I dial the emergency number she gave me without thinking. I wait while it rings once, twice, three times.

"Chester." The voice sounded like Dr. Larunda. "What happened?"

That's what I like about this woman. There's no need for small talk and avoiding the obvious. She gets a call from me in the middle of the night and gets straight to the point.

"Everything's falling apart, and I don't know what to do."

"Did you stop taking the pills?"

"I did a lot more than that, I flushed every single one down the toilet." I sigh. "And I can't remember how or where I found them." I press my fingers against my temple and massage the skin. "I feel like I'm not in charge of myself anymore."

"But you are." Her voice is soft and comforting. "You mustn't forget that."

"It doesn't feel like it anymore."

"Might not feel like it, but that doesn't make it so." Her silky comfort washes over me and I wonder if she's using some sort of spell on me.

I take a moment to let her soothing ways clear my head. "I've finally met my invisible friend in my dreams. But tonight, *he* took over. He made me destroy the pentagram under my bed and tried to make me stab my..." I shake my head, trying to forget what happened. I don't want to mention the damned feathers either. "I've ruined the protective circle under my bed and Elvi got really upset. I don't know how much more of this I can take."

"You're very close to figuring everything out, aren't you?"

"I feel like I'm going crazy." For someone who's spent most of her life battling the whispers inside her head, this seems redundant.

"You're not crazy and—"

"Why did Mum make me feel like I was?"

"She couldn't come out and tell you the truth." Dr. Larunda sighs. "If she had, you probably would've fallen into a severe depression, or suffered even worse anxiety than you already do." She's quiet for a moment. "Maybe you would have done something even worse than that if you knew everything. She couldn't risk it. Surely you understand that."

"Why are you protecting her?"

"Trust me, Philomena Warden doesn't need my protection."

"What are you saying?" I'm sick and tired of people tiptoeing around the truth.

Another sigh. "All I'm saying is that you should cut your mother some slack."

"But she lied about everything!"

"There's a good reason for—"

"You know what she did, so why am I this way?" A hollow sensation opens up in my stomach, like an abyss waiting to consume me.

"Yes, I do but—"

"Do you know so much because of the blue creature that hovers around you?" A cool breeze raises my hair. Nobody steps closer and I lower myself onto the grass so I can wrap an arm around her warm body.

"So, you saw her?"

"Yes."

"You're stronger than we suspected," she says. "And all of this is normal. The fact the voice is trying so hard to get you to eliminate the safeguards and hurt your guardians means he knows he's at risk of losing you completely. He's going to push harder and won't stop. You have to be prepared. You have to use every defense Mena taught you. You need to make sure you stay strong and don't fall apart, and you need to figure out who your father really is before you're ready."

"Before I'm ready for what?"

"Knowledge is your first step. Before this is over, you'll have to go against your biggest foe. Now that she's gone and your guardian obviously can't handle this as well as I thought she might, I'll guide you. Find out who your father is and call me."

"I already know he's some kind of freak," I say, and the journal entries echo inside my head. "And the fact I've been vomiting black feathers has to mean something…"

She's quiet for several moments, but I hear muffled sounds as if she's trying to keep me from listening to someone else. "I'm not supposed to tell you specifics, but I think this one thing might be allowed." She takes a breath. "You're purging feathers because you're rejecting him."

A sense of relief flows through me. I'd honestly thought it was for the opposite reason. "Really, are you sure?"

"I'm positive because I've consulted with my partner, and he agrees."

"Hold on, I thought they were a she."

"I'm not talking about Foras."

"Now I'm just getting more confused."

"Chester, don't concern yourself with the small details and start looking at the big picture. Now that you have some insight into your mother's past and where all of this began, start to frame things in the only way they matter."

"Okay." But my mind stumbles over her suggestion because I have no idea what she means.

"You're very clever but in order to figure everything out, you need names. Without names, there's no power."

"I'll keep reading." I probably shouldn't have, but I leafed ahead and noticed the notebook was only halfway full. And a lot of the stuff towards the end can probably be skimmed because it's written in point form, rather than the narrative she adopted at the beginning.

"You do that." She's quiet for a moment and I'm positive someone is whispering to her.

"Can I ask you something, Doctor?"

"You may."

"Why can't you tell me what you know?" She's dropped hints but hasn't come out and told me exactly why.

She pauses long enough that I think the phone is dead.

"It's forbidden," she answers. "I can't interfere. There's only so much I can reveal, and it's all in relation to how much you've learned."

"That makes some sort of weird sense, I suppose."

"Stay focused, stay strong, and the next time we see each other, I'll tell you everything I know in relation to this. *Everything*."

"I can do that." Not that I have any other choice. Things are falling apart and if this crap doesn't stop soon, I'm going to totally lose my mind.

"Oh, did you name your familiar yet?"

"No."

"You should."

"Is she a demon?" I glance at the cute puppy sitting so close beside me that I can feel her every breath.

"Give her a name and find out for yourself," she says. "Oh, and Chester, whenever the voice takes over, stop thinking of the experience as a loss of control. Watch and listen, learn what you can about him, because I doubt there's anyone else in this world who knows his weaknesses better than you."

"All right, bye."

The call disconnects and I shove the phone back into my pocket.

I stare longingly at Mum's chair but no matter how desperately I want to go and sit, I decide not to. I think it's time to start taking things seriously and like the doctor suggested, maybe use others' weaknesses against them. It worked when I used it against Elvi.

Nobody whines and I hug her tighter. She licks my face and I swear the sting of the slap fades instantly.

"Let's go inside."

When I reach the sliding glass door, I catch my reflection on the surface but it's not entirely me. Another shadow stands close, several inches taller and curvier. Behind that, a horned woman with a tail peeking around her waist towers over both of us. I still can't make out her face, but I know she's the one I saw on the street and the darkroom inside my head. Looks like Shiny Pictures is here to stay.

The most disturbing reflection is the one superimposed over mine. A large, feathered body shimmers in and out like a crackling image on screen. Big and glossy, wings spread out on either side, with a sharp beak and shiny eyes glaring into mine. Menace and hunger emanate off this creature so deeply, I can feel the desire crawl over my skin.

I have a feeling the voice has finally decided to reveal himself to me. And he's not a freak or a corrupt man, he's so much more.

Even Nobody appears different. She's huge and half of her face is melted off, so one side is ebony and the other ivory. She reminds me of a chessboard. I pat her head and a thought strikes me—one that will hopefully lead to the perfect name—and I can't help but smile. I close my eyes for a second and when I open them again, it's just me and a cute dog standing together.

MUM'S (DREADED) NOTEBOOK
January 6, 2000

We did it. We *finally* got away from him.

We're totally free.

I'm writing this while my partner in crime is taking a shower. Even after driving for eight hours straight and crossing several state lines, it took a long time for her to fully understand what we've achieved. She was jumpy all the way here, watching for cars following too close. And when we paid for this shitty room in a random motel off the highway, miles away from the compound we'd known as home for so many years, she still couldn't quite believe it. This made no sense since she's the one who's good with spells and concealed us from everyone. Actually, even the woman behind the counter in this motel will have a hard time remembering us. She probably already forgot all about the two random, very forgettable girls.

This is a welcome change after being watched every minute of the day. I don't want to stand out again. I want to be an average person, doing her own thing, going about her boring life. Being categorized as 'special' isn't as exciting as it's cracked up to be. Just now I've switched through the channels and started watching at least three different movies and shows where the main character was the *Chosen One*.

No one should ever have to carry such a burden.

This room hasn't been redecorated for decades and there are a few mossy stains in the bathroom, but the sheets are clean, and the pillows aren't too bad. It's safe here, no one knows where we are and even if they did, we've smudged our location.

Besides, the one person who could hurt us won't be able to track us down. He's gone. I still can't believe he's *really* gone. Not dead, because someone like him never truly dies, but he's definitely not in our world anymore.

As soon as we got the blood tests back and they confirmed we were both pregnant, we made fast arrangements to prepare for our escape. We packed bags full of everything we could get our hands on and stuffed them into one of the smaller, older cars. He kept a closer watch on the more expensive models. No one gave this car a second glance, so we slowly packed it full of supplies. Even when I snuck out one night, took the ugly thing out of the compound and parked it on a dirt road, no one noticed.

It was agonizing to wait out the week until the ceremony, but we made it. I don't even know how we survived letting him touch us for even another second, but we endured all the extra visits. Now, we're finally away from his clutches and can give the babies growing inside us a real chance at life. But that will entail more sacrifice. I know she wants to totally walk away from this life and never touch the demonic again, but we have one more thing left to do.

We don't have any real-life skills and will never get the kind of jobs we need to totally blend in and support ourselves. But if I do this *one last thing*, I'm sure we can survive. It's cheating and I'll probably have to spend the rest of my life paying penance, but it's a sacrifice we have to make. As long as we can be together, stay safe and raise our kids, we'll be okay.

I can still feel the heat of the fire on my face, but at least none of us got burned. And a lot of the other people got out too. I didn't want everyone to suffer, just the ones who deserved it.

The last thing I want to do is remember what happened, but I have to write it all down before I forget...

As we dressed in our ceremonial gowns, so we looked like nuns from the neck up but with an open robe from the shoulders down, we snuck nervous glances at each other. I love this girl with all my heart and soul, so I couldn't wait to be free of all the bullshit.

The ceremony was to take place inside the barn behind the house. For all that he loved to call it a compound, it was just a farmhouse and a handful of barns. The biggest one was the temple. With the huge windows and the light of the moon framed within its boundaries, we were to lay on our backs with our knees up and legs spread.

A circle of fire was lit around the three of us, and while he was supposed to take both of us—one after the other—we made sure only one would suffer his touch one last time, and that was me. I needed him to be close, and she had to focus on backing me up.

He spoke in a guttural language he'd yet to teach anyone and was already naked, revealing the long sleek frame of his muscular body to his followers. We all watched as he grew taller and sprouted black wings. As his human head was engulfed by a giant beak, to be replaced by that of a giant crow. His body had become a crow's, with sharp talons at the ends of his clawed feet. He was majestic, terrifying and was already approaching me with an erection that didn't belong on any bird I'd ever seen.

Everyone gasped, but I'd already seen his demonic form many times before.

As he lay on top of me and pretended to take my purity in front of the others, I watched his true form because I refused to look away. This black feathered creature kept his beady eyes on me the whole time. Little did he know he'd already impregnated me.

He made a show of his overacted climax, and a sharp pain tore through my insides as I dug my fingers into the dirt and hay. My lower abdomen hurt but I bit away the sting as clapping erupted. I couldn't afford to stall and stabbed him in the gut with the athame I'd dug out from the earth beside me. He was too full of his own pride and triumph to do anything but cry out as I squirmed from underneath him and invoked the imps and minions. So many they filled the circle of fire almost completely. That's when my backup sprinkled our former lover with what would entice them the most.

These creatures were vermin and all they desired was to consume the blood of the rotting. He might not be rotting, but she'd covered him with enough blood and guts to ensure they thought he was. The pests were on him in seconds, engulfed him instantly.

I plucked a feather and stuck it within these pages for safekeeping.

When I sent the minions and imps back to where they belonged, they took him with them.

Once he was sucked out of this world, the fire dwindled, and we ran. We didn't look back at the pandemonium of smoke we'd left behind, kept going until we ran out of those wretched gates. We jumped in the car, and she drove as fast and faraway as possible.

Now we're finally sharing a bed without him.

Now we can finally rejoice in our shared news.

Now, the real story of Elvira and Philomena can begin, without Raum.

Fourteen
Before
One month ago, April 2018

Mum hugged me so tightly I thought she might suck the breath out of me.

"I can't... *breathe*."

"Sorry, I miss hugging you." Her arms kept me stuck to the spot and my chin awkwardly dug into her shoulder.

"What do you mean? You hug me all the time!"

"Not like I used to when you were little," she said with a smile as she pulled back and held me at arm's length. "Look at you now. You're maturing into such a beautiful woman, but I can still remember when you were such a tiny little thing." Her voice rises and she chokes on a sob.

"Stop saying little! Besides, you still hug me *way* too often." So much that I had to constantly squirm my way out of her arms. When I was a kid and would wake up from a bad dream, she would run into the room and hold me until I'd stop crying and fell asleep in her arms. Sometimes she told me stories about the fair maidens and the evil Crow King who tried to peck their eyes out. Other times she told me the tale of the evil minions who served their purpose and helped two princesses escape from the demented king who wanted to steal their children.

These were creepier tales than the Disney movies we enjoyed and were more in league with the Brothers Grimm fairy tales Elvi read to us. But she'd always said children needed to hear the darkest of stories so they could be aware of the dangers lurking in the dark.

My favorites were *The Girl with Two Shadows* and *Alice in Wonderland*. I had multiple copies of Alice, but never did find any editions of Two Shadows. That one was Mum's original.

"Hey, where did you go?" Mum's question roused me back from my story-time musings.

"You reminded me about the creepy stories you used to tell me."

"What about them?"

I shrugged and untangled myself from her. "They were so dark, but I loved them."

"Sometimes I wondered if they made your nightmares worse—"

"No, they did the opposite. I used to find courage in them."

She rubbed her arms and sat down on her chair. "The weather's changing." She tilted her head back and stared up at the sky. Grey clouds were collecting faster than the white puffy ones, streaking away the blue. "The older you get, the faster the seasons shift. Winter will be here in no time."

"I don't mind winter," I said. "I get to steal all of Dar's fluffy socks to keep my feet toasty around the house."

She laughed and I handed her the throw blanket, which she draped over her jeaned legs. For all her talk about the shifting seasons and time, both her and Elvi were in her thirties. They'd had us very young and neither ever spoke about our fathers. Actually, *these* were stories both of our mothers avoided and refused to answer. So, Darwin and I didn't know who they were.

I lowered myself onto the table next to her chair as carefully as I could because this time, there were a bunch of books piled on top. I pushed them to the corner and watched her for a few silent moments. Her black hair was pinned up in a messy bun, she was wearing a sweater and even had her sneakers on. This was her autumn gear, so she wasn't kidding about the weather transition.

"I strengthened the safeguards around the house yesterday," she said.

"That's good." Sometimes, I didn't know how to respond to her stranger comments. She'd always tried to include me in the so-called safeguarding of our home, but I was never really interested. Even so, she made me go around the house with her, carrying salt and crystals while she chanted words I half-listened to.

"You don't have to be patronizing about it." Her gaze caught mine. "You know there's a reason for making sure this gets done every season."

"I'm not being anything, Mum."

She narrowed her eyes. No one could do the squinty-eyed glare like my mother.

"Don't look at me like that."

She sighed and smoothed out the blanket on her lap. "If more people bothered with psychic protections, maybe the world wouldn't be in such a sad state."

I rolled my eyes. "Oh no, have I set you on the path of analyzing what's wrong and right about our planet?"

"No," she said. "I'm just saying that if we were all aware of what positive and negative energy can do to our planet, maybe we wouldn't say and do some of the hurtful things we do to each other. And really enjoy every moment as if it's our last." She sighed. "You never know when that will be."

"That's so depressing!"

"Being aware is not depressing."

"You're talking to the girl who can't remember some of the things she does and randomly wakes up all over the house."

"Don't say things like that, Chester." Her eyes darkened and her face paled. "Never talk about your condition as if it's a joke or something to be taken lightly. What you're suffering from is serious and I've spent a long time trying to find a cure."

"There's no cure for crazy."

She took my hand. "You're not crazy, okay?"

"I know you're trying to make me feel better, but normal people don't hear multiple voices inside their head." Her combative attitude towards my *condition* was an issue I had trouble dealing with. While she continuously tried to make me feel as if my problems weren't abnormal, the way she compulsively took notes and dragged me to see new doctors cancelled out all her good intentions. Her obsession with questions about my pill-taking and headaches and itchy skin didn't help.

Mum sat forward. "We all hear at least one voice that isn't our own, and it's called our instinct or conscience—an inner voice. The one that puts all our thoughts together and makes some sense out of them. So don't ever feel like you're so different from the rest of us."

"But I am. Other people don't pass out and wake up with broken things around them." Talking about this made me feel uncomfortable, but for some reason I couldn't stop. "And they don't hear multiple whispers and suffer from strange headaches. They also don't argue with the strongest voice." Or still remembered their invisible friend because she used to feel so real.

"I know. Trust me, I know." Her eyes filled with unshed tears. "There's a reason why I do all of this"—she spread her free arm in front of her— "I love you more than anything in this goddam world, and I've dedicated my life to keeping you safe. But I won't be around forever, and that's why it's important that you learn to protect yourself."

"You're not going anywhere, are you?" This wasn't the first time she'd said this, and I didn't like it. Being at odds with her was a constant in my life, but I never wanted her to leave. I needed my mother because in spite of how I acted, or how many times I complained about her nagging, her presence was a constant sense of comfort. And safety.

"I don't want to..."

After her cryptic answer, we both sat quietly for several minutes because I didn't know what to say.

"So, you know how to douse the outside of the house with salt?" Mum asked, breaking the silence. "And you can tell if it actually worked?"

"Mix salt and warm water in a bucket, pour enough around the front and back yards so that it meets in the middle until your ears pop."

"Good girl." She closed an eye. "What about the windows?"

"Sprinkle a line of salt outside the windowsill with every season change and keep your favorite crystals on each inside corner."

"Not your favorite crystals," she said with a shake of her head. "The ones you specifically need for each stage of your life."

"Um, okay."

"I'm serious. You need to learn the properties of each one."

I groaned. "Don't I have enough stuff to memorize for school?"

Her face softened and she patted my hand. "I know it's a lot to take in, but it's all things you need to know."

"But why do I have to learn when you're the one who takes care of all of this?"

"I've already told you I won't always be there." She sighed and avoided my eyes. "And I need to know that I've equipped you with enough knowledge to take care of yourself, without me being around to hound you about everything."

"Can you please stop saying that?"

"Stop saying what? That I want you to understand—"

"No, that you're not always going to be here."

"But honey, it's the truth," she said. "You're going to turn eighteen this year. You're not a kid anymore and can't keep depending on me to take care of these things."

I groaned. "I realize that, but the way you say it sounds so..." *Ominous. Sad. Confusing.* "Final."

"Maybe I *am* being a bit melodramatic, but I want you to understand how important this is. You're my daughter and I want the best for you, that's all."

I rested my head on her shoulder. "I know, Mum."

"So, what about the spirit bag, do you feel confident enough to make your own?"

I thumbed the one she'd helped me make last month. "Yep, especially if you're going to supervise."

"Could you do it on your own?"

"Yeah, I reckon I could."

"And the pills, you're still taking them even when I'm not on your back about it, right?"

"Yes." Yet, that was a bit of a lie because I'd gotten so used to her telling me when to take them that if she didn't, I'd forget.

"What about the mind exercises? Do you practice how to shut the whispers out of your mind if they feel like they're taking over?"

"Sometimes." I found it hard to control my rampant thoughts, let alone attempting to lock someone up behind the many doors I imagined lined the corridors inside my mind.

"Chester, this is important." She shrugged me off her shoulder and grabbed my chin, forced me to meet her eyes. "Let's give it a try."

"Now?"

"No time like the present."

"But Mum, I don't want to feel like a freak."

"You'll feel like a bigger freak if you let negative energy seep into your brain."

"Ugh, you always have to go for the guilt trip, don't you?"

She flashed me a toothy grin and squeezed my chin. "Whatever works, baby."

I pulled out of her grip and sat up straighter. "Okay, let's give it a try." The sooner we got this over and done with, the better. "But I have to tell you, I'm kinda crappy."

"That's why you need to practice." She sat back in her chair. "Okay, let's get started. Are you comfy?"

"Yep."

"Close your eyes and feel your surroundings."

I did, but a laugh bubbled out of me.

"Chester!"

"Sorry." I closed my eyes and attempted to push away everything swirling inside my head. At least the voices were quiet this afternoon.

"Let go of every thought and concentrate on your surroundings. Feel every noise and sensation nearby."

The rush threatened to consume my mind—how open Darwin and Su were about their relationship since I'd confronted Darwin, so we were back to being a comfortable trio, that I hadn't even bothered thinking about the spirit bag until Mum mentioned it, how I hated when she said she wouldn't be here forever...

This is impossible.

"I can't, everything's circling around—"

"Don't fight. Let your thoughts flow *into* your mind and move through you, then release everything slowly." Her tone was soft and comforting. "If you push things away, you'll never be able to think clearly."

"Ah, so that's what I've been doing wrong."

She sighed, and this time sounded annoyed. "We've been through this before, many times. Haven't you learned anything?"

"I have, but there's so much to remember."

"Stop using that as an excuse, life is full of *things to remember*. Our brains are made to store relevant details and discard what we don't need. If you don't deem what I'm trying to teach you as important, you'll never get the hang of it."

Ouch!

I took a deep breath and let it out slowly. "I'm ready."

"Let the thoughts flow through your mind, acknowledge and expel them."

I let the tide wash over me, paid attention to every single thought that surfaced.

"Open your mind's eye and see yourself walking down a corridor full of doors." Mum's voice was soft and relaxed. "Are you there? Can you see them?"

As strange as her instructions sounded, I found myself strolling down a white corridor lined with doors on both sides. "Yeah."

"Are all the doors closed?"

"They are." Was this really my mind?

"Make sure they're completely shut because sometimes it feels like they are, but they're not."

I pressed a hand to the nearest door, and it was closed. So were the next six, but the seventh was opened a tiny crack. My hand shifted at its own accord, and I pushed the door inwards enough to find a red room in front of me. I stood in the doorway, taking in all of the photography equipment and the blank papers hanging on the line attached across the room.

Something shuffled in the corner, and I heard the *swoosh* of a tail, followed by the sound of hooves. I shut the door, and it bounced off the frame, but I walked away.

"Are they all closed?" Her voice seemed to boom down from the ceiling, as if she was talking through speakers.

"Not all of them."

"You have to make sure they are."

I shut my eyes tight because it was getting hard to keep this imagery alive, especially since every step seemed to get me farther away from the pristine corridor and into a shabby, abandoned one. All the doors might be closed, but the scratching noises coming from the other side weren't my imagination.

"Don't get overwhelmed, stay calm," Mum said.

I breathed in and exhaled slowly.

The splintered door at the end of the corridor was rotting and wide open.

"Did you make sure they're all closed?"

"There's one that's still wide open."

"Why?"

"I don't know," I whispered.

"You have to shut it."

"I don't want to touch that door. I can feel someone watching me."

She sighed and the action shivered through me. "That's the whole purpose of this exercise. You don't have to touch any of the doors. You can shut them with your mind."

"I can't."

"That's right, Chesty. You can't close the door on me and never will."

I slammed my fist against my head and for a scary moment, I wasn't sure if the real me was walking down this dark place, or if I was still sitting in the backyard and only visualizing this nightmare.

"Don't do that," Mum said, and she must have grabbed my hands to stop me. "That's only going to hurt and scare you in the wrong direction. Take small, shallow breaths and concentrate on *closing the door*."

My feet slid when the floor shifted beneath. There was nothing I could do to stop my destination because the ground was taking me there.

"That's it, come closer so I can see you."

"No."

"Chester, who are you talking to?" Mum sounded frantic, and a lot closer than she was before.

My stomach twisted into knots because whoever was hiding in the darkness ahead made a scary rustling sound.

"Shut the door."

"You're a work of art," the voice cooed, *"the perfect combination of both of us."*

"I don't know what that means."

"Shut the door, now!"

The tip of a black, feathered wing extended past the doorway and I was going to plunge headfirst into the darkness. But I refused to go to him, wouldn't. I concentrated as hard as I could, collected the strength of every thought and pushed them away out of sheer terror.

The door slammed shut between us.

"Chester, come back!"

My eyes snapped open, and I sucked in a pained breath, struggled to breathe until it turned into a coughing fit instead.

Mum seemed agitated. "Are you okay?"

"I am... now."

"I'm sorry I put you through that." She kneeled in front of me and smoothed the sweaty strands of hair away from my face.

The coughing was subsiding, but I felt lightheaded.

"Oh, honey." She rubbed my back until I felt a lot better.

"I closed the door on the... feathered monster."

"I'm so sorry."

"Don't be," I said. "That's the first time I've ever done that."

Tears slid down her pretty face and I reached up to wipe them away.

"You really closed it on your own?"

I nodded. "I shut him out."

The color had completely drained from her face, and she drew me into her arms, squeezing so tightly I could barely breathe. But I didn't mind this time, actually fell into her embrace because the love of my mother was the most powerful weapon I had on my side.

"You did it," she cried.

"I did."

"At least I can breathe easier knowing you're capable of shutting him out."

When she pulled away, I met her eyes. "Mum, who is he?"

"Someone you need to make sure never gets anywhere near you again."

"Okay, but I'm sure he's gone now."

"He'll never be gone," she said with a shake of her head. She sat on her chair and smiled through her teary face. "I'm so proud of you." Her eyes searched mine. "I need you to know that, okay?"

"Thanks." I pushed a hand through my tangled hair and groaned. "I think I need to take a shower or relax in the bath for a bit. I feel like I've run a mile."

"Go on, you deserve it."

I stood, stretched, and surprised *her* by wrapping my arms around her neck and kissing her cheek. "I do appreciate everything you've taught me," I said. "Even when you make me feel like a total freak."

"Don't ever forget how strong and brave you really are."

I smiled and she reached for her trusty journal and a pad of pink sticky notes. "I love you, Chester."

"Love you too." I left her sitting in her favorite chair while the tears dried on her face, and she took notes. I paused at the sliding door and took one last look before stepping into the house. I liked how things kept shifting between us, bringing us closer together.

"Hey, what were you doing outside?"

I swiveled so quickly my neck jolted. "Dar, you scared me!"

"Sorry." He stood in front of me munching on a sandwich and blocking my way. "Didn't mean to spook you."

"That's okay." Besides, I was already spooked.

He glanced over my shoulder. "Who were you talking to?"

"I was hanging out with Mum."

"Oh yeah, where is she?"

"Sitting in her chair," I said. "Why?"

"Huh." He took another bite and swallowed. "She's not out there anymore."

"What? But I was just with her."

"Take a look for yourself." He pointed out the sliding door and whatever was in his sandwich came very close to slipping out and onto my head.

I went to the door and checked the backyard and sure enough, her chair was empty. I stepped outside again and scanned the rest of the yard, but she wasn't there. The lights were on in the shed. "She's probably gone to the workroom."

"Yeah, probably," he said, popping the rest of his sandwich into his mouth.

A sudden chill filled me from the inside out and I caught movement from the corner of my eye. When I checked to see what was there, I found nothing but skittering outlines. Dark ever-changing swirls on the grass that were too fast to catch.

I spun around and headed into the house but as I stepped inside, a sense of inertia made me stumble forward. Something struck my shoulders hard, and the weight pressed down on me with so much intensity, it took my breath away. I winced but the sensation was gone in seconds.

"Hey, what's wrong?" Darwin stood in front of me, leaning down with a concerned expression on his face.

"I, uh..." I straightened. "Nothing's wrong."

"Are you sure?"

"Yeah, I must've tripped on the way in."

"If you're sure..."

"Yeah, everything's fine." But it actually wasn't. I'd left my mother in the backyard but now she was gone, and something definitely smacked into me. I didn't want to burden him with more weirdness.

"So, what're you going to do now?" Darwin asked. "Want me to make you a sandwich?"

"No, I'm not hungry. Think I'll take a bath." I definitely needed to clear my head and the grimy sensation the birdman had left behind on my skin. "What about you?"

"Just gonna finish up my homework," he said with a shrug.

"No big make-out sessions planned for tonight?"

"Ha, ha." He made a face. "Did you want to finish our chess game after that?"

"Uh, yeah, sure..."

"See you then." He walked out of the kitchen, but I couldn't leave yet.

I went to the sliding door and stared outside, trying to figure out how she could be there one second and gone the next.

You're worrying too much. She'll walk back inside with Elvi soon.

I sighed and decided that as soon as I was done taking a bath, I'd probably find Mum in the kitchen, and we'd all sit down for a nice meal together.

Mum's (Dreaded) Notebook
June 1, 2000

<u>Possible Baby Names</u>
Drusilla   Chester
Adelaide   Edgar
Hazel   Kirk
Nora   Jack
Dawn   Nicholas
Willa   Atticus
Ophelia   Darwin
Lavender   Charlie
Evelyn   Lucas
Rose   Ronan
Daisy   Nathan
Annabelle   Caleb
Bindi   Bodhi

    These are the names that made the cut after Elvi and I threw a bunch of possibilities at each other last night. I grabbed my grimoire and wrote them all down before we forgot any. Now that they're in here, I like the way they all sound. We don't know if we're having a boy or a girl because we decided to leave it to chance, but we need to have some idea of what to call them. Not just because it's something to put on their birth certificates, but because these two special babies need to be named instantly.

It's too risky for their souls, otherwise.

The father bit is going to be a lot more complicated, but I'm sure we'll get around it somehow.

Anyway, I'm leaning towards Chester and Ophelia. Elvi likes the sound of Darwin and Adelaide. ~~These must be places she wants to visit.~~

Oh, okay, she just slapped my arm and said she likes the names not the locations, so I'm crossing that comment out. ~~I mean, she's making me cross it out.~~

The last six months have been a scary, but fun ride. There were a lot of tears, a lot more fears and so much nausea. *Ugh.* Nobody ever tells you that morning sickness is actually a whole day, everyday thing. Or that it continues *all the way through* the pregnancy. Not to mention the myth about eating whatever you want—**such lies!** Elvi could barely keep anything down for several weeks and ended up in the hospital for a few days on a drip. I hate almost everything but force myself to eat a bit of whatever I can manage for the baby's sake. And the smells are really bad. There are so many foods I used to love but now can't even think about without feeling ill.

Both of us were put on iron tablets, and we're now at that whale-sized stage where the baby can come any day. I feel like I can barely walk. Let alone get—no, roll—out of bed in the morning.

As soon as the babies are born, at least one of us is going to have to get a job with a real income. But with no life skills,

I don't know what we're going to end up doing. That's a bit of a lie. There's one thing we can certainly do, but Elvi is against the idea. Well, she *was* against it the first time I mentioned it. Now she simply doesn't like it, but I'm sure I can change her mind.

Eventually.

I have to make her realize how right I am about the path we have to take. The only reason we've survived this long is because I stole a bag of cash from Raum's safe before we left, and that's almost run out. I know it's cheating and there'll be sacrifices and consequences, but it's the best way to get instant wealth, skills, and qualifications. To start living the lives we've both been dreaming about for so long.

Elvi wants to make things with her hands—namely, furniture.

I want to design things—furniture and rooms.

Problem is, neither one of us has the abilities required for these occupations. But if we can get instant funds, the documentation to back it up, and manifest the ability, we'll be able to start our own business. We won't have to answer to anyone and can set up shop in our own home. We've been renting a small apartment, and the lease runs out in a few months. I saw the perfect house the other day. It's an Edwardian and has three bedrooms, a huge backyard and it's in a nice suburb. There's a school nearby for the kids and several shopping centers within driving distance.

I have to make Elvi see things my way. I'm sure she'll agree as soon as I tell her the plan and show her the house. If it was just us two, I'm sure we would be able to do things the tough way and get a proper education to save up for a house and everything else. But we're soon going to be joined by two babies, two new people. There's no way we can provide without some sort of cheating. Our love is strong, a very true and powerful thing that has kept us together and happy for a long while now, and I think we've got what it takes to keep it alive for the rest of our lives—but kids cost money and time.

We *really* have to think about this.

But I can't now. I think Elvi's going into labor and I don't feel so good...

*

June 14, 2000

Well, we went into labor at the same time, but I gave birth first because the nurses stopped hearing the baby's heartbeat. What followed was a messy and bloody C-section. I nearly died in the process due to severe hemorrhaging.

Of course, I don't remember any of this, but the nurses relayed most of the information because I wouldn't stop asking. I'd wanted to enjoy the birthing process, but it was taken away from me.

Not much later, after only four hours of mild contractions, Elvi gave birth to her son.

Our babies came into the world under very different circumstances, but my daughter and her son are both healthy. No, they're OUR kids. *Our daughter and our son.*

CHESTER WARREN was born on June 6th at 11:56 pm.

DARWIN ARDEN was born on June 7th at 12:07 am.

*

June 16, 2000

Now that I've had time to think about Chester's actual birth and how hard and violent it was, I'm worried that I took too long to name her.

Elvi told me she whispered Darwin's name as soon as he was born, but I was passed out and hours went by before I told the nurse what I wanted to call our daughter. Could that have given *him* enough time to locate her? Raum is her father, after all.

I feel heartsick thinking about it and will safeguard little Chester her whole life if I have to.

*

June 19, 2000

I've done some research about our future plans, and I think these are the demonic possibilities at our disposal:

Amy

Vassago

Orobas

As long as we stay away from Raum and anyone he's affiliated with, this should work.

*

June 20, 2000

Chester was born two weeks ago and I'm still tired and sore. She doesn't sleep much and cries a lot. Elvi is tired too, but Darwin sleeps through the night and rarely cries.

*

June 22, 2000

We did it! After a lot of convincing, and making her realize this was the right thing to do, Elvi FINALLY agreed. We did this for our children but might have damned them in the process.

Last night was the Winter Solstice and I invoked a demon. I asked her to grant us several wishes. Amy is known for granting skills and treasure, so she was perfect. It was a bit like summoning a genie, but then everything went wrong. The money magically appeared in our accounts, the skills we dreamed about were suddenly at our disposal... but someone hijacked the otherwise successful encounter.

Raum somehow snuck through, piggybacked into the transaction. But I didn't know until it was too late. I knew what the payment would be. The required payment is always the same when dealing with the demonic, and no amount of protection is going to spare you when you're dealing with anyone from the Goetia.

So, I was prepared to give up my soul to Amy. But she wanted Chester and Darwin. By this stage, I should've realized she wasn't in the driver's seat anymore. Raum somehow managed to boot her out of the invocation and took over. Still, after everything he's done—passed himself off as a man of dignity, took my innocence, lied, and impregnated us—I was still prepared to give him my soul. If that's what it took to get what we wanted and keep our children safe, I'd give myself to the Devil. But he didn't want it.

He desperately wanted the kids. I never quite understood what his obsessive offering entailed because he kept those details well hidden, but since he faded away because of me and lost his ability to become human, he probably wants new vessels to stow away for future use.

Most demoniacs can't survive in our world in their own form. They can switch and change while they're in our minds, but not outside of them. There's only a dozen out of the seventy-two listed in the Goetia who can actually do that. He's not one of them. But they can still possess humans and wear them like an outfit, use them up for fiendish purposes and toss them aside. I don't like the idea of him doing that to me, but doing something so vile to our children is never going to happen. Plus, there's also the matter of one's soul. Human souls are a huge trade for demons, and if he can take two for the price of one, why wouldn't he?

But we're not giving him our kids. So, we tried to do something that would ensure they got the protection they need for the rest of their lives. Unfortunately, it only worked on one of them. Luckily, Elvi had a backup demonic waiting in the wings, and we invoked her, just as Raum was preparing to take Chester.

Orobas saved my daughter, but she too will expect payment. She'll be back to collect when Chester turns eighteen, which is also how long it will take for Raum to fully reclaim his former glory and be able to become a real threat. In the meantime, I know they'll both influence her in some way, but I'm going to do whatever it takes to empower our little girl with the strength to keep every demonic at bay.

This is my fault and I intend to keep her safe. No matter what it takes, no matter what happens to me, I will make sure Chester is okay.

She will be okay.

Fifteen
BEFORE
Five months ago, December 2017

"What's it like?" Darwin's voice sounded steady, but he avoided my gaze and seemed too focused on the chessboard lying on the floor between us. Still, I could feel the uncertainty vibrating from him.

"What's what like?" I knew exactly what he wanted to know, but it was fun to make him squirm until he spelled it out. Avoiding my eyes and trying to pretend my condition didn't freak him out wouldn't get him a ticket on easy street. Not when I was constantly living through this insanity. I did feel bad because no one was more unconditionally supportive than him. He was always there to help, no matter what strange situation I found myself in.

He propped his hands behind his head and sat back against the side of his bed. He surveyed the chess board. "What does it feel like when the voices speak to you?" The question finally slipped out, but he still didn't meet my gaze.

I shrugged and crossed my legs, sat up straighter while trying to figure out his next move. Chess might be my nickname, but he was the one with the tactical brain. And right now, he had way too many of my pieces on his side.

Sometimes I felt like the most vulnerable chess piece. The King was under constant protection by those around him but as hard as everyone tried, someone would eventually checkmate, or stalemate him. The King needed to be protected by others, the same way my family tried to protect me. Their attempts to keep me safe were pure and strong, but I would eventually be captured. Whether I wound up institutionalized or something worse, my internal problem would catch up with me eventually.

"You can't run away from a checkmate."

"But you can reach a stalemate," a soft feminine voice whispered in my ear.

I glanced over my shoulder, where a soft breath had left a shiver.

"What're you looking at?"

"Huh?" I turned back to Darwin, my mind reeling from the delusional episode.

"Why do you look so spooked?"

"No reason," I said, probably a little too loudly. "Thought I heard something."

"Mum's still away and Ma's in the workroom."

"That's exactly why I was wondering what that noise was." I sounded paranoid even to my own ears. I told him about a lot of the stuff I imagined, mostly because he was there to see me struggle through the odd incidents.

"You want me to go and check?"

"Nah, don't worry about it."

"Good, because I don't want you cheating while I'm gone."

I rolled my eyes. "I don't cheat."

"Sooooo," he drew the word out. "Are the voices loud?"

"It's mostly one that's the loudest, and scariest." Darwin had known about my inner struggle since we were kids and he caught me doing weird stuff I couldn't remember. He was also there when my head hurt so much, I'd lie down for most of the day. He'd stayed with me the whole time on most occasions and didn't ask many questions.

The unspoken rule was something only my mother broke. She didn't care about subtlety or hurting my feelings, she asked as many questions as she could and bossed me around when she didn't like the answers.

"Does he sound like a monster?"

"I guess so," I said. "Kinda sounds like those movies with the possessed people."

He laughed, but stopped when I didn't join in. "You're being serious?"

"It's really scary when he tells me he's going to hurt me, or you guys." I conveniently left out the actual threats—when he told me that no matter how hard I tried, I would end up hurting Mum, Elvi, and Darwin. We might not be blood relatives, but our mothers were now married and had been together since we were born.

We're a real family.

As I stared at this boy I considered my brother, I doubted anyone would ever be able to make me hurt him. *He's too good, too pure of heart.* Aside from my friend Su Kim, Darwin happened to be the only person I'd ever considered a true friend.

"That's never going to happen." Darwin finally dared to look me in the eye. "No matter what he says to you, he's only a voice and voices can't hurt people."

"No, but the people they command can." The whisper slithered into my head like an unwanted snake.

I shut my eyes, trying to block out the pain. Sometimes, when the voice lay dormant for a while because I'd remembered to take my medication, and then did something stupid like forgetting, the pain was immense when he awoke.

"Hey, don't get upset."

I opened my eyes slowly.

"I won't let him hurt you." Darwin took my hand. We used to have the same sized hands, but now his engulfed mine.

"Thanks." I couldn't help but recall what Su told me about him the other day. She said she had a crush on him and constantly blushed when the three of us were together. I often wondered if she'd eventually tell him how she felt. I hoped so, they were both awesome and if they found joy with each other, it would make me happy too. As long as they didn't forget about me or left me out of the loop.

"I'm serious," Darwin said, squeezing my fingers. "I won't let some bastard voice hurt you."

"That's very sweet, Dar, but we both know he's already hurt me."

"I'm saying that if it ever gets so bad you feel like this thing is completely taking over, but you're afraid to say so because this monster tells you he'll hurt me if you do, I still want you to tell me."

"Okay." I wasn't sure I could, but I wouldn't say otherwise. Not with the conviction shining in his eyes and his hand anchoring me to reality.

"You have to promise."

"I will."

He let go of my hand. "Let's make a pinkie promise."

"Are you serious?" I couldn't help but laugh. "We haven't done that since we were like five."

"What?" He shook his hand in front of my face. "I clearly remember making a pinkie promise when we were ten to never tell our mothers we broke the lip off that ugly vase in the hallway."

My eyes widened. "You're right!" During one of my *incidents*, I'd held onto the vase while passing out and chipped a chunk off the top. When I'd regained consciousness, we'd superglued the fragment back on and rotated the vase, so the broken bit faced the wall. Till this day, no one knew but us. "We pinkie promised never to tell."

"I never told, did you?"

"Of course not!" I said, aghast at the accusation. "Okay, so we haven't made a pinkie promise since we were ten."

"You're wrong there too," he said. "Don't you remember when we were eleven?"

The frog statue we couldn't fix.

"And when we were twelve?"

The magnifying mirror in the bathroom, the one we threw away and pretended we didn't know what our mothers were talking about when they'd asked. "Those seven years aren't up yet."

"Luckily, we're not superstitious." He sighed. "Do you want me to keep going?"

"No, I get the picture." I got it loud and clear, because every single time we'd found ourselves in a sticky situation it was because I'd passed out and smacked into something. Well, except for the time we were six and we broke a picture frame because we were playing chasings around the house.

"Anyway, now that I've stated my case, are you going to leave me hanging or are we going to make this promise?" He wiggled his pinkie at me.

"And here I thought you might suggest we cut our hand and become blood brother and sister." I laughed, hoping to drown out the voice's sudden interest at the mention of blood.

"I'm not a barbarian," Darwin said with a shake of his head. "Besides, we're already brother and sister, as well as best friends. So, we don't need to do something so gross to prove a point."

I smiled and hooked my pinkie around his.

"If you ever feel like it's all too much, I want you to tell me right away. I don't want you to suffer alone." He sighed. "I know Mum's always keeping an eye on you and carting you off to doctors while making sure you take your meds, but she's so determined in that one quest that she misses a lot."

"What do you mean?"

He shrugged. "Whenever she asks you a question, she misses all the most important bits of your answer."

"And you don't?"

"Not usually." Darwin looked thoughtful before answering. "Like the other day, when she made you take your pills and you opened your mouth to show her, I could tell you hadn't swallowed them."

"How?"

"I could just tell," he said. "Besides, I followed you into the bathroom and saw you spit them out into the toilet before you flushed."

"Are you following me around the house?"

"No, of course not," he said a bit too loudly. "And when Mum asked if you were hearing whispers this morning and you said no, I knew that meant you were."

I looked at him for a moment, trying to work him out. "How could you know that?"

"I hear the things you leave out, or the tone you use." He laughed, but there was no humor in the sound. "Not to mention that fidgety glaze you get when you're leaving something out. She doesn't spot the shine, but you shouldn't feel victorious about fooling her if the voice is speaking to you again. Is he here now?"

"It's not a radio I can switch on and off."

"Have you ever tried to figure out who he is?"

"I don't need to be on a first name basis with the creepy voice."

"That's not what I mean."

"What *do* you mean?"

Darwin glanced across the room, stared at his hidden wardrobe. "Have you ever tried using a Ouija board?"

"No, why would I do that?"

"So, you can find out his name."

"Wait a second," I said, holding up a hand. "Who do you think this *thing* is?"

"I don't know, but I want to help you figure it out."

"I'm not possessed," I said.

"That's not—"

Now that he'd brought this up, I couldn't let it go. Why would he think something so bizarre? I was mentally ill, not possessed by a demonic entity. This wasn't *The Exorcist* or *The Conjuring*. I didn't need an exorcism. Yet… "You think performing a séance might help us label whatever is causing my illness?"

"Chess, can you calm down?"

"Don't tell me to calm down."

"No one should ever tell you to calm down," the voice whispered.

"I'm sorry I said anything, okay?" Darwin looked crestfallen as he ran a hand through his hair and avoided my eyes.

"Yeah, well, it's too late because the voice is here." I hated throwing this at him, and sounding smug made my gut clench. What was happening to me?

"Really, he's here right now?" He searched the room, as if he was expecting to find an entity materializing inside his neat and tidy room.

I rolled my eyes. "He's not floating around us."

"This boy is a problematic idiot, and one day you're going to have to do something about him."

"No," I whispered. *I will never hurt him.*

"You love him, do you? I thought you were incapable of falling in love with anyone. How many times have I tried to make you kiss or touch someone, and you're just not interested? It's so frustrating."

"Shut up."

"I can't wait to take over your youthful body and put you through so much wicked sin." A moan echoed through my skull. *"And we'll start with him."*

I fought against the action, but still felt my tongue run over my bottom lip as I stared at Darwin. *Stop it.*

"What's wrong? Are you talking to me or him?" Darwin asked.

I pointed at my head in response.

"Tell the asshole to leave you alone, or I'll make him pay."

Maniacal laughter rang inside my ears, making them ache.

"You should tell him I can hear everything you can."

I shook my head because I refused to allow him access to Darwin.

"You think that's how it works? I don't need your permission."

The impulse to slap Darwin swelled up inside me, made my right arm flop at my side because I wasn't going to do that.

"Are you okay?" he asked, concern darkening his face.

"I need to... go." But my legs refused to uncross.

"Slap him as hard as you can."

"No."

"Do it!"

"I won't!" I was fighting the impulse so hard, sweat dripped down my temples.

I struggled to catch my breath while wondering why I did something as stupid as refusing to take my pills for four days in a row. I'd allowed the voice to get stronger, to gain passage.

Why can't I just be me?

"Because you're mine and I'll never stop until you give up."

"What's going on?" Darwin was on his knees in front of me. The chess board was magnetic, so the pieces were holding their positions.

"It wants me to…" I gritted my teeth and shut my eyes, but this made everything worse because reality was slipping away.

"*Take a nap while I take the driver's seat.*"

No matter how hard I tried to resist the darkness closing over me, I wasn't strong enough to fight. A warm trickle slid from my nose before I was pushed into nothingness.

Not exactly nothingness, because I was suddenly inside a dim room where the walls were made of splintery wood and the floor was covered in dirt. I tried to get my bearings before I slid sideways and found I was inside a different room, one with a red light so bleak it stung my eyes until they adjusted.

A sink was positioned against one wall and several trays were laid out on the opposite counter. I backed away and was slapped on the back of the head with something hanging overhead. It took me a second to figure out these were black and white photos pegged to lines running from one side of the room to the other. As I shuffled closer, I spotted pictures of Su smiling and Darwin laughing.

There were others still developing in the trays filled with chemicals.

I'm inside a darkroom.

"This is a safe place to fall," someone said.

I spun around and found a dark figure hiding there. The red light didn't spread far enough. *What does she mean by that?*

"Exactly what I said."

"Are you reading my mind?"

"You speak too loudly to ignore."

"What am I doing here?" More importantly, why was I here?

"Look around, don't you recognize the fragments?"

I might be confused, but still understood these weren't photos. *They're my memories.*

The way my mind had captured Su's smile the other day when I told her something she thought sounded dorky. The memory of Darwin laughing at one of my lame jokes. Further away, I spotted the sandcastle the waves destroyed all those years ago.

"These are all pieces of my life," I said. "But..." I couldn't bring myself to admit these snapshots were the good times trapped inside my mind.

"Yes, they are, and you must always protect them from him."

"You're talking about the voice?"

"He'll stop at nothing for total control, and if you let him in here..."

"Who are you?"

"Someone who wants to help," she said. "I'm someone who's *always* wanted to help."

"But you can't tell me your... wait a minute." She sounded so familiar. "Shiny Pictures, is that you?"

"That's as good a name as any, I suppose."

"Why and how is this possible?"

"One day, very soon, you'll find out."

I opened my mouth to protest but a bright flash filled my vision. Several blinks and tears later, I slowly started to get my vision back and could hear someone cursing nearby.

My ears popped.

"What happened?" The words slid between my lips as I looked around. My heart stopped for a moment when I spotted Darwin cowering at my feet. "Dar, are you okay?"

He flinched when I reached out, so I pulled back.

"What's going on?"

"Is that you, Chess?" He peeked through his arms. "Are you back?"

"Yes, it's me. Why are we here?"

Before I'd slipped away, we'd been sitting near his bed but now we were all the way across the room. One of the wooden walls wasn't sitting properly, as if the wardrobe hinge was broken.

"You slapped me."

"No, I didn't." My stomach twisted.

"You hit me so hard I flew across the room and landed here."

"No." I didn't want to believe I would do such a thing to him.

"When I tried to get away, you practically leaped across the room and pushed me down." His eyes were shiny, sad. "You were about to kick me but froze."

I crouched down in front of him and reached for the red finger marks on his cheek but stopped myself. "That wasn't me."

"I know it wasn't." He sighed. "Your eyes were completely black. And the expression on your face was like a statue. I've never seen you look like that before."

"I'm so sorry."

"It's not you that needs to be sorry."

"I never want... to hurt... you." Tears dribbled down my face and caught in my throat. "Never!" How could I have allowed myself to lose control like this? I might not have been the one in the driver's seat, but my hand had done the damage. I'd temporarily given control of my body to someone else, an entity who wanted to consume me and hurt the people I loved.

I can't let this happen again.

The taste of blood was inside my mouth and my upper lip felt dry. When I wiped the back of my hand under my nose, it came back red.

"Your eyes were black before they switched to white," he said.

"What?"

"I don't know why, but I saw the change just before you came back."

I didn't know what to say and instead offered him my hand. He hesitated but took it and when he was standing in front of me, I threw my arms around his midsection and clung to him. "I'm so, so sorry, Dar. I didn't do this. It wasn't me."

All I could think about was the mark on his face and the horrified glint in his stare. I'd actually hurt him. I was absent during the ordeal, but there was no denying the voice used me to hurt him.

"I know."

"I didn't want to..." The sobs were catching in my chest, making it too hard to speak.

"I know you didn't." He held on tight and rested his chin on the top of my head. "But we can't let this *thing* get control of you again. You're like the Hulk. We can't let you get this angry because when you do, this thing is ready to take over."

I sniffed against his bright yellow T-shirt. "Can't believe I hurt you."

"*He* did. Not you."

"It's still—"

"How about we finish that game of chess?"

I pulled back and rubbed my nose, and noticed I'd stained his tee. "Shit, I got you all dirty."

"Don't worry about it," Darwin said with a lopsided smile. "I'm used to you ruining my clothes."

S IXTEEN
NOW

Saturday, 3am
May 19, 2018

I try to rollover in bed but jolt awake.

My heart hammers inside my chest when I find myself staring down at my bedroom.

Where the hell am I?

I stretch my hands out on either side of my body and find the ceiling pressed against my spine.

How did I get up here?

What is happening to me?

Why am I stuck on the ceiling like some sort of insect?

After trying to mentally run away from the words I read in my mother's grimoire and reliving the one time I hurt Darwin because of the voice, I shouldn't be surprised to find myself in such an impossible situation.

I'm the daughter of someone—no, *something*—dark and horrible, but now I have his name.

Raum.

Even sounding it out in my head sounds gross.

Orobas has to be Shiny Pictures, the horned woman. Except, she's not a woman. She's also some sort of demon who is probably trying to get inside my head so she can beat my father to the punch. Everyone wants to take over my mind and spirit, but I still don't know why.

Although, that's not true either because Mum had theories, and it sounds like Darwin is involved in this raw deal as well. But that's even more confusing because he's never suffered from the delusions I have. He never complained about whispers and certainly didn't randomly pass out all over the place. All the freaky behavior skipped him and latched itself onto me.

But right now, thinking about all of this crap isn't going to help.

I need to get down from the ceiling and I have no idea how to do that.

Just relax, I hear Mum whisper in my ear.

She's right. I have to stay calm or I'm going to hyperventilate and I'm not ready to deal with whatever that leads to. I'm awake and have to get myself back to terra firma.

I use my fingertips to help glide myself along the ceiling, let the momentum push my shoulders across. It takes a long while, and I'm sweating by the time I make it to the light fitting, but I feel accomplished when I can wrap my fingers around something that isn't a smooth surface.

"*It's not going to be that easy,*" the voice says.

My body shakes and my legs flop down so that the only part stuck to the ceiling is my torso. It feels like I'm being bent out of shape and hurts so much a frustrated scream tears out of me.

Nobody raises her head and leaps off the bed. She races across the room and growls when she finds me dangling like a useless chew toy. She barks too loudly, and I try to shush her because I don't want to wake the others. Especially Elvi, not after what happened only hours ago.

"Get rid of the mutt."

"No!"

My mind skips a beat and I'm propelled into darkness.

The world spins upside down and when I'm back, I find myself scuttling across the ceiling like a spider. Shifting like the shades crawling inside Dr. Larunda's office. When I think of her, I reach into my pocket, but my phone isn't there. It's on the carpet below, must have fallen out when I floated like a balloon.

My arms and legs are shuffling at their own accord and when I come to a complete stop, I push all the willpower I can summon into forcing my limbs to keep going. At first, nothing happens because he's in control of my bodily functions, but my arms take me an inch further.

His anger rips through my insides hard enough to feed pressure into my skull, but I push ahead. And stop in the corner of the room. Where the ceiling meets the wall, he forcibly spins me around in a painful twist. My hips pop and ache.

My spine is pinned like a helium balloon to the ceiling again.

"No!"

Nobody runs from one side of the room to the other, jumps to paw at the wall as if she's trying to get to me, but she can't reach.

When a bark tears out of my mouth, I fade away.

Between blinks, I wane in and out.

Saliva dribbles from the side of my mouth the next time I manage to suck in a breath.

Every breath is sticking inside my chest.

I need to get down, but there's nothing to hold on to.

Nobody is barking so loudly it reverberates through me.

When Darwin races into the room, I'm not surprised but want him to leave.

"Calm down, girl." He makes a grab for Nobody's collar but can't get a grip before she squirms away from his grasp.

"Darwin." His name barely bubbles out of me, so he doesn't hear me. Not when the puppy is still going crazy and he's trying to calm her down.

His attention turns to my bed. "Nobody, where's Chess?"

"I'm up here," I struggle to say.

My throat closes up and I feel like I'm about to pass out, so I swallow my breath and words. Try to stay calm, but it's hard to do that when I'm basically panting like a wild beast and can't catch a proper breath.

Darwin finally looks up and when he sees me, he jumps. "Oh, fuck! What the hell are you doing up there?"

I don't reply because I don't want to give Raum the opportunity to take over. Not when Darwin is this close, and I know how much he wants *me* to hurt him. I won't let this asshole push me around. Darwin and I were born into this nightmare, but he's somehow been spared from the worst of it. I'm going to do whatever I can to make sure it stays that way.

If someone deserves to be saved, it's him.

Darwin licks his lips and seems to get a grip because he's now heading towards me with both hands extended upwards, in my direction. "Come on, reach out and I'll get you down."

A terrifying growl roars out of my mouth when he nears.

"Chess, it's okay. I'm not going to hurt you."

I want to tell him it's not me doing this, but Raum won't let me. He's put a gag on me and the only sounds I can make are guttural. I spot my shadow in the adjacent corner. She seems to be in the same position, but is rotating head over heels, reaching towards the same spot Darwin would be in if he were on that side of the room.

Except, that's not me. She's the one that keeps skittering away from my body because she's somehow connected but isn't.

"Reach out," he says. "Come on, I can grab you."

I close my eyes and remember what my mother told me to do that day in the backyard, when she was trying to warn me about the awful things to come.

Accepting every thought inside my head isn't hard but letting them go takes a bit more effort. I let all the horrible truths I read about in her journal flow through me, imagine everything finding its way into one of the many rooms I have inside me, so I can store everything for another time. I take all the fear and let the sticky residue flow out of my fingertips.

When I visualize myself reaching for Darwin, my eyes snap open.

Our fingers connect.

He grabs my hands and pulls, but ghostly wings wrap around my midsection and pin me to the spot.

Darwin's not a quitter and he puts up a fight.

When I'm floating closer, Raum takes over. He makes me bark like a rabid dog, but Darwin still drags me down until my toes finally touch the floor.

"Thank you," I whisper and throw my arms around his neck because Raum's presence has slipped from my limbs.

I'm so grateful, I cling to him like he's my lifeline and he does the same. His arms are tight around my waist, and I never want him to let go. We've always been two peas in a pod and I've never felt closer to him. He saved me from myself. His body against mine feels so good, and right.

Suddenly, his being this close makes me feel… *strange*.

"Are you okay?" He pushes back enough for me to see his face, but his hands linger on my waist. "What did he do to you?" His jaw clenches so tightly the muscles twitch.

A new trail of bruises runs up and down my arms, but I know they're all over my body. It's Raum trying to punch his way out.

I shrug.

Darwin checks for injuries and cups my face in his hands when he's done. "This has to stop." His thumbs are rubbing my jaw in a way that sends shivers down my spine. "I'm not going to let him hurt you like this anymore."

I don't know how he can possibly keep me safe but don't focus on that. I stare into his beautiful chocolate-brown eyes and wonder how I've spent my whole life gazing into them and never realized how he really makes me feel. A burning sensation spreads below my bellybutton and a sigh escapes me.

This can't be happening.

I can't let it happen.

"What's wrong?" He looks worried—always so worried about me. Even after all the times when I've scared him half to death, and he's had to hide truths from our mothers because of me, he still cares enough to check up on me. Every single time.

I'm so grateful and I love him so much. There's only one way to show him how much he means to me. I close the distance between us, press my body flush with his and press my mouth against his. This is my first attempt at a kiss, so it's clumsy and forceful. So very strange.

"Whoa, what're you doing?" He pulls back quickly, but his hands are still on my face. Our bodies are pressed so tight I can feel his heartbeat.

I kiss him again, a lot softer than my first attempt. This time, I feel his lips quiver in response. When we part, because Darwin jerks away from me, he stares into my eyes and seems dazed but doesn't say anything.

Then he's the one who kisses *me*. I don't understand what's going on or why we suddenly find ourselves here, but his hands are wound tightly around my back and our lips set a frantic rhythm. When his tongue slips inside my mouth and collides with mine, I feel an electric shock run all the way to my toes.

I lose my fingers in his thick hair and love how our bodies fit together.

And I suddenly imagine doing so many wicked things with this boy, they run through my mind like they've already happened. I never imagined a kiss could feel like this, more than physical and wrapped up in such intense emotion. A desire I've never known.

I open my eyes for a split second and find his are closed, and his breathing is getting heavier. The way we're kissing is frantic, as if we can't get enough of each other. As if we've been holding back this lust for so long it's ready to burst.

"Chester," he whispers against my mouth.

"Darwin," I whisper back.

He presses his forehead against mine and his heart beats fast, so our thuds echo each other. Our lips join again, and I can't believe we're doing this, but refuse to stop because it feels too good.

"What in the hell do you think you're doing?"

Elvi's voice cuts through my murky thoughts of desire hard enough to break us apart. Our arms drop to our sides, and I notice his cheeks are flushed, eyes dark.

Darwin shakes his head, looks confused but he doesn't break eye contact.

I wipe my mouth when I realize what I've done. My lips feel tingly, but the fervor is fading fast.

What did I do? I crossed a line that should never be crossed. All I can do is remember my mother warning me about developing feelings for Darwin. But everything I told her back then was true, is *still* true. Yet, as I stare into his eyes and see the desire reflected inside, I realize my wickedness has affected him. Muddled his brain and emotions. Did Mum fear something like this would happen eventually?

"That felt really good, didn't it, Chesty?"

I try to back away, but Darwin takes my hand.

"I'm sorry," I say.

"Don't be." His fingers are warm.

My whole body feels cold, arctic.

I look past him, at Elvi and she's both sad and mortified. But when her eyes stray to the floor and I follow her gaze, I spot the open grimoire. It must have fallen when I floated to the ceiling. Before I can stop her, she reaches the book and peeks inside before snapping it shut and running her fingers over the cover. I can practically hear her mind working overtime, trying to figure out what Mum's notebook is doing in my bedroom.

"You're shaking," Darwin says.

My attention goes back to him, and I feel bad for what I did. I have no right to confuse him like this. I'm weak and allowed Raum's poison to infiltrate too deep. "I'm so sorry. I didn't mean to…"

"I told you not to be sorry."

With his hand still holding mine, I can't help but flash back to how good and tingly he made me feel when we kissed. I enjoyed the way our lips worked in tandem and how his hands were all over me. His tongue was a surprise I'd never expected… And I suddenly remember Su. I kissed her boyfriend. Even worse, I kissed someone I've always referred to as my brother.

"You two, in the kitchen now," Elvi says as she heads for the door.

Nobody is licking my free hand and whines.

"But Ma, can't you see—"

"I've seen plenty already. Now come to the kitchen where I'll brew us some tea."

"I don't think tea—"

"Darwin, I'm not asking. I'm telling both of you to come to the kitchen. *Now*. There are some things we need to discuss and after what I've witnessed, it looks like it's well overdue." She leaves the bedroom without a backward glance.

We're both silent in the tense air trapped inside this room.

I don't want to apologize again or talk about what happened, even if the details are still whizzing around my brain. What I did is wrong. I enjoyed kissing Darwin, but this can never happen again.

It wasn't me. *Raum* made me do it.

"But you're the one who enjoyed it so much."

I don't know who's thought this is.

"Let's go and see what she wants, huh?"

I nod, grateful Darwin doesn't say anything about what happened.

Even though Raum knows what we mean to each other, he still made me do this.

"If that bitch hadn't interrupted, you and the pest would've been doing a whole lot more by now. Don't you wish you'd gone all the way with him?"

I ignore his intrusive suggestion, refuse to respond to his taunts.

"I should've thought of this a long time ago," he coos. *"Nothing pushes a weak person over the edge as quickly as carnal sin."*

"Shut up!"

Darwin tightens his grip around my hand as we leave the room. "Don't let him get to you more than he already has."

I meet his gaze because I feel that on some level, he totally knows what happened between us was out of my hands. Out of his too. Whatever Raum did, it bewitched both of us. I wish Elvi hadn't seen us kissing because she's already angry with me. What did she call me earlier?

"An abomination," Raum answers.

She's not wrong. Not after what I did. What I enjoyed doing and didn't want to stop.

As we pass under the doorway, I spot the shadow sink into the ceiling and still don't know if she was trying to help me or not. Or even if this was really Mum.

Seventeen
NOW

Saturday, 4am
May 19, 2018

By the time we reach the kitchen, I'm not shaking as badly.

Elvi is standing behind the kitchen counter while the kettle boils behind her. She's thumbing through Mum's diary—grimoire—and I feel a violent need to rip the book away from her grasp. I don't, because I've already done enough to hurt her and don't know if she'll ever forgive me.

Nobody is by my side, a comforting ball of fur I'm starting to get used to. The way she reacted when she spotted me on the ceiling only confirms she can tell when I slip out of my body and become someone—*something*—else.

How much of me was in control when I kissed Darwin? Who was in the driver's seat as I thrust my fingers into his hair and swept my tongue over his? Not me because I would never do that to him, or to myself. Yet, the tingle on my lips confirms that no matter who was in control at the time, I didn't think it was awful. I suppose the part of me who has always hero-worshiped Darwin is trying to make me feel better about this disturbing situation.

"Don't lie to yourself, you've always wanted him for yourself."
No, that's not true.

Even as the thought leaves my mind, I wonder if the voice is partly right. I remember the day I saw him making out with Su, and how betrayed I felt when they snuck around behind my back. Until that day I thought it would always be Dar and Chess against the world, but when he got romantically involved with our friend, everything changed.

"You want him to be yours," he taunts. *"But you're both mine."*
We don't belong to anyone but ourselves.
"That's what you think."

I risk taking a peek at Darwin and when he catches my eye and offers me a shy smile, I feel the strength to push the voice away. I refuse to let Raum get the upper hand again. He made me crawl along the ceiling, to bark and groan like a beast, but I refuse to allow him the satisfaction of thinking he knows anything about my emotional state.

Nobody growls beside me. She can sense I'm still struggling.

"Are you okay?" Darwin asks, squeezing my hand.

I nod quickly, while psychically trying to shove the voice back into his room at the end of the corridor. But he's loose now and the barn door won't fully close.

Darwin runs his thumb over the back of my hand, and I use it to ground myself. His shiny eyes make me feel as if something has definitely shifted between us, and I'm not comfortable with that. Not entirely. Can a few kisses change everything forever? According to some of the books I read and the movies I watch, they usually do. But I don't want to ruin our wholesome connection. He's the only person who truly understands me, and the last thing I want to do is cloud his vision about what we are to each other.

"You've been reading this." Elvi's statement is devoid of all emotion, so flat I think it couldn't have possibly slipped from the mouth of someone as seemingly together as her. When I don't answer she looks up, and I manage a nod.

A shiver runs through me, and Darwin helps me into one of the kitchen chairs. He takes the one beside me and drags it closer.

Elvi places a mug in front of each of us and in the process smacks them harder against the table than necessary, some tea spills down the sides.

"Drink this, it'll help," she says.

I'm not sure how anything will help but I'm glad for a distraction and take a sip, let the smooth chamomile taste slide down my throat. I can also detect a hint of honey and maybe even peppermint, plus something else I don't recognize. Either way, I drink half before I put the mug down.

Darwin sips his cautiously.

Strangely, Elvi isn't drinking at all.

Nobody sits under the table near my feet and finally seems settled. I take her reaction as a good sign and allow myself to sit back on the chair.

Elvi is upset for good reason, but I want to clear the air. Our mothers aren't innocent in all of this. They might be a happy, married couple who gave us the same surname and formed a family after a turbulent time in their young lives, but when we both turned six, they decided to stop raising us together. They sent Darwin away to boarding school, splitting up our happy family.

Now I can't help but wonder if separating us was because of all this demonic crap. Did our mothers fear what happened in my bedroom only minutes ago would happen someday? Did they know the demonic influence might push me into Darwin's arms because he was a kind and nice boy always willing to comfort me? Suddenly, Mum's accusation about Darwin comes to mind. Did she ask because she was worried about Raum's influence, and not because she was concerned about the two teenagers who got along so well?

She's not here to ask, so I'll never know.

"How long have you been reading Mena's grimoire?" Elvi asks, breaking the silence.

I blink away my thoughts and concentrate on that word again. *Grimoire.* Mum's journal is actually some sort of ritual book, even Dr. Larunda called it the same thing. I don't like the word because it sounds witchy but after reading her rantings, also seems fitting.

"Chester!" she snaps. "I asked you a question."

"Um..." I lick my lips. "I started reading it about a week ago." I avoid Darwin's eyes but feel him shift in his chair.

"Why didn't you tell me you'd found it?"

I meet her eyes. "I don't know."

"I've been looking for this darn thing everywhere, hoping it might shed some light about what's going on and where Mena went."

"You didn't know where the notebook was?"

"A grimoire is a very personal item." She pushes a strand of hair away from her face. The messy bun is collapsing around her face, but she makes no effort to fix it. "It feels wrong to take a peek now, but I know a lot of what she keeps inside. I was there when she wrote most of it. We've often recorded similar information."

"You have a Dreaded Notebook too?" Darwin asks after taking a slow, slurping sip.

"All practitioners do."

"So, you're into demonology too?"

She glares at him for several silent moments. "How do you know about that?"

"My therapist mentioned it," I answer. "So, I spoke to Dar about it."

She's quiet for a moment, and I can tell her mind is racing too fast to express everything she wants to say. "Looks like you two have been keeping a lot of things from me during the last few months." She's fidgety, uncomfortable. "What I walked into back there, is that something you two do often?"

"No!" we both answer at the same time.

"Are you sure?"

"Ma, we've never..." He glances at me then looks away.

"That's never happened before," I whisper. Maybe I should add that it shouldn't have happened at all, but the words won't come out.

"You can pretend all you want, but I know what you felt and how much you enjoyed having his hands all over you and his tongue in your mouth."

I shake my head.

"You wanted him to fuck you, didn't you?"

"Shut up!"

"I'm sick of reading your silly thoughts about not wanting or needing intimate contact," Raum says. *"Everyone craves a connection. I showed you what it feels like, but you did most of the work. And I know you liked it. Admit it."*

Strong hands stop me before I can hit my head.

"Chess, it's okay." Darwin's voice is like music to my ears. "Open your eyes, he's not here. *I'm* here, and so is Ma and Nobody."

I slowly open them and find strength in him. I remember what I did the last time I stared this deeply into his eyes and I'm relieved that I'm not compelled to throw myself at him.

"That's it, you're back now." His fingers caress my face and I automatically lean into the connection.

"He's getting stronger," Elvi says.

Darwin is kneeling in front of me, and Nobody has her head on my lap.

"I'm fine, I'm back."

"Are you sure?" he asks.

I nod.

"Why didn't you tell me about the journal?" Darwin whispers, and the hurt on his face makes me sad. "I'm not angry, just trying to figure out why you wouldn't at least mention that you brought it inside." He stands, sits back down beside me.

"I..." First, I look at Elvi before flicking my gaze to him. "I wanted to share something with my mother, alone. She was always writing in that thing and seemed more interested in filling those pages than anything else." I shrug. "I'm sorry." I hold his stare as my next words tumble out. "I've been doing a lot of weird stuff lately, and I've involved you in enough already."

"I don't mind, I never did. Don't forget our pinkie promise." He taps his shoulder against mine. "I want to help you through this, through everything."

"Can you two please stop acting like a pair of lovesick birds?" Elvi shuts the book and stands straighter, crosses her arms over her stomach. "You both denied kissing before this incident, yet your body language and the way you talk to each other negates that."

"I don't know what you mean." Darwin shakes his head. "We've always been this way. We're best friends No, much closer than that. We're—"

"Siblings?" she cuts in.

He nods quickly but doesn't hold her stare because we all know siblings don't kiss each other. My stomach lurches at the thought of how I've altered everything.

A dry chuckle escapes her. "All I see is *you*, Darwin, going out of your way to help Chester out of her latest problem. Every time. You bend over backwards, always have. I used to think it was because of your kind nature, because you thought of her as your sister. When you started seeing Su, I was happy to be wrong about…" She shakes her head. "But my worst fears were confirmed earlier."

"I'm sorry, okay?" I snap at her. "I didn't mean to kiss Dar like that. He helped get me down from the ceiling and I was so grateful… Something took over, made me…"

"I know, honey." Her eyes are shiny, unshed tears swimming inside. "I understand how hard this must be for you." She abandons the grimoire and comes over to sit on my other side. Elvi takes a couple of short breaths, seems to be collecting her thoughts. "I know why you did it. It's for the same reason you came at me with scissors, the same reason why you scratched away the protective circle…" She pushes the hair away from her face. "I was stupid enough to think this would never happen, but it has. It's such a shock to find the kids you think of as your own kissing like that. I've seen some awful things in my life, but when I walked into your room and found you two… it shook me to the bone."

"Ma, stop making her feel guilty."

"That's not what I'm doing."

"Can you maybe spell out what you're trying to say, then?" Darwin takes another sip of his tea.

"Chester, someone is compelling you to do bad things," she says. "But what I'm specifically talking about now has to do with Darwin."

He sputters, almost chokes on a sip. "What about me?"

"At first, we sent you to boarding school because we needed to watch over Chester very closely, to make sure nothing demonic slipped through. Since you didn't show any signs of disturbance, sending you away seemed like the best option. And you still got to spend holidays at home with us, you always loved spending time together."

"That's why you send me away to school?"

"Yes, we're not proud of it but when you were about to start high school and wanted to come home, we thought it would be safe. I was still worried that when you both hit puberty you might start getting confused, but Mena told me not to worry. She didn't seem to see the way you looked at each other, or how your overprotective nature towards Chester could become more." She meets his gaze. "Darwin, I've suspected for a while now that you might be…" She pauses and sighs. "That your feelings for Chester might run deeper than they should."

"What?" I can't believe she would say such a thing.

"Ma!" he yells. "I have a girlfriend."

"You have a safety net, a way of guarding your true feelings."

He shakes his head. "That's not true."

"You're wrong," I tell her. "Mum asked me about this already, but I told her the same thing I'm going to tell you—you're totally wrong. Darwin is happy with Su, and I'm happy for both of them."

She considers her son. "I saw the way you kissed her, how you held her." She turns to me. "Although you were compelled, demons can only manipulate and exploit feelings and desires that are already there."

"You're really grossing me out." Darwin can't look at either of us. "Can we talk about something else? Let's go back to the journal conversation."

"It's okay." I take his hand and lace my fingers through his. He doesn't resist but his body is rigid. "Elvi's right."

"What? No, she's not—"

"She's right about my own feelings being manipulated by some asshole demonic entity, so why can't she be right about him doing the same to you by using me?"

He shakes his head. "I don't understand."

I have to face some hard truths. It's not fair to make him feel bad because of something I did. Raum has weaved his way in and out of my head for as long as I can remember, so he knows how much I love Darwin. He's also good at twisting everything good into something perverse. I sigh and stare at our joined hands.

"The voice has been with me for a long time, and he knows how close we are. He also knows that I love you and depend on you"—I spare a quick glance at Elvi— "so, of course he tried to manipulate me at my weakest. And he compelled you to react in the same way. We've always found comfort in each other. He just pushed us over the edge, exploited what wasn't even there."

His expression softens, but he doesn't say anything.

"There's a very good reason why I'm pointing this out," Elvi interrupts and shifts in her seat. "Chester, if you've read far enough in Mena's grimoire, you probably know what I'm talking about."

I nod because the horror has already started seeping in.

"Minus the demonic disturbance, Mena and I have been as honest as we could with you kids." She stops to wring her hands together, nervously. Her energy is frenetic. "We've been a couple since we were your age, so I know what hormones and spending countless hours together can do to two people. It's why I'm not being as harsh as I should be, not with everything else that's going on." She sighs. "But our honesty had limits for some very horrible reasons, and we left out a few things or hinted at others, without actually spelling anything out."

"You're talking about our father." The words almost make me choke, but I manage to get them out. I reach for my spirit bag and my breath catches when I can't find it. I search my PJ pocket but it's empty. Where did it go? No wonder Raum can come and go as he pleases. When was the last time I replaced it? I can't even remember.

Laughter echoes inside my brain, spreading through the vacant corridor. I hold on tight to Darwin's hand.

"You mean our *fathers*?" He squirms beside me.

"I first met Mena when we were fifteen and my parents decided to join a *movement*. They were tired of city living and demanding jobs, decided it was best to escape to the country." She laughs, but there's no humor behind the sound. "That's a flashy way of saying they joined a cult. They sold all their belongings and we relocated to a commune of farmhouses. The closest town was over an hour away, and only a select few would go to get supplies when needed. We didn't need much because we lived and hunted off the land." She shakes her head. "Not long after we arrived, the leader spoke to my parents and told them I was going to become one of his brides. He took two at a time and I was to be the second one. It was a big deal."

"Why have we never heard this before?"

"I'm sorry, Darwin, it was too hard to talk about."

"Please, keep going." I knew some of this story, but not all of it.

"Of course, they agreed. They were both beyond brainwashed by this stage and ironically had new jobs to keep them busy. They also saw this opportunity as an honor. I moved into his house, where I shared a room with a feisty brunette. We became friends and the more time we spent together, the more we fell for each other. It wasn't supposed to go that way. We were to be his brides and at constant competition with each other, only devoted to his needs, not each other's." She sighs. "We spent so much time alone that it was bound to happen. Two girls weren't supposed to fall in love in the cult. They could engage in activities to entertain the leader, but never for each other. That didn't stop us. Isolation, comfort, and love wrapped us so tightly we kept our relationship a secret and escaped when things got really bad."

"Who was this guy?" Darwin is still holding my hand, but his other arm is thrown over his belly in a defensive manner.

"He was a God to all of us. Raum the Prophet was believed to be a smart and powerful man, a visionary. One who would teach us the proper ways and lead in rituals and ceremonies to transform our lives. His followers would be equipped with skills that would carry them forward in this life and the next. None realized they were signing themselves over to eternal damnation." Elvi gets a faraway glint in her eyes. "We soon realized that being his brides was a sham too. He said we would become his true wives after he took our purity during a very important ceremony. One of us would get pregnant and we would be one big happy family. But because he snuck in and out of our beds... we both fell pregnant beforehand. And he lied about needing two of us, too."

"Mum wrote about that," I say.

She nods. "You share the same father."

"*What?*" Darwin yanks his hand away and stands, puts a bit of distance between us.

"You and Chester have the same father," she repeats. "It's why it's time I get this out in the open. You can't be together because you're half-siblings."

"No, that's not possible! You told us—"

"I'm sorry, son, but it's the truth." She sighs. "Well, it's as true as he wants it to be."

He stops pacing. "What the hell does that mean?"

"He wasn't human," I answer.

Darwin glances at me and sighs.

"Raum is a demon who flows in and out of this world." Elvi looks sad. "When he was with me, I was with a beautiful man—tall, dark, and handsome. The same man who could charm everyone out of their money and belongings. But when Mena was with him, he was something else entirely. With her, he was himself."

"The giant crow-man?" It's a testimony to how much crap we've been through that I can actually say this with a straight face.

She nods. "And for that reason, you two share the same father but at the same time, don't. Raum is a multi-faceted demoniac who wears different skins."

"Wait a minute, so if he was two different people when we were…" He gags. "God, even thinking about this makes my skin crawl. If he was dressed as a different guy, we can't be brother and sister."

"Maybe not technically, but it's a stretch," she says.

He sighs and it's a full body thing. "So, we're not siblings." When his gaze drills into me, the spark I noticed after we kissed is flickering through. Finding out we're half-brother and sister sort-of is disturbing, but he seems relieved at the possibility that we're not.

"Why did Raum have access to me since I was born?" The hints Mum mentioned in her account were devastating so I shouldn't chase this, but I have to know.

"We think it's because Mena was impregnated by his true form, so their connection wasn't completely severed. But I did something to ensure he couldn't get to Darwin."

"What did you do?" he asks.

She glances at her son. "As soon as we got back from the hospital, we performed a guardian angel ritual. It worked on you but not on Chester." She shifts her attention to me. "We were forced to call on another darker guardian to protect you." She sighs. "There was nothing else we could do to protect you from him."

Darwin stops pacing. "Wait a minute, what *darker guardian?* What does that even mean?"

"He wasn't going to stop until he got what he wanted." Her face is sadder than usual. "There was no other way."

"Why didn't you try harder to find a guardian angel for Chess?"

"We did, we tried so many times, but…"

"I understand," I say, putting a hand over hers. "I'm glad you were able to spare Darwin from all of this. Glad he didn't end up like me." And I mean it with all my heart and soul. I got Shiny Pictures out of this deal, but I'm still not sure how much defending she'll be doing.

He sighs and sits down again, takes my hand. "Don't say that."

"It's the truth," Elvi says. "I didn't want you to suffer through the endless possibility of demonic possession."

"But—"

"Darwin, we couldn't take that chance."

"Did he get his clutches into me because of the final sacrifice my mother made before leaving the compound?" By the horrified shock in her eyes, she knows exactly what I mean. "It is, isn't it?"

She finally says, "We think so."

"What am I missing?" Darwin asks, but we don't answer.

Elvi pushes the chair back and stands. She goes to the sink and stares out the window, into the night. "It's too painful to go into, but yes. Mena and I believe that was the case and Larunda confirmed it."

Was there anything my mother hadn't sacrificed? She'd insisted he take her first during the ceremony because she didn't want Elvi to be violated again and made her unborn child vulnerable. Raum had access to me from conception. It's a miracle he didn't make me one of his human puppets years ago. It also speaks volumes about her tenacity to never give up.

"She put both of you at risk because of me." Elvi turns around and tears are streaming down her face. "I know this situation is totally fucked up and some of what we've done is unforgivable, but we have to stick together. We need to find Mena before it's too late."

"Who has her?" I ask.

"I don't know."

"But we can figure it out, right?" Darwin adds.

"I'm not sure."

"Then I have to keep reading her grimoire," I say. "It's what Dr. Larunda told me to do. She said to find answers, and names, to contact her so she can fill in the rest."

"Larunda said that?"

I nod.

She picks up the grimoire and brings it over. "Go to the last entry."

I open the book at the bookmarked page but flick past most of the entries. They're much shorter, and every drawing is now precise and artistic. She wrote a random paragraph here and there about how old I was, and how many times I heard voices or woke up from nightmares. According to her notes I've been doing it since I was born, and sleepwalking started as soon as I could walk. One particular time she claims I wrote RAUM on the wall using crayons and Darwin kept asking what that meant.

"Even as a baby I was messed up." How did they put up with me? Why didn't Mum give me up so I would stop tormenting her? "She should've let him have me."

"Chess, what the hell?" Darwin says.

"Mena loves you very much and spent her life trying to right what she believed was her wrong." Elvi sighs. "We both love you and will do whatever we have to."

Mum goes on to state she told us stories to keep us interested and pushed our imagination in other, safer directions. There are lists—so many lists—and dates where she's marked the pills I took. She even mentioned when I appeared to feel fine against when I didn't. She says things like *'distracted'* and *'angrier than usual,'* or *'scratches at her skin and doesn't even realize it.'* She also kept a register of doctors.

"Two pages are doctor names." I recognized quite a few.

"You didn't go to all of them, some were potentials."

"This isn't revealing much," I say.

"It reveals a lot more than you think." Elvi sighs. "She wanted to monitor you, make sure Raum was kept at a distance for as long as she could before telling you everything. And she was, you know. On your eighteenth birthday, she planned to tell you exactly what all the risks were and how to combat him. She was going to tell you about Orobas, too."

"I already know about Shiny Pictures."

"Who?" she asks.

"It's what I used to call her…" I pause when I reach the next page.

"What is it?" Darwin asks.

"It's a letter from Mum."

"You don't have to read it out loud." Elvi's hand is on my shoulder, and I like the comfort she's offering. Even after every uncomfortable thing she's seen and we've discussed, she's still by my side.

"I know, but I want to."

MUM'S (DREADED) NOTEBOOK
A Letter from Mum

March 7, 2018

Dear Chester,

This is a letter you might never see. No, it's a letter I hope you NEVER have to read.

Yet, it's still important that I write it because if something happens to me, you need to know a few things. There's so much I haven't told you. So much I've wanted to share, but I was too afraid that knowing the awful truth might push you over the edge. That it might make it easier for him to get a total grip on your mind, body and soul.

I know you're strong, stronger than you know, but he's always ready to strike. It's unsettling, but I can tell when he's watching me behind your eyes. Just like I could always tell when Raum was watching me from across the room.

So much of what I want to tell you about him is terrible and unforgivable, but he wasn't all bad. When he lived for any amount of time amongst people, he softened slightly. He would fixate on someone and do whatever he could to please them, even if it were because he wanted something in return. Unfortunately, I was that fixation for a while. He bathed me with attention and love, made me feel special for several happy months of my life. Long enough for me to fall for his trickery and believe he was all I needed. Or wanted.

Until he brought Elvi into the house, I thought my life was set. But meeting her changed everything. Made me see things for what they really were, to the point where I started really looking into the man I was so in awe of, and discovered he wasn't really a man at all. He was so much more. An entity I'd never considered existed. I always associated him to be more god than devil. It was a shock, but enough to wake me up to the truth.

Of course, it wasn't early enough to stop him from planting his seed. Yet, I don't regret that either. If I hadn't fallen pregnant, I never would've had you, or met your bright soul and seen your beautiful, perfect little face.

I've achieved some good things in this life and have so much more to be ashamed of, but <u>YOU</u> are the best of everything. The love I felt for you the first time I held you in my arms was something I will never be able to sum up in words. The feeling was instant and strong, and I vowed to protect you for as long as I could. No matter what the cost, I was prepared to make sure you survived and lived a normal life.

It didn't always work out that way, but I really tried. I tried. So hard.

I'm sorry that I couldn't fulfil my own goal, but I need you to know that I did everything I could. I even considered an abortion before you were born. Well, we both did. But it was something we couldn't do, something that I'm glad we only considered as a passing thought. The happiness, joy, and pride you two kids provided us with is immense. I wouldn't trade that for anything.

But you need to accept that I'm the sole reason why your life has been so hard, unstable, and full of moments where you aren't even sure if you're yourself anymore. You have no idea how much it tears me up every time you pass out and wake up somewhere else. Or when you've scribbled a message on the wall that means all kinds of awful things, but you can't remember doing it. The worst is when he completely takes over and sends you climbing the walls and hides you so deep inside your own mind that you send messages to me via slashes on your skin.

I'll never forget when you wrote HELP *across your belly. It was so clearly your childish handwriting, but so alien at the same time. I can't forgive myself for those sheer terrifying moments, but at least I can rest assured that you don't remember them. I think that will probably change the older you get, because soon you'll hold onto some of the horrible things. He'll make sure you do.*

The mental scars I've accumulated throughout the years are nothing compared to your suffering, but I suppose the one saving grace is that you don't remember doing half of the things you've done. There are a lot of terrible things he's made you do to try and consume your soul, but I've done what I can along the way to keep him out. The salt pills, baths, the doctors, and the psychic safeguards might all seem like a waste of time and fill you with anxious energy, but it was all necessary. All these combined have made life easier for all of us. Even the pentagram under your bed, the one you don't know about.

The worst of times were during your toddler to kindergarten years, when you didn't understand what was going on and he used you like a ragdoll to get back at me. To haunt me with sadness and make me feel useless. That's when you often turned to Orobas. You called her your invisible friend and said she reminded you of a pony from TV. I can't remember what you called her, but you made up a name.

I need to tell you about her. She's a strong demon, but one of the good ones. She'll have your back and will assist you, but you have to understand that she too will require payment. And the demonic only accept one currency—souls.

Orobas will be there when you need her, but her payment is steep. So, don't call on her unless you absolutely have to.

After all the research I've done, I've come to the conclusion that she's a much better option to tie yourself to than Raum. He will suck you dry, but she'll work with you. And if you plan to accept her help, tear off the folded sheet of paper glued on the next page and read the instructions to protect yourself. To take control of the situation. It's a way to make a bad situation better—if not bearable. Memorize the words and get rid of the evidence. But you can't show or tell anyone what you read. That's a secret weapon only you should have.

You'll know when the time is right.

I've done all I can to keep Raum away from you and nothing's worked. I don't like what I have to do next, but it's necessary. A lot of what I did to try and keep you safe involved research in demonology circles that most try to stay away from because they are on the fringes of society, but I sought them out because they offered detailed occult assistance.

After everything we did, it always leads back to him.

Yes, your father found me. No matter how many religious and non-religious exorcisms we tried, none of them worked. Expelling a demonic entity that creeps into your body is one thing, trying to get one out that's inside your head and has been a part of you since birth is another. At least all those experiences were erased, and you'll never have to endure them, but they happened, and I'll never forget.

Anyway, every bit of experience I've accumulated came with an uncomfortable payment. One of those payments is now due, and I have no choice but to honor it... I have to leave.

There are a lot of things I'm ashamed of, but I hope you understand that everything I've ever done was to keep you safe. All the nagging, endless questions and the pill-popping were for your own good.

Chester, you are my heart and soul. I want you to be happy and to have a normal life someday. That's all I ever wanted, but I'm afraid that's not possible. There's only one way to release you from all of this, and that's to give myself over to the shadows.

I hate to leave you, but there's no other choice. It breaks my heart that I'll never see Elvi or Darwin again either, but you'll all be stronger without me. Tell Elvi I've left her a letter in the workroom on my favorite shelf, she'll know which one that is. And tell Darwin that I'm very proud of him. He's a great kid and I'll always owe him for the sacrifices he's made for you. He never complained or got angry, not even when you beat him up because of Raum. He took care of you. He's a wonderful person to have as a friend and it was an honor to have him as a son.

Now, I only have one thing left to say. Remember what you did this afternoon? I'm so proud of what you did, glad you can finally block that son of a bitch out of your mind. You need to accept how much this ability can help you overcome him. And use it to your advantage.

When you hit puberty, you developed your own strength and he's finding it harder to overcome, so don't let him. Don't ever lose that skill and fight, fight, FIGHT. Don't shy away from your bravery.

Chester, I love you more than anything.
Forever hugs,
Mum
PS. You can trust Larunda and Purson, completely.

Eighteen
NOW

Saturday, 4:05am
May 19, 2018

"... you can trust Larunda and Purson, completely." As soon as I say the last word out loud, I burst into tears. Every emotion I've been bottling up bursts out in great big sobs.

Mum wrote this letter before she disappeared. Was that why she was so persistent about practicing my mind exercises that afternoon, when she kept saying she wasn't going to be around forever?

The words written in her grimoire blur through my tears. A very important piece of this puzzle is still missing and my chest heaves, making me feel brittle. I've never felt such weakness, like sodden paper that will tear easily.

Darwin throws his arms over the backs of my shoulders and Elvi joins the family hug. I try to find comfort in them, but it's hard.

Despite all the bleak stuff she mentioned in her letter—most I don't even remember—we had great times too. Now that I know as many truths as I can handle, I refuse to let our story end like this.

I can't let my mother sacrifice her own soul to a demon she banished, but never gave up searching for her. That he sought her out through me after everything they endured to escape him, makes my skin crawl. I'm not sure if the payment she had to make is to him or not, but I need to find her—save her. I know what Raum is capable of and don't wish that on anyone, especially not my own mother.

I don't care if I have to drag her out of hell, he's not keeping her.

"I need to call Dr. Larunda," I say, wiping away the tears dripping off my chin.

"What's that going to do?" Darwin's arms are still around me and I'm glad. The comfort he provides is fueling my determination.

"She told me to contact her when I was ready." And I'm ready now.

I'm done being scared and confused. It's time to take charge of the situation.

Elvi steps out of the embrace and her eyes are shiny with tears. "Okay, so you call her, and then what?" At least she understands the situation we're in. She's protective of us too, but she was right when she accused her son of being *overprotective*.

"She told me to contact her as soon as I knew everything, right?" An uneasy sigh escapes me. "Now, I need to know why, and how she can help us find Mum."

"But honey, you read the letter, she's—"

"I don't care what the letter says." I untangle myself from Darwin and stand. "I need to talk to her."

I leave the kitchen with the grimoire in hand. My phone isn't in my pocket, so it has to be in my room somewhere. I probably dropped it on my way to the ceiling. The thought makes me cringe. Did I float up there like possessed girls do in the movies? Or did I climb the walls like some freaky insect?

Before anything else, I stop in the middle of the hallway and yank the small, folded piece of paper Mum stuck to the page after her letter. My pulse quickens, but I read every word enough times to summarize what I need to say and do, before scrunching it up into a tiny ball and shoving it into the pocket of my sweatpants. I hug the notebook to my chest and make my way along the carpeted corridor.

The dark corners of the ceiling shift like smoke so I walk faster. Still, when I catch movement out of the corner of my eye, I look up.

My shadow is crawling over the ceiling, but away from my room.

"Where are you going?"

She pauses and motions for me to follow. That's when I understand she isn't me. This is definitely the piece that keeps splitting away.

"I can't go," I say. "I need my phone."

She shakes her head and skitters away, disappears into the kitchen.

A second later, Nobody wanders into the corridor with me. Her eyes are glowing as she glares into the darkness ahead. I lose my fingers in her fur, find comfort in her presence. She's much taller now and barely resembles the small Staffordshire Bull Terrier I found in the bin. She's tall and bulky, brings to mind a full-grown Rottweiler.

If she's supposed to be my guardian, companion or familiar sent by some mysterious *person*, it's time to make sure I treat her like one.

We step forward, matching each other step for step.

The silhouettes and unidentifiable swirls shift overhead, and they remind me of the ones I always spot in Dr. Larunda's office. But these seem different. Their actions are languid, like tentacles stuck to the walls and barely bothering to reach out. And there are whispers too, nothing I can decipher but plenty of sound fills my ears with an irritating buzz.

Even from here I can feel the wrongness around me.

Our house, this hallway, my bedroom, none of these spaces have ever felt so foreign. As if whatever these things are have taken over. When the thought creeps into my brain, I pause. Because isn't that exactly what's happening? When was the last time I bothered with the salt protection or checked to make sure crystals were still on my windowsill? I'd promised Mum that I would take care of all that but hadn't.

At least I still have my spirit bag.

My heart falters, because when my fingers reach for its familiar weight around my neck and find nothing there, I remember that I've lost it all over again. All of my protections and safeguards are disappearing fast, and I know who's erased them. Maybe when I wasn't aware of what I was doing, but it was still me.

You had to let go of the barriers to face the truth.

I'm not sure if that's my own inner thought or not, but I'm glad it doesn't sound hostile.

The pup growls, a more guttural groan than usual.

"What is it?"

She responds by overtaking me, running into the dark.

I catch up and she barks a warning at me, telling me to stay back. But I'm not going to stop now because I have to get my phone. And more importantly, I need to see what's happening inside my bedroom.

Something awful is in there, bad enough to make part of my shadow run away.

I take a deep breath, release it and rush forward.

The edges of the doorway are caked in black tar that's slowly extending into the hallway ceiling. I don't know what this gooey stuff is, but I'm sure it's the same liquid rotting the wooden walls of the abandoned place I constantly find myself in when I'm asleep.

It feels like real life is being eaten away by my nightmares, and the scary places usually pushed deeply into the confines of my head are spilling out. Everything is merging into one big sticky mess. I might not fully understand how something this strange is possible, but I won't let this nightmare get any bigger. I don't want any of this to infect Darwin or Elvi.

My socked feet sink into goo as soon as I enter my room.

Nothing looks as it should. Everything is *wrong*.

The black liquid is dripping from the ceiling, engulfing the walls. The ripped rug is squishy under my feet. All the pictures and knick-knacks on my shelf and desk are facing the other way and my bed has been thrown against the other side of the room. The wooden frame is splintered, the mattress lying sideways. The pentagram I destroyed is gone, replaced by a black hole.

My head is buzzing, and my nerves are wound so tight I can't believe I can actually move my legs. But I somehow dare to get closer. I peek into the abyss, but quickly back away because someone—or *something*—is staring back. And there's a horrible smell spilling out from all that blackness. It's a combination of rotten egg and spoiled meat.

Nobody stares inside for a while longer before she starts barking like crazy.

"Get away from there." My voice is barely a breath because fear is gripping my entire body. If I felt like paper before, now I'm an old guitar string close to snapping.

A hot wind blows out from the crevice, and I step away from the edge, taking the pup with me. I grip her collar, while holding the grimoire to my chest. But I'm glad to have something solid and real in both hands, because nothing about this room feels right.

I glance at my bedside table and desk but can't find my mobile. The disturbing imagery is everywhere, but the creepiest are the dolls. All my plushies, dollies and action figures are lined up in front of the floor and are facing the grimy walls. They're a clear reproduction of me, how I wake up too many times.

"Where are you?" I know Raum is here. If my bedroom has been turned into a hellmouth, he's got to be nearby.

"I'm inside your head." The laughter rings in my ears, but also echoes out of the dark crevice on the floor.

"Chess, what's going on?"

I spin around and find Darwin standing in the doorway.

"Stay there!" I yell.

He surveys the room, and I wonder if he can see everything I can.

"Don't come in!" I search the shelves and every surface for my mobile, but it's nowhere. "I can't find my phone."

"Don't worry about your phone, get out of there."

I snap at him and instead of a response, an unexpected growl slips from my throat.

"Calm down," he says, with one hand raised in front of him.

My fingers slip from Nobody's collar and so does the notebook. My feet aren't on the messy floor anymore, I'm hovering and don't know how this is possible.

Nobody snaps at me, as if trying to catch hold of my pants. My vision is suddenly covered by a slimy filter causing everything to blur. My body rises and it's so disorienting. All I can do is stretch my arms out in front of me, trying to grab at the air.

"Chester, fight him!"

I don't know who said that, but it's not Darwin.

My head rolls along my shoulders until I hear a creak.

"This body is going to fit me very well."

My legs dangle like useless lumps but he's spinning my hands in directions they're not supposed to. He's going to break my wrists.

Stop it!

"Now that I've finally got you, I'm certainly not going to stop."

Leave me alone!

My breath is coming too fast. I'm panting and know that tiring myself out like this isn't going to help anyone but him, but it's hard to get control back when someone is taunting me mentally and physically.

I inhale and actually feel like my lungs might be coming unstuck. I can't make this easy for him. I need to fight.

My mother's words tumble into my brain: *"Don't ever lose that skill and fight, fight, FIGHT. Don't shy away from your bravery."* Right now, nothing ever made more sense than those words.

I let every thought crowding my head flow through me. Everything packed into my brain shifts in quick succession—losing control, kissing Darwin, listening to Elvi's explanation, Nobody's loyalty, my mother's letter and all the things she endured. I keep her secret instructions locked tight because Raum's too close.

I imagine all the thoughts sliding out of my fingertips like glitter. When I manage to release everything and clear my mind, I'm still floating in mid-air. I reach out for the ceiling, or what I'm sure is the ceiling, and start spinning head over heels. I'm not sure if I'm actually doing this, or if it's all in my head.

Saliva dribbles down my chin and the next time I focus, can barely make out Darwin and Elvi standing in the doorway.

"I have to help her," he screams.

She's holding onto his arm. "No, you can't."

"But he's going to hurt her."

"You can't help," Elvi says.

"Don't say that, Ma!"

Elvi looks right at me. "Chester, honey, if you can hear me, you have to save yourself. Mena believed you could, I know you can, and Darwin definitely believes in you."

The cozy sensation of love surges, cocoons my body and soul.

After my next blink, I'm no longer floating or even inside my room. I'm casually strolling down familiar corridors. I'm inside my mind and some of the doors are slightly open, but most are locked tight.

As I pass one that's ajar, I can see the red tinge seeping out and stop. I push the door until it bounces off the wall. I need this to be wide open.

"Shiny—" I cut myself off to call her by her real name. "Orobas, I need your help. Can you come out when I call on you?"

Two horns separate themselves from the darkness, quickly joined by a tail. "Thought you'd never ask."

My vision is clear and has adjusted to the dark, so when I notice a single photograph hanging beside several blank sheets, I focus on it. *Mum.* That's a photo of my mother sitting in her favorite chair in the backyard while writing in her grimoire.

This is the last time I saw her. When I walked away and didn't know she would disappear by the time I reached the sliding door.

"Memories are some of the most powerful tools humans have at their disposal," Orobas says. "Don't ever forget that."

I nod and accept her enigmatic comment before turning away.

The walls on either side of me are changing. The white is slowly getting darker with gooey streaks that feel alive. If I stare too long, I can see a multitude of eyes staring back, but I know what I need to do and don't waste any time analyzing my unstable surroundings.

"It's time for you to go back to your room," I say.

"I'm not done having fun, yet."

Between blinks I'm back in my bedroom, hovering in mid-air while my hands continue to twist unnaturally. The pain is immense, forces a scream out of me. Then I'm back in the corridor, standing near the spreading goo. Back in my bedroom, one of my hands sits at a weird angle and Darwin is shouting my name. In the corridor, I'm getting so close to the open door I can feel his evasive presence.

"Come now, come a little closer so I can get inside you."

"I'll never let that happen."

"Never say never," he coos. *"Bet you didn't think you'd enjoy kissing your brother."*

I shake my head and go back to my bedroom long enough to spot the glint of something familiar on the floor, near my desk. At least my eyes are no longer filtered. A second later, in the corridor, a large glossy bird is framed by the doorway.

"That's it! You're so close I can taste you."

In the room, I finally find my phone.

"Wait till you see the things we can do together."

"No thanks, I'm happy with what I can do alone."

His laughter echoes up and down the corridor, which seems to be closing in around me.

"You'll never do anything without me again."

I grin, an actual smile, and feel the shine of his cocky desires glow all over my body. Mum always said I was stronger than I thought, and I've spent most of my life watching her make things to enforce the positive energy around me. He might have burst a few of those bubbles, but I still have some up my sleeve.

"As soon as I take over, I'm going to find Philomena and tear her to shreds."

"I don't think so." A surge of anger threatens my control, but I reel it in.

When his wings extend and morph into arms tipped with talons, I imagine flinging him back inside. He doesn't expect it and is sent flying through the air.

He smashes past the doorway.

The door slams shut between us and chains pour out of the doorframe.

Raum is trapped.

When I blink, I'm kneeling on the floor of my bedroom. Nobody and Darwin rush towards me, but I raise the hand that still works properly to block their approach.

Papers are floating everywhere and my sweaty hair flies over my face. The bruising on my arms has doubled and my left hand is limp, but I banish the commotion until everything circling the air crashes onto the floor.

"Chess, are you okay?" Darwin drops in front of me and puts his hands on my face. His brown eyes search mine, as if he's desperately trying to make sure I'm still alive. "Are you back?"

"Yes." My throat feels hoarse and the skin around my mouth cracks when I speak. I hope I didn't throw up again. "What happened?" I survey the room and the bedframe and mattress are still here, lying like discarded toys. Papers and so many other things are everywhere, but the gaping crevice is gone. Did anyone see the abyss but me? Was it ever really there?

Nobody licks my face and whines.

"That's what I want to ask you," Darwin says. "What happened, Chess?"

"Did you see the gaping hole on the floor?" I have to check, need to know.

"What gaping hole?"

"It was over there…" I stop because it was right where he's kneeling. The abyss is obviously a manifestation I witnessed but was never there. At least I know.

Darwin's eyes swim with tears. "I thought you were gone, that I'd lost you this time."

"You'll never lose me." I hate that I'm responsible for the dark circles under his eyes. If I could take all the pain and worry away from him, I would.

Tears fall silently down his face.

"I have to call... Dr. Larunda."

"I think we've gone beyond calling," Elvi says from the doorway. "Let's go to her office." She leaves and Nobody trots after her.

"You scared me," Darwin says when we're alone.

"I scared myself." I gasp. "I think my hand is... broken."

He tries to cradle it, but I wince. "I've never felt more helpless in my life. I wanted to help, but there was nothing I could do."

I catch my breath. "This is something I have to face on my own." I attempt a smile even though my insides feel queasy. "But I can't do it without you in my corner."

"I'll never leave your corner."

I try to stand, but he stops me.

"Chess." Darwin holds onto my arms and stares into my eyes. "About all the stuff Ma told us and what we did—"

"I know, and I'm sorry that I made you feel weird and confused."

He shakes his head. "It's not that. You didn't... argh."

"What is it?"

"I know it's all kinds of wrong and it's going to sound creepy, but I need to tell you something." Darwin sighs, licks his lips. "When you kissed me, I... I..."

I search his face. "Yeah?"

"Shit, okay. Hold on." He sucks in a quick breath and lowers his voice to say, "I *wanted* to kiss you back, and enjoyed it too. I know that sounds awful and probably makes me a creep, but something came over me and..." He pauses. "It sounds bad to admit this, but I needed you to know."

My heart is beating too fast when I say, "I liked it too." He's right, the admission sounds awful and wrong on so many levels, but I refuse to lie to him when he's being honest with me. Besides, the same thing that pushed him to respond was what made me kiss him in the first place. We weren't in total control, but it wasn't entirely out of our hands.

For a second, I think he might be inching closer, so I lean away.

"But we can't do that again," I say. "I can't keep confusing you like that, and there's also Su to consider."

We stare at each other for a few silent moments, and I can read all the muddled emotions he feels. How a part of him wishes we could pursue whatever this is, how he wants to get another small taste, and thinks that might help us figure out if it was the demonic influence or not. Or maybe these are my thoughts.

Either way, I can hear the imprisoned asshole slamming against the chained door inside my head. I can feel him trying to scratch his way out because this is definitely an exchange Raum could use to his advantage.

"Everything's so messed up," Darwin says with a shake of his head.

"You can thank me for that."

"No, it's our family. You heard all that crap Ma told us, and what Mum's letter said... of course, we'd turn out weird too."

"Oh, Dar, you're not weird, you've just spent too much time with me." I lean forward and give him a quick peck on the cheek.

"Darwin! Chester! Come on," Elvi calls.

"We better go..."

"Yeah," he says.

The rueful smile on his face makes my stomach twist because something has definitely shifted between us. But I won't let it change what we are, or our true connection. Though for the first time in my life,

I suddenly realize it's wrong to put so much dependency on him. He deserves to have his own life, without the taint of Chester hanging over him all the time.

Darwin gets to his feet and holds out a hand.

"Wait, I need to get my phone." I crawl over to my desk, yank the mobile from the floor and pocket it.

"You could've used my—"

"Larunda's emergency number's on here."

"Oh, yeah."

"I need to stash Mum's Dreaded Notebook somewhere safe." I tuck the grimoire into my desk drawer and cover it with the contents. "That'll have to do for now."

I take his offered help with my good hand and stand.

We leave my bedroom together, and I refuse to look back at the destruction Raum caused.

When we reach Elvi, she holds up a roll of bandages and motions me over. "We've got to strap it," she says. "We should go to the emergency room, but... this will do for now."

I nod and wince every time she curls the bandage around my fingers, palm, and wrist. I'm not sure what's broken—maybe every bone—but she's right, keeping the hand strapped tight will help until I can get a proper cast.

If I make it.

"Thanks," I say with a smile.

"Let's go."

The four of us leave the house and she locks the door. A few minutes later, with Darwin's help, because he insists on sitting in the back with me, we're all strapped in and driving down the dark roads. With Nobody on my left and Darwin on my right, I dial the number on speed dial.

"We're coming to your office," I say as soon as she picks up.

"We know."

NINETEEN
NOW

Saturday, 4:30am
May 19, 2018

The building where Dr. Larunda's office is situated looks different at night. The giant white cross affixed to the exterior seems to glow like a beacon, and there are more shadows crawling over the red brick façade than there should be.

When I mention this to Darwin, he shakes his head and claims he can't see anything. Maybe I'm the only one who can see uncanny movements in the dark. I've been known to see things that aren't really there my whole life, so it's not surprising.

Not after seeing a black hole open up in the floor inside my bedroom. One that magically disappeared and only I could see.

My brief conversation with Darwin keeps echoing inside my mind, as well as his reaction. I try to focus on what I said to him. I've hurt him too much already and if I make it out of this alive, I've decided it's time to enforce some boundaries between us. We're almost eighteen and are at the cusp of spreading our wings—as much as the imagery makes me shudder—and it's time I let him go.

"Are you okay to take the stairs?" he asks near my ear.

I nod. My legs are weak, my thoughts keep swaying in and out and my hand hurts like hell, but if I focus on my next step, I'm fine. I might have decided to eventually get some space from Darwin, but for now he's got an arm hooked around my waist as the four of us skip the elevator and take the stairs to the second floor. Elvi's in the lead and Nobody races up to beat her to the top. I'm leaning too heavily on Darwin, so I'm grateful that we don't have to go too far, and sigh in relief when we reach the landing.

Elvi glances back and frowns. I don't know what she sees when she looks at us anymore, but I feel bad that she has to deal with this alone. Mum's attempts to save me actually meant abandoning *everyone*.

"We're almost there." Darwin clutches me against his side.

His mother reaches the office entry and before she touches the handle, Dr. Larunda's assistant swings the door open. Elvi shrieks but stands her ground.

"I'm sorry to have startled you," the man says, sounding apologetic. "But I heard when you entered the building." He changes before my eyes—bearded man one minute, lion riding a bear the next. His eyes are twinkling in the bleak light as he holds the door open.

I almost trip over one of the couches in the waiting room but Darwin catches me and helps me sit. I slump back like a useless lump and sweat coats my neck. Every time I close my eyes, I feel like I'm weaving in and out of my body. I don't understand why this is happening when my mind, although flaky, is considerably stronger. I feel feverish and scratch at my skin hard enough to leave red marks over the multitude of bruises.

"She's in a worse state than I suspected." Dr. Larunda materializes wearing her usual business attire, as she walks perfectly on the tallest heels I've ever seen.

I roll my head to focus on her. "I don't feel so good."

"Purson, please get her something to drink." She motions for her assistant and a second later he's holding a glass of water.

Purson?

You can trust Larunda and Purson, completely. That's what Mum wrote in her letter. Isn't Purson the one who supposedly sent me a familiar? Purson is the doctor's assistant, the ever-changing man?

Larunda crouches and holds the glass under my nose. "Here, drink this."

"What is it?" Am I heading into Wonderland like Alice? In some sick and depraved way, I totally am. Out of all the stories my mother told me as a kid—not including the ones she made up—I always liked *Alice in Wonderland* the best because I could relate to her trippy adventures.

"It's something to help you get your wits back." Her face is incredibly close and her skin shimmers, as if it's lit beneath the surface. She covers my good hand with hers and a soothing sensation smooths away my twitchy nerves. "Drink it so you can see things clearer."

I take a sip and nearly spit it out, but I don't want to be rude and could definitely use something to perk me up. I hold onto the horrid liquid, swish it inside my mouth for a second before swallowing. Whatever she gave me stings all the way down like the time Darwin and I dared each other to taste vodka. It takes me a moment to recognize the aftertaste.

"You gave me salt water? I thought you said—"

"What I advised still holds true. No salt tablets. But he's eating you up from the inside and if you don't have salt, it's only going to get worse." She meets my eyes but all I can concentrate on is her calming ambience. "There's more than salt in this solution, but nothing harmful. The right dosage to get the outcome your mother always wanted." Her lips aren't moving for the last part. I'm sure of it.

I feel the scrunched-up piece of paper burning a hole in my pocket. She even knows about *that*. I guess Mum wasn't kidding around when she said I could trust Larunda and Purson completely.

"Chester, do you understand?"

All I manage is a nod.

"What do you mean he's eating her up from the inside?" Even though we're sitting next to each other, Darwin sounds like he's not in the room, but talking through a speaker. "She was getting better before."

"Well, I wouldn't say that exactly," Elvi says. "But she did seem to be more focused."

Dr. Larunda gives Elvi her full attention. "What happened?"

"You can ask me," I whisper. *I'm right here.*

She pats my hand, as if to hush me.

"Her bedroom was destroyed, and we found her floating in mid-air." Elvi crosses her arms and sways slightly. "That's after trying to stab me with a pair of scissors and throwing up feathers." She stares at me with what can only be described as pity. "But she's fighting so hard. She even came out of the trance before he could completely take her."

Larunda looks thoughtful for a moment. "The house has become an annex to his power." She does something she's never done before, and the doctor places a hand on the back of my neck. "You have to drink all of it." She helps cradle my head so I can swallow the rest of the water. "The house is where she spends most of her time, where he's managed to worm his way in. Her leaving the premises is weakening him, making Raum fight twice as hard to reach her." Her eyes are on mine. "Did you lock him up tight?"

"Tighter than usual," I say, toying with the bandage on my hand.

Darwin squirms beside me. "Are you saying we could've moved away and none of this would've happened?"

"Not exactly. While relocating might have helped at the beginning of this ordeal, the shift would end up harming her further." She takes the glass when I'm done and passes it to Purson, who is suddenly standing behind her. "Chester has done everything she can to keep this demonic disturbance from taking over, but it's not enough. There's only one thing left for her to do."

Elvi steps closer. "What's that?"

"She has to face her demons in the most literal sense." Dr. Larunda takes her time focusing on each person in the room. She's now holding my broken hand softly, so the touch doesn't hurt. "If you don't battle and defeat him inside the domain he's trying to rule, you'll lose this fight."

"In my head," I say.

"She's in no state to fight anyone," Darwin says. "Can't you perform an exorcism, or something?"

"I'm afraid not." Larunda shakes her head. "The function of an exorcism is mostly a fictional creation. No one can drive a demoniac out of your head but yourself. That's the only battleground left, because if the demon seeps into her soul, she'll be completely lost."

"But—"

"You discredit her by even suggesting such a weakness." Larunda lays my injured hand carefully on my lap and straightens. She still resembles a tall insect. "She's merely going through withdrawals, as any addict would."

"She has to purge him?" Elvi is biting her thumbnail.

"It's more complicated than that, but yes." Her eyes are bright and so clear they're almost see through. The demon attached to her torso shimmies into existence and she's beautiful, but I think she might blind me with her glow. Like usual, she has a hand cupped over the doctor's ear and is whispering. "She'll be tested like never before, but I know she's more than ready."

I take a shallow breath and my chest doesn't stick. Actually, I feel a bit better. The nausea has settled to a dull disturbance, and I can at least hold myself up. Darwin is still there to lend support, but I no longer feel like I'm about to float away.

"Are you sure she's ready?" Elvi seems worried, her eyes skirt from me to the doctor. "She's already been through so much. I don't want anything more to happen to her."

Larunda shrugs. "The worst that can happen already has."

"It's okay," I say, using Darwin to sit up straighter. "I can do this."

Elvi and Darwin don't appear to be convinced, but Larunda and Purson are standing side by side with matching smiles on their faces. They probably want to appear encouraging but look downright creepy.

"What do I need to do to get my mother back *and* get rid of this asshole for good?"

Her eyes are positively sparkling. "Interesting that you should concern yourself with your mother's wellbeing before your own—"

"She's suffered enough, don't you think?"

"I would say you all have." Larunda takes her time considering Darwin and Elvi, before returning to my side. "What do I have to do?" I shiver, and I'm not sure why.

"I mentioned the annex is your abode, well my office is the apex."

"What does that even mean?" Darwin's heart picks up. I can feel it thumping against my side and it's both comforting and disconcerting.

"It means Chester will have to enter my office and can't come out until she's completed the task of eliminating the parasite leeching off her." She holds up a hand before his protests begin. "No matter what the outcome, she won't be able to leave until this is truly over."

"I'll go with her."

"You'll do no such thing," she snaps. "There'll be no white knight in this story. Here, the princess must save herself."

I can't help but laugh, and that becomes a coughing fit. When it's over and Darwin has rubbed my back until I feel whole again, I push off the couch and with his help find my feet. I certainly don't feel like a princess, but I did read a book with a similar title once.

"Let's get this done," I say.

Raum isn't the only one who wants this shit to be over. Dr. Larunda is right, I need to face my demons because if I don't, I won't be able to put up with more of this. The temporary strength I felt in my bedroom has leaked out of me, and I'm afraid that if I don't complete the task tonight, I never will.

I don't feel like giving up my soul to this bastard.

"If I come out of that room with black eyes and wings, I want you to take care of me whichever way you have to." The words taste bitter in my mouth, but the good doctor knows what's at stake. "I don't want to become his puppet. I'd rather die."

"No," Darwin says.

"Yes, we'll take care of you, if things don't go as they should." It's Larunda's assistant who answers. "Being possessed is no life at all."

"Thank you, Purson," I say.

He nods.

Darwin steps in front of me. "Over my dead body."

"If it comes to that—"

"Hush now," Larunda shouts. "We'll do what needs to be done." She glares pointedly at Darwin. "But we're not going to make any rash decisions until it's necessary." She reaches for my hand and hers feel so cold, I shiver. "Let's get you on the road to recovery."

I let her lead me to her office door without looking back.

"Whatever you see in there, half is real, and the rest is pure delusion. Raum is very good at making people see what he wants them to. Stay focused and don't let him overrule your mind completely."

"I'm not sure how to do that, but I'll try."

She leans into my ear. "You're more than capable of putting him in his place, but your familiar and demoniac know how to end it completely." She slaps her thigh once and Nobody appears beside me. "But if she doesn't have a name yet, she'll be useless." Her eyes are shiny. "I know Mena told you what needs to be done to get Raum out of your life forever and paid dearly for such knowledge. Don't waste the opportunity."

"You know where she is, don't you?"

"Shortly, you will too." Larunda caresses my temple and backs away. "Say your farewells and go when you're ready."

Elvi is suddenly there, crushing me in a hug so tight my spine curves. She kisses both of my cheeks and grips my shoulders as she stares into my eyes. "You can do this. I believe in you. I always have." Her eyes are shiny with tears. "Go and show Mena that you're stronger than all of us."

"Thanks." A tear escapes and she's gone too quickly, so Darwin takes her place.

"Hey," I say.

"Hey." He's standing close but for once, we're not touching.

"This isn't goodbye." I'm not sure if that's true. But I can't leave him thinking this might be the last time we see each other. Not after everything we've been through and what he's put up with because of me.

"I know it's not." He takes my good hand. "You're going to kick his ass." He steps closer. "And when you do, I'll be here waiting for you."

"I know you will." Another tear slides down my face.

Darwin cups my face and kisses my forehead. "I believe in you."

"Thank you."

I slip from his grasp and turn away from the people I love and believe in me unconditionally.

It's time to exit the light and embrace the dark.

Twenty
NOW

Saturday, time slips away
May 19, 2018

I bury my good hand into the fur between Nobody's tense shoulders and we walk into the office together. I can't believe I found her in the garbage only weeks ago because so much has happened, and she's now tall enough to reach my thighs.

"Are you ready, girl?"

She barks a response.

The corner lamps are switched on and provide a circle of illumination barely able to penetrate the filing cabinets lining the opposite wall. The two red armchairs we sit on during my sessions are in their usual spot. Everything is in its proper place, even the curtains are held open on either side of the window framing Dr. Larunda's monstrosity of a desk.

Outside, the sky is black and studded with shiny stars, but I feel like I'm in an entirely different world.

Swirls churn above, concealing the ceiling. They always squirm and skitter like spiders weaving a web but now they're somehow heavier, and I can feel their many stares. A multitude of eyes blink in the darkness and their glaring sight scrapes against my skin, to the point where I want to gouge scratches in my arms to stop the disturbing sensation.

"Where are you, Raum?" My pulse is out of control but there's no point in prolonging the inevitable. I'm done with this shit. I might not feel as strong as I did before but drinking the salt water, while embracing Darwin and Elvi's love—as well as the faith Larunda and Purson seem to have in me—is enough to harden my resolve.

No matter what, I refuse to let anyone down.

Especially Mum.

I need to get this done, to wrench her out of the shadows.

The room spins upside down and my sense of equilibrium is thrown completely off balance. My legs jolt but I keep my feet glued to the harsh surface. The recognizable room might have flipped completely but I'm still the right-way up, and this isn't Dr. Larunda's office anymore.

I'm back in the abandoned room, facing the rotting wall.

"Nobody?" She's not beside me, but I hear her bark in the distance.

"She can't help you."

I try to turn, but of course, I can't. Every damn time I find myself in front of this wall, I'm completely stuck.

"You can change that now," someone else whispers in my ear. And it's not Raum or even Orobas. It's my mother, I'm sure of it.

My shadow has returned and she's facing me. But for the first time since all of this deteriorated, I realize something. Shadows are supposed to be distorted in their own uncanny way, but this one continually shifts independently because she's not an extension of me. If I hadn't been so terrified of being lost in this nightmare world and wanted so desperately to break loose, I might have faced the truth sooner.

"Mum, is that you?"

My shady reflection nods.

"It's been you all along?"

Another nod.

"But how is that even possible?" The skittering, and the way she always separates herself from me whenever Raum appears, now makes sense.

"You remember the story about the girl and her two shadows, don't you?"

I nod. The girl who was born with a shadow like everyone else, but also had another attached to her. One that was powerful enough to trap others if they weren't careful. I never thought the story was remotely true, but she's telling me *I'm* that girl.

"How do I get you out of here?"

"Face him and we'll make it out together."

"Where is he?"

"Right behind you!"

She's suddenly sucked into the wall and disappears into the crevices.

"Mum!"

She doesn't respond and I can't feel her or see where she went.

"*She* can't help you. She never could."

Anger makes my blood boil and I force myself to spin around. I'm so surprised when I actually move, that I almost tumble into him.

"Impressive." His grating voice echoes around the chamber.

I glare at him. He's really here, in front of me.

Finally.

His gaze falls to my injured hand, and he smiles. "Once I take over your body, I'll be able to repair that"—his wriggly fingers sweep over the air between us— "as well as all your other unfortunate ailments."

"You did this to me."

Raum sighs. "The act of possession is such a messy business." He's still mostly concealed but has materialized as an actual entity, not a disembodied voice. "It's unfortunate, but the merchandise has to be damaged before being repaired."

"I'm not *merchandise*."

"Ah, see, that's where you're wrong. That's exactly what you are."

"So that's what you want from me?" I ball my hands into fists, ignoring the pain. "You want me to sign my body over and vacate the premises." A horrible thought strikes me. "What would happen to me, to my soul?"

"At first, you would linger because I like to show my hosts how badly I can fuck up their simplistic and useless lives." He considers me with those unsettling, shiny black eyes. "Imagine if I go back to wearing your petite body and throw myself at that boy you're trying to save. He would be so easy to corrupt." A satisfied moan escapes him. "If I get you, I'll definitely acquire him too, because he'll surrender willingly if *you're* the one doing the begging. As a bonus, I'll finally get my hands on those two bitches too." A snicker fills the air between us. "Then, when I'm completely done with you, I'll move on and add your soul to my collection."

"This is what you do, collect souls?" I refuse to focus on what he said about Darwin or my mothers. They've all been through enough. I won't let this monster hurt my family.

"I can do a great many things," he answers. "But I like to cycle back to the human world, where I can hunt down new followers and ensure my name isn't forgotten."

"No one remembers or worships you."

"No one you know, but there are plenty of people who are still in league with me. How else do you think I found my way back to you?" He steps forward and I spot the crow feet, slender and taloned.

"It wasn't because of your connection to my mother?"

"Well, there *was* that, but I couldn't find my way back to you directly. I had a bit of help with that task." He laughs and it stirs gooseflesh over my body. "Don't look so distraught. It's not anyone she knows personally." A huge wing touches the tip of his beak. "I think Elvira knew him *intimately*."

The thought twists my stomach and confuses me. "Are we going to stand here and chat all day, or are you going to end this?"

The space between us stretches until we're suddenly standing in the middle of my mind's corridor. The walls are white and pristine, rooms line both sides and most of the doors are closed.

"What's keeping you from ending this?" I take a step, followed by another. Until I pass the darkroom and notice it's empty, but I can feel the usual presence lurking inside.

"*Soon,*" Orobas murmurs in my ear.

I keep moving because this time there's no escaping until this is done.

Raum stands in the darkened doorway at the very end, waiting for me.

One step before I reach him, the corridor spins around several times. When it's right-side up again, my feet are firmly on the floor, but Nobody is on the ceiling. We're on opposite ends. I try to grab her, but my fingers aren't long enough.

She's barking at Raum.

"You can't reach her," he says. "You don't share the same space anymore."

I look down and there he is, still in the doorway. Waiting.

"*I'm* here now." It seems like such a stupid thing to say, but what else is left?

"I can see that." His beady bird eyes glare at me as he shuffles on those spindly black legs. When he crosses the threshold, his beak opens wide, and a human head pops out from within. The beak slips down until it becomes the high collar of a feathered coat. His face is pale and handsome, his bare chest is all smooth, and his abdomen tight. I can see why people fell for him, but I had the misfortune of meeting all the awful and scary parts first.

He won't charm me, even if he *is* my father.

"I'm not going to let you have what you want." I shake my head. "My mother fought too hard. I won't surrender to you."

"No matter how, I'll have what I've always wanted. What I was promised."

All the knowledge I'd read in Mum's grimoire circles inside my brain like an endless database of information. "You wanted an offspring, and you got two. Why did you only try to invade one?" I wouldn't wish this on Darwin but need to know the truth.

"That boy is not my offspring."

"Yes, he is."

His chuckle echoes up and down the corridor. "Is that what they told you? That you two are siblings because *I* fathered both of you?" He laughs again. "You understand less than I thought you did."

I have no idea what he's talking about, so I bite my tongue and glance quickly at Nobody. She's still on the ceiling, barking without sound.

"I might be *your* father because I impregnated your ungrateful mother, and laid claim to you during the ritual when you were already a tiny fetus growing inside her. But that boy's not mine." He spits the admission like it's the most horrid accusation.

I cringe at his description. He makes everything sound so dirty.

"Did you think that boy cared so much because you're *both* my offspring?" Raum smirks and it darkens his pale features. "No, it's because those truly touched by the demonic can influence others very easily. Didn't you enjoy having total and utter control over the pest?"

"No, I didn't do that to him." I never manipulated Darwin. Yet, that's not true because in a way, I've been unwillingly affecting him for years. "You made me do it."

"Ah, humans are so easily fooled, and like to fool themselves the most."

"Shut up."

He's quiet for several moments. "I suppose I can't blame the girls for thinking I'd fathered both of their kids. They were so wrapped up in each other they didn't notice what was going on half the time." He raises a hand and he's suddenly right in front of me, cups my chin. "I went to Philomena, but Elvira was never good enough to receive me. So, I sent one of my devotees to her. You're the one I marked, the one who was supposed to make way for my rebirth." He pinches my chin. "But that ungrateful bitch ruined everything."

"My mother's not a bitch."

I try not to reveal my thoughts, but Elvi's revelation about Darwin being protected by a guardian angel finally makes sense. I'm the only one who was ever affected by this demon before I was born. At least this confirms Darwin isn't like me and never was. He's a pure soul, my complete opposite. And if I don't establish some distance between us, I'll corrupt him.

Raum's eyes are blazing.

"She outsmarted you, defeated—"

His sharp talons pierce my skin. "You need to watch yourself." He lowers his face until we're eye to eye. "Or I'll destroy your body. I can repair you when I'm in control, but for now... I can cause a lot of pain."

Warm blood trickles down my jawline. "You can't have me."

"A mere child isn't going to stop my plans."

I don't know why I do it, maybe it's to get him back for the hurt he's inflicting on my face or because I hate him so much, but I raise a hand and slap him. One second, I'm glaring at him with hateful intentions in mind, and the next his sharp talons are out of my skin. He has no respect, only contempt for humanity. Yet, still wants to be one. He wants to wear me as an outfit and I'm not going to let him.

He recoils and when he meets my gaze, the same hatred I feel is reflected back at me. "You dare strike a greater being! I'm an Earl!"

"I don't care what or who you think you are," I spit. "You're not getting your grimy paws on me. I'll die before I let that happen."

"Very well," he says. "I thought you might want to make it easier on yourself by signing your body over willingly, but now I understand that's not going to happen. So, we'll have to do this the hard way. I can beat you to a pulp and when you're down to your very last breath, I *will* take you."

"No. You. Won't."

I don't see him coming because it's not his hand that smacks me, it's the tip of an ebony wing. He hits the side of my head so hard, that it sends me flying across the room. My spine impacts a wall that's not supposed to be there.

"Fight him, you know you can."

"I don't think I can, Mum." I taste blood in my mouth, must have bitten my tongue or the side of my mouth. When I try to stand, it takes all the energy I have because for a second, I forgot my left hand is still screwed up and keep trying to use it.

"You're another ungrateful little bitch," he shouts, and the walls shake. "You're all the same, skin and bones with no real marrow!"

"Bring him to me," Orobas whispers. *"I'm ready."*

I shut my eyes and visualize the red room.

When I open them, he's standing in front of me and kicks out with those clawed feet, slamming me hard in the gut. I trip but something stops me, and I manage to grip the sharp edge of a counter. It takes a moment to notice the overhead light is red and the trays are filled with chemicals. It worked!

All the photos, except for the one featuring my mother, are gone.

"What is this place?" Raum screams as he scans our new surroundings. Several black feathers fly into the air as his body ruffles in outrage.

"This is *my* room." I spit blood on the tiled floor and my stomach feels like its engorged, but I stay on my feet.

"Any time now, I'm ready," she whispers.

Raum rushes me, but I scoop up a white tray and we strike at the same time. I splash the chemicals into his face, and he wallops me on the side.

I stagger and smack the back of my head on the way down.

"I can't see!" He flails and screams while rubbing his glossy eyes. "What did you do to me?"

"Nobody!" I shout.

My dog races into the room. She's no longer on the ceiling or somewhere different, she's with me.

I slam the door shut with my mind. The world is slanted, but it's not from some delusional demonic trick. It's because I've smacked my head and I probably have a concussion.

Raum wipes the last remnants of chemicals from his deranged face and storms ahead, but Nobody blocks him.

"Get out of my way," he says. "This fight has nothing to do with you, Okuri-Inu."

She barks at him, saliva frothing at her mouth. There's a crimson sheen to her eyes I've never noticed before, and one side of her face has melted away.

"Fair enough, I'll make you."

Nobody rushes him, clamps onto one of his wings with her sharp fangs, shakes him violently until she plucks a large section of feathers and flesh. Raum screams in frustration.

While he's occupied with my dog, I inch closer to the patch of darkness on unsteady feet and a wobbly mind.

"Orobas, I need your help."

She separates from the wall but remains concealed. "Are you willing to pay the price?"

I nod, even if I've got Mum's trick up my sleeve. Or, tucked deep inside my pocket.

"Say it."

"Yes, I am."

"Let's do this," she says.

Raum slams me hard between the shoulder blades and when I collapse in agony, Orobas reveals herself.

She's grand and beautiful, takes my breath away. The two gnarled horns at the top of her head are glossy and brown. Her hair is a combination of burgundy and ginger. Her shapely legs end in hooves, but she has hands with black talons on the end of each gnarled finger. Her eyes are white, and her body is covered from head to hoof in an intricate network of dazzling, kaleidoscopic tattoos.

It's no wonder I called her Shiny Pictures when I was a kid.

"Hello Raum," she coos. "Long time, no see."

"Not seeing you has always been a godsend."

Orobas giggles like a kid, and I remember that resonance from when she used to spend time with me inside my room.

"Godsend?" she teases. "You shouldn't be using such filthy words, should you?"

His chest is heaving, and feathers have almost concealed his human face. "And you shouldn't dare to show yourself in my presence!"

"I think it's time for you to leave the girl alone."

"Make me." Raum kicks me aside and charges the other demon.

Twenty-One
NOW

Saturday, time slips away
May 19, 2018

Orobas and Raum clash in a tangle of horns, hooves, beaks, and feathers. It sounds like two trucks colliding and feathers fly all over the darkroom.

The combination of weak lighting and my brain not working properly doesn't help me keep track of what's going on. One second, she's on top. The next, he's pulling on her horns and hair as she screeches like a banshee and rattles the walls.

I crawl under one of the benches and hide as the two demons battle hoof to talon. With the many injuries I've accumulated, I'm useless in this skirmish of wits and brawn. Still, it's not easy to watch because unlike in movies or shows, the two fiends strike so fast I miss half of the action between every blink.

The darkroom is getting destroyed, but I don't care. I'm not even sure I'll need this place after this battle.

Besides, I know Orobas—like me—won't be able to defeat this creature on her own. There's only one way to do that, it's what my mother's note told me. We must beat him *together*. But I have to wait until the right moment, because we'll only have one shot at this, and I don't want to screw it up.

I hunch down, catch my breath, and press my face into Nobody's fur. I try to muster as much courage as I can but feel like a weakling who's come too close to losing her body to a demon. I'm not a hero and I think at least one of my ribs is broken, my wrist is swollen, and this concussion isn't getting any better.

"The girl is mine," Raum growls.

A wave of dark blood spills over the counter and onto my head. I scoot forward enough to catch a glimpse of the action.

"The girl doesn't yet belong to you or me, or anyone else."

"She belongs to *me!*"

Orobas punches him in the face. "Grooming human children doesn't make you keeper of their offspring."

Their exchange is as gross and uncomfortable as every word they fling at each other, so I decide not to stall any further. They could keep this up for hours, and in the meantime, I'll probably pass out.

I push past my dog, slip on a puddle of blood but cling to the counter to keep my footing before hitting the ground. On shaky legs, I make my way behind Orobas and hope Raum hasn't noticed. I press my good hand against the base of her spine, above her tail.

Mum's first instruction—*physical contact with Orobas.*

"Orobas, the fifty-fifth spirit of the Goetia, Great and Mighty Princess, I give you passage to my soul." I say the words as loud as I can manage because even my throat hurts.

Raum tilts his head, hollers and objects tumble, shatter all around us. The floor quakes and several tiles shatter, opening a pathway to the darkness below.

"Let's get rid of him together," I say. This seems risky and I suddenly feel stupid for even trying, but Mum and Dr. Larunda and Purson have faith in this process, so who am I to question it?

"What we can't do alone, we can do together," she whispers.

"Yes."

Orobas blinks out of existence and reappears behind me. Both of her hands are on my shoulders, and she towers over me. One second, she's physically there and I can feel the weight of her presence, the next she's vanished and is occupying my body. My skin feels too tight with both of us in here, but I don't waste time feeling awkward. All my worries, concerns and fatigue have fallen away.

I stare at the room but feel like a passenger watching through the windshield of a vehicle, as someone else takes the driver's seat. I don't like how this feels because it reminds me of the times I've woken up and don't remember how I got there.

Yet, this is different.

Raum won't stop yelling when Orobas uses my still-working hand to grab a good grip around his feathered neck. My fingers are much longer and have talons on the ends, and when I take a step, I have hooves instead of feet.

I'm graceful and strong on unfamiliar limbs.

"Focus, Chester," Orobas whispers inside my head.

I want to be free of Raum and his poisonous voice.

I want to be free so I can finally get to know myself.

I want to be free to become who I've always dreamed I could be.

"You will be soon enough," Orobas says using my lips and voice to speak.

The now familiar silhouette hangs upside down from the ceiling, as if Mum's shadowy legs are somehow secured to a trapeze. I know it's my mother but I'm not sure if the only reason I can see her now is because of Orobas, or because I'm focusing instead of hiding.

My mother has a part to play in this, but I don't know what that is yet.

"Chester, open the door."

I concentrate and follow Mum's instruction because that was definitely her talking. I can clearly see where this bastard belongs, and we need to put him there together.

"No, not that door," Orobas echoes. *"The other one!"*

Orobas takes control, snaps my head up and glares at the spot where she always hid from me. That's when I realized, she didn't stand on the same spot out of habit or convenience, the demon was protecting a pathway. A door that will save me from eternal damnation and get rid of a malicious being.

One she couldn't open, but I can.

"Can you take us closer?" I ask, using my voice. It's so strange to vocalize two different thoughts.

"I'm a bit busy." She's holding tight to the sharp tip of Raum's wing with one hand while squeezing his throat with the other. He's using so much energy trying to shake her off that we're all vibrating. Any second now she's going to lose her grip and our opportunity will be lost.

I let all the crazy thoughts, aches, pains, and strangeness flow through and out of me. Orobas sighs, so she must feel the moment everything leaves my system. I zero in on the spot on the wall, past the darkness until I can clearly visualize a doorway.

A creak is shortly followed by a hot blast of air.

"You done it!" I say, with her voice.

Raum unhinges a wing and gets loose. He smacks us in the face but Orobas is fast and even tougher than he is. She's already standing in front of the door, clutching him tight. She throws him toward the open doorway, and he lands with eyes wide, full of horror. Where does this lead? What place could be so bad that such a malicious demon is terrified of going?

"Chesty, you can't do this to me," he says. "I'm your father."

"I'll give you points for trying, *Daddy*."

He glares at me, and I can see the hatred, the promise of revenge burning within.

Orobas cackles.

"You're nothing to me." Those are my words and my voice, no one else's.

"Do the honors," Orobas says.

I glare at Raum one last time, trying to remember the horrible, feathered giant he could become while forgetting the beautiful man he became. I despise this creature for everything he's done to my mother and Elvi. For all the hell he put me through, and how he made Darwin suffer along for the both of us.

"I've finally got you where I want you," I whisper. "Checkmate."

Orobas is the might behind the momentum and the speed, but *I'm* the one who barrels into Raum and shoves him into the pathway to oblivion. He shifts back into his crow form and caws, tumbles, and the grating sound he makes echoes as he's swallowed by the darkness. A darkness that isn't actually a pathway, but a mouth.

He's devoured by a bigger monster than him, and I don't want to know who or what this is.

I feel nothing.

No guilt, no remorse, not even victorious.

I mentally shut the door that'll keep him out of our world and the frame disappears, as if it were never there. It might not be forever, because Raum will probably try to claw his way back into our world, but he won't have access via *my* body. I've shut him out forever.

I'm Chester Warden and I might be the daughter of a demon, but he'll never possess me or own my soul.

"Well done," Orobas says inside my head. *"Now it's time to pay up."*

Twenty-Two
Now

Saturday, 7:35am
May 19, 2018

"Yeah, I suppose it *is* time to pay up."

"You did the right thing."

I feel like an inmate in a fictional asylum—one body, two entities.

"I'm *about* to do the right thing," I say.

"What are you talking about?"

"Nobody, come here." The emotionless name sounds awful, and I feel bad for making her carry this meaningless title for so long. I haven't been fair to my familiar, but I finally have the perfect name. I crouch in front of her and say, "Your name is Gambit, because you're not nobody. You're definitely somebody very special. I'm sorry it's taken me so long and promise to be a better companion from now on."

She's the epitome of what a gambit is in chess. A move made at the beginning of a game with only one purpose—an advantage.

The dog almost doubles in size and although I can still see the precious canine I've grown to love, she's completely different. Her eyes are black with crimson pupils, her muzzle is slightly longer, and her mouth is crowded with too many sharp teeth. One side of her face is no longer melted away.

"*Chester, what are you doing?*" Orobas can't use my mouth to speak anymore, because I won't let her.

I breathe in, roll my shoulders, release all thoughts, exhale, and eject her from my body. She drops out like a superimposed picture and lands on the floor behind me with a clang of horns and hooves. I turn to face her.

"Gambit, it's time for you to do your thing—guard, protect, *become* my familiar."

She steps between us and paces in front of Orobas like a jittery tiger watching their prey.

"What's going on?" Her white eyes are wide, panicked. Even cut, bruised, and swollen, she's beautiful. I'll forever be grateful for her help in eliminating my father and tormentor, but I can't give her what she wants.

I refuse to.

Gambit stops, barks, and exposes her large fangs to keep Orobas in check when the demon attempts to stand.

"You know I mean you no harm." She raises both palms and they're full of shifting tattoos. "I never have."

"I know you have good intentions, but you still want a payment I can't give you." I sigh. "We've reached a stalemate, and thanks to my mother, I know a way we can both win."

"You knew the deal before—"

"And that's why I'm doing this."

"Doing what?"

The invisible tether between us solidifies as I chant the words I memorized. Thick chains seal our connection, extending from my palms so the ends coil around her neck. These remind me of the chains

I used to secure Raum's door. I've made sure they're nice and strong, visualized and psychically enforced every metal link to be sturdier than any demonic entity.

"You can't do this." She tugs at the collar, but she won't be free until I choose to release her.

"I just did."

"Chester, you have no idea what you're doing."

"Actually, I do." I pause to consider my next words because I don't want to screw this up. "Orobas, the demon who has tasted my soul and I have tasted your essence, I bind you to me. My soul belongs to me, and I'll always be in control. But should you require my help, all you have to do is ask."

The noose around her neck tightens and clicks into place.

There's a part of me that hates doing this to Orobas because she helped me more than once, but I will *not* risk becoming someone else's tool. I refuse to pass out and lose time because a demon decides they want to make me their personal robot.

It's time to be me, myself, and I. No one else.

"I'm not like your familiar," she says. "I don't want to be roped in for whatever purpose you desire."

"No, you're not like her," I say. "Gambit *chose* me and has never had any delusions of controlling me. Unlike you."

Her eyes blaze with anger and she groans, stamps her hooved feet a few times before she starts to laugh. "You're one clever little bitch, aren't you?" She shakes her head and makes the chains rattle between us. "Are you sure you want to do this? You could banish me the way you did Raum, that might be easier."

"Why would I do that?" I shrug. "You freaked me out a few times with your sudden appearance and darkroom dramatics, but you've always helped me. For that, I'm grateful." My voice drops and I'm filled with emotion. "For most of my life I've been attacked by unwanted whispers, blackouts, and sleepwalking. I want a chance to take responsibility for all my actions, so I can't give you total control. But I don't mind sharing this space." I tap my temple. "What do you say? Do you want to be my imaginary friend again? I promise to visit."

A smile spreads over her pouty lips. "I think I can handle that."

"Good, now get my mother down from there."

She glances at the ceiling. "I—"

"It's okay, I know you're the one who kept her hidden in my memories." I grin and hope it looks authentic. "I'm not angry. You all had a part to play in this pantomime that's called *Chester's Fucked-Up Life*, but at least I've finally found her." Is everything really working itself out in the back of my head, or am I smarter inside than out? It's a scary thought.

"Can't get anything past you, huh?"

"Used to be that anyone could get *everything* past me, but now... I'm not that shy, uninformed girl anymore. From now on, I'm going to pay attention to everything."

"Good for you." Orobas picks up Mum's photo off the blood-stained floor as she stands. "You can come out of hiding now, Philomena." She throws the photo into the air and the shadow dives from the ceiling, falls headfirst into the paper.

"What just happened?"

She catches the photo. "Take this with you and she'll be restored when you reach the office."

"What about you?" I grab the sheet of paper and glance at the picture of Mum sitting on her favorite chair.

"I'll be here when you need me, and if I need you"—she tugs on the chain— "I'll give this a yank."

"You won't materialize in the real world, right?"

"Never wanted to before... so why would I want to do that now?"

"But I saw you in the street that day," I say. "And I thought you were a pony when I was a kid, and you came to my room."

"I hate to break it to you, love, but I wasn't actually there."

"But I saw you."

"I was in your head. I still am. You're the only one who can see me." She winks. "You've always been particularly vulnerable to seeing what others can't. Once you've been touched by the demonic, you never miss us. It's a perk."

"Or a curse."

"Either way."

I nod because this revelation makes freaky sense.

"Now, get out of here and take the pooch." She pats Gambit's head. "Purson really does provide the best familiars."

"His delivery service sucks, though."

"Well, he's not known for his subtlety."

I hesitate. "So, you're not angry with me?"

"It's not the best way to spend my time, but it could be worse." She shrugs. "You have no idea what some conjurers expect from their demons. At least I know you won't be *too* demanding."

"I'll hardly bother you at all."

Orobas dips her horned head.

"Uh, how do I get out of here?"

"The same way you always do." She points behind me. "Open the door, get out into that corridor of yours and will yourself back."

"Oh, okay." I head for the door with Gambit beside me.

"And Chester, don't forget to close the door."

I nod, leave the darkroom, and shut the door behind me.

The sudden gleam of white is too bright, but I ignore the stinging tears and hug Mum's picture to my chest. I release my tangled thoughts—there are way too many now—from my mind and close my eyes.

When they snap open, I'm back inside the doctor's office.

The photo has slipped from my grasp and is on the floor, but it's a blank piece of paper now.

"Chester!"

I spin around too fast and my head spins, but I don't care. "Mum!" I limp to her side and fall into her open arms. She's actually here, inside this office and not as some skittering silhouette or an image in a photograph.

"What did he do to you?" She pulls back, surveys the damage while holding me at arm's length. Her eyes rove over my face and arms before she frowns. I must look like a total mess and now that I'm standing still, every inch of my body hurts.

"He slapped me around a bit, but I'm mostly all right."

She holds on tight, and I wince. "You did it, you found me. I knew you would!"

My skin tingles from all the bruising, my left eye is swollen and makes my vision slant sideways. My head is throbbing, there are cuts on my arms and legs, the bandage on my hand is unravelling, and I feel like I might pass out any second… But I feel stronger within than ever, and I'm happy to have my mother back.

I also feel lighter.

"I missed you so much," she says.

"I missed you too." And I did, much more than I ever expected to. After seeing her as the pain in the neck reminder of everything that was wrong with me for so long, I didn't realize what losing her meant. I love this woman with all my heart and learning about her struggles when she was my age, and how hard she tried to keep me safe, slashes at my very soul.

She hugs me again and I hold on tight until she squirms under the strain but doesn't pull away. "I'm so sorry he put you through all this." A sob catches in her throat.

"No, *I'm sorry* you've spent all these years trying to hide me from him." I lick my lips and taste blood. "I didn't understand anything until I started reading your grimoire and dared to ask Larunda real questions." I feel like a spoilt brat for ignoring and resenting her every attempt at protection.

She smiles when we pull back. "It looks like you've learned quite a bit. I can't believe you used that spell on Orobas."

"I learned from the best." Besides, there was no other way. As much as I liked having access to her strength, I was done sharing my body with anyone. I meant what I said to Orobas, though. If she needs me, I'll be there.

Maybe one day I'll ask Mum how I can release her. But not today. Her smile widens.

"I can't believe you were that pesky shadow."

"It was the only way to make sure I was completely out of his clutches, and you were free to face your destiny." She makes a face. "I sound like a character in one of those movies you and Dar love to watch."

The sound of his name makes my heart skip a beat because I've finally realized that whether intentional or not, I've manipulated him to my side all of our lives.

"I don't understand how you ended up on photo paper." My eyes stray to the blank sheet on the office floor. Gambit patiently watches the scene without making a single sound. She's the best-behaved companion.

"It was hard and took months of preparation, but by using *your* shadow and the flimsy control you learned to keep him out of your head, I was able to anchor myself to you." She stares into the darkness. "As well as some heavy artillery from Larunda and Purson, of course."

"But I don't understand why you were trapped *in my head*."

"Chester, I just told you. A little prep work while teaching you control, some persuasion from Larunda during your sessions, and you were able to take a snapshot strong enough to shelter me away." She sighs. "That I was able to find Orobas instead of Raum when I got there was pure luck, but she completed the rest of the cycle."

"So, you *were* trapped? Inside me?" I can't help but remember the afternoon I finally listened to her instructions, and she was happy about my progress. I didn't realize back then that I'd captured her essence but do remember she disappeared as soon as I walked away.

"It's a lot more complicated than that, but essentially, yes."

"That's so freaky and disturbing." I shake my head. "I think I'm done with sharing my headspace, though."

"I think your time of possession is over. From now on, you'll call the shots."

"Did you see and hear everything that went down in the darkroom?"

She nods. "I know about everything—inside and outside of your head."

My cheeks warm when I remember that Darwin and I kissed.

"I'm sorry that I hurt you too." Tears blur my vision.

She wipes the tears away from my face and although it hurts, I don't flinch. "Raum lied and manipulated, he influenced my life for many years in the worst way possible. I was blinded by his beauty and knowledge, but none of that matters because he gave me a wonderful gift—you. And I'll *never* regret having you in my life."

"Even with all the trouble I've caused?"

"You kept me busy." She sighs.

I nod and Gambit makes her way over to lick my injured hand.

"Purson really came through with this one." Mum offers her fingers and my familiar smells her skin, inhales her scent.

"Gambit's the best."

"How about we get out of here?" she says. "As nice as Larunda's office is, I really want to go home."

"Yeah, me too." We head for the closed door on unsteady feet, but I don't care because my mother's finally back and my head feels nice and quiet. I peek at the ceiling and the feeling of being watched, as well as the constant scampering of tiny feet is still present. I feel like I'm connected to whatever's up there, somehow.

"You will always be kin," a voice whispers in my ear.

I freeze, wondering if it's in my head.

Mum pats my back. "Don't worry, I heard it too."

We follow Gambit and leave the office.

As soon as we step into the reception area, we're bombarded by Elvi and Darwin. They throw their arms around us and mutter words I can't understand because they're talking at the same time. I'm hurting all over and the contact isn't helping the pain, but I'm too grateful to pull out of the family hug.

There are tears and smiles, and eventually we branch off into twos. Elvi drags Mum across the room where they whisper to each other, hug, cry, and kiss. Repeat. I stay with Darwin, and he stares at me like I'm a broken doll he isn't sure how to approach. Or fix.

"It's not as bad as it looks," I say. "You should see the other guy."

"Don't joke about this." His fingers hover over my eye and jaw but settle on my good hand. It's still bruised and stained with blood, but it's the least tender part of me.

"I'm serious. You should see the other guy! He got sent back to hell." I smile but even this makes my face strain.

"Did Nobody help?"

"Her name is Gambit."

He nods approvingly. "A chess term, I like it."

I nod too, and don't know what else to say. Not now that I've made a personal resolve to let him go and haven't told him yet. It's time for Darwin to pursue his many personal goals and walk down his own path, away from me. I've held him back for too long already.

He runs his other hand through his hair. "I'm glad you're okay."

"Dar, I have to tell you something."

His eyes are bright and all I want to do is wrap myself in their chocolaty goodness, let him comfort me like he always does.

No, I must stop this. Stop sucking away his kindness and strength.

"What is it?"

I look away before settling my gaze back on him. "Now that all of this is over, I think we should stop living in each other's pockets."

He makes a face, seems confused. "What do you mean?"

"I think it's time you spread your wings and I learn how to preen mine."

"Chess, you're not making any sense."

I sigh and pull my hand from his. "I don't want to bring you down anymore, okay?"

"What? Is this because of what Ma said earlier? Because if it is—"

"No and yes. She's right about my dependency on you, but it's more than that. I know you refuse to believe this, but I've been dragging you down since the beginning and I'm done doing that to you."

He leans closer and whispers, "Is this because we kissed?"

"It has nothing to do with that," I lie. But, of course, it does because his reaction made me understand how easy it is to lead him down any path I desire. I can't do this to him. I refuse to.

"Are you sure? Because that was the demon and—"

"What happened was more than just the demon and we both know it," I cut him off. "You're the best and kindest person I've ever known, and you've helped me every step of the way since we were kids. You've been my anchor forever, and I've always appreciated the sacrifice that took. Don't look at me that way, you know it's true."

"You're not a burden."

"I'm a troubled soul and although Raum's influence is gone, this isn't over for me." I sigh, trying to make him understand what I'm trying to say. "The demonic problems will never leave me, and that's why it's best if you stop acting like my keeper."

"That's not what I am."

"School's almost over and you've got ambitions you need to pursue. Forget about me and get on with your life. You have Su, and so much to live for."

He grabs my hand again, squeezes. "I won't turn my back on you."

"I don't want you to," I say. "We'll always be family and I love you. You're my brother. I want you in my life, but what we've been doing is too much. For both of us."

For the first time, I feel as if his mind has finally cleared, and he understands what I'm saying. "I'll always look out for my older sister."

I grin and nod.

"Let's go, kids," Mum calls. "I need to wash away all of this hellish grime."

Elvi takes her hand. "That's going to have to wait. We're going to drop the kids off at home and go to the police station to report you as *found*."

"Damn, that's right." She doesn't look happy about it, though.

"And we really need to take Chester to the emergency room…"

Her brow wrinkles. "We should go to the ER first—"

"No, we need to deal with the police first," Elvi interrupts her.

"Shit, you're right," Mum says. "But what the hell are we going to tell them?"

"We'll think of something."

She nods and together the reunited couple head for the door, where they meet Dr. Larunda and Purson. Mum hugs them both and whispers something to the doctor, who glances my way before heading back towards her office.

I call out, "Wait, Dr. Larunda, do you have a sec?"

She stops.

"I'll take Gambit and meet you outside," Darwin says as he leads the hound after our mothers.

I watch them leave before facing Dr. Larunda and Purson. The tall, pale thin lady and the stout, dark bearded man stand side by side, their gazes pinned on my approach.

"You knew where she was the whole time." It's not a question or an accusation, it's a clear statement. I'm not angry.

"Yes, we did." She doesn't look apologetic, but when did she?

"But you couldn't tell me because I needed to work everything out for myself."

"Exactly."

I glance at Purson. "Guess I should thank you for sending Gambit."

"You're very welcome." He bows his head. "She'll make a wonderful familiar."

"So, even after all this is over, she'll stay with me?"

"She had a task to fulfil and was free to choose her way afterwards." He glances at the door. "The fact she's still here and glamoured to look like a canine, makes her intentions very clear. She's chosen to stay with you."

"But why did you dump her in a rubbish bin when she was so tiny?" It wasn't the first time I thought about the many variables that could have led me to *not* finding her.

"I don't choose the location. I summon and send the familiar to the recipient." He reaches out and pats my shoulder lightly. "I hope you're able to live a much more fulfilling life now." With that, the bearded man walks away.

"He's a good assistant."

"Purson is my partner in every sense of the world. We're equals." Larunda watches as he steps behind the reception desk. "We love to put labels on everything, but sometimes there are none."

I nod because she's right. I've spent my life stressing because I couldn't find a way to describe who I really am. Now, it all makes perfect sense.

"We're both very proud of what you've achieved." Her eyes are wide and bright, and the slight twist of a grin is definitely on her lips. "You often seemed to be non-responsive to my advice, didn't seem to be listening. The ease in which I was able to help you should have confirmed your ability."

"You haven't been messing with my brain like everyone else?"

"I did most of the listening, Foras"—she pointed at her left side—"took care of making you more open to what was to come, and what was to happen to Mena. I'm sorry I couldn't tell you about that. I wanted to, but it would have ruined everything. The only person who could send Raum back was the one he wanted to possess."

"But he's not gone forever."

"No, no demon ever is. He'll be back, but it will take hundreds of years before he can even come close to manifesting on this plane of existence again. You won't have to worry about him again." She clicks her tongue. "Well, unless you make a deal with your devil and expand your lifespan."

"Is that what you've done?"

She shrugs. "I might tell you my story someday, but we need to focus on yours first."

"So, therapy isn't over?" It couldn't be because I still had Orobas to deal with.

"Therapy is essential to help you learn about the bargain you made." She glances at her closed office door. "Binding Orobas was essential but is a bigger deal than you might realize. She's a good demoniac and will be happy to remain in the background until she grows restless. You must work together and not against each other."

"Will she resent me?"

"Not if you don't forget about her."

"What do you mean?"

"You must learn everything you can about her—what she likes, dislikes, the powers at her disposal—and use those to keep her entertained." Dr. Larunda caresses the air beside her. "Having a bound demon can be used to our advantage, but you can't neglect them."

"Foras helps you with your patients."

"She does indeed, and Orobas is a great and mighty entity who can help *you*."

I shake my head. "I don't want to use her to get advantages in life."

"Don't ever think you're above such a thing," she says. "Even your mother took what she could to gain wealth and experience, to ensure her family survived. Never shun what you have. You, of all people, should know that."

I understand exactly what she means and haven't even considered this.

"So Foras is bound to you?"

"The same way Orobas is to you." She nods. "That is why it's essential that we continue to see each other. But this will be more like training than counselling."

"I like the sounds of that." I remember Orobas telling me to visit her, so everything the doctor is saying makes total sense.

"Give me your broken hand for a moment."

I do, and her warm touch instantly soothes away all the pain. I can feel the bones knitting together, see the bruising and swelling fading away from my arms.

"Now your mothers will only have to concoct one story."

"Thank you." I can't believe that every injury is gone—my skin is clear, and my hand is back to normal. "Thank you so much!"

"Well, take care young Chester, and I'll see you next week for our scheduled appointment."

"Sure," I say, stepping away, but pause in mid-step. "Oh, and Dr. Larunda?"

"Yes?"

"You can call me Chess, that's what my friends call me."

She smiles and Foras shines through in all her cerulean goodness.

"Also, what're all the swirls in your office?"

"They're another story I might tell you one day."

"But... are they dangerous?"

"Only if they need to be," she responds. "We'll discuss this and so much more in the months and years to come, but I'll tell you one thing. Not everything that thrives in the dark is out to hurt you. Sometimes, they're looking out for you. It's up to you to work out the difference."

All I can manage is a curt nod because what else can I say to such a bombshell? What if the writhing darkness in the hallway was never trying to *get me*, and weren't even connected to Raum? My own mother had been one of them and she'd been trying to communicate.

"See you on Monday."

I walk out of my therapist's office with a head full of shadows, thoughts and voices that are all my own.

AFTER
Six months later, November 2018

"I hope you have an awesome time with your mum," Su says after she hugs me. She knows the many ups and downs I've suffered with my mother through the years, so she's happy about how everything worked out. She might not know about the demonic family problems and the many issues we suffered along the way, but she understands what she sees on the surface.

"Thanks."

Darwin steps in next, and although we've hugged a thousand times before, this time feels different. There's a distance extending between us that wasn't there before. One I established and he's adapted to better than expected. He no longer wakes up in the middle of the night to find me facing a wall or has to watch over me because I might throw up or break something after an unexpected collapse. I'm not his responsibility anymore and although he won't admit it, he physically looks healthier. The dark circles under his eyes are gone, he sleeps without that sixth sense of interruptions, and doesn't seem to be haunted by never-ending worry.

Letting go of my dependency on him was hard, but necessary.

"You take care out there and don't get too *New Age* on me." He kisses my forehead as he untangles his long arms from my waist. "I'll miss you," he whispers.

"I'll miss you too." I bite my lip to keep from crying. "And you enjoy working the summer away like a Capitalist slave."

"Ouch," he says with a smile as he steps back and throws a casual arm over Su's shoulder.

I watch them for a second and take a mental snapshot of my two best friends, happy together.

"What?" Su asks.

"Nothing, I'm going to miss you guys." I *will* miss them, but the truth is, I'm happy to put some distance between us. Not only because Mum and I are going away for a month and staying in an isolated cabin near a lake in north NSW, but because I need to get to know myself without Dar and Su. "So, don't have *too* much fun without me, okay?"

"We'll miss you too," she says. "And will try not to have too much fun!"

Darwin laughs. "Yeah, we'll try really hard."

After getting through the Raum mess and settling back into our lives, I made a promise to myself. I was determined to keep my spirit clean and safe, as well as actually paying attention in school. Now that our Year Twelve exams are done and our last year of high school is over, I need to concentrate on my future. I tried my hardest in every exam and don't have to worry about the results yet.

Either way, I've decided to take a gap year to clear my mind and take control of my life before deciding what trade I want to concentrate on. The only new skills I'll be learning now will be from Mum.

Darwin and Su both applied to University—Dar is hoping to get into law because he wants to help people. Of course, that's *so* Darwin. While Su wants to pursue a career in engineering, I can't remember which one. I'm sure they'll both get into their courses, and I hope their relationship survives. Even if it doesn't, they'll still find their separate paths to happiness, and I intend to be there to share everything with both.

"Hey, kiddo, are you ready?"

As ready as I'm ever going to be.

Mum's already behind the wheel and leans over the passenger seat to get my attention. Gambit is in the backseat like a good familiar, with her head hanging out of the half-open window. I pat her head, and she licks the back of my hand.

As soon as I turned eighteen in June, I registered her under my name.

"Yeah," I say. "I'm ready."

After more shared smiles and awkward waves, I jump in the car and strap on my seatbelt. I nod at my best friends and at Elvi—no, at Ma, because I want to get used to calling her what she is—who is coming up behind them and has been crying all morning because she's fearful of *any* time away from her wife.

"Have fun, you too," she says.

"We will," Mum calls as she reverses out of the driveway. "Love you!"

"Call or text every day!"

"We will, Ma," I say, even though I don't know if there's service where we're staying. "And we'll be back with plenty of time to get ready for Christmas!"

I take one last look at the people I love and the house I've never left for longer than several hours at a time, and never overnight. I didn't go to sleepovers at Su's place because my mother was afraid about what would happen.

"Hey, are you okay?" Mum asks.

"Yeah, I'm looking forward to learning about demonology." It sounds like a prerecording, but I mean it. It's time to delve into the world my mother tried to escape but is forever tied to. If I'm going to protect myself and use the demon bound to me in the safest and most mutual of ways, this is necessary.

Besides, Orobas and I have already made quite the connection.

"Are you ready to add more info to your grimoire?"

"Yep." I actually started my own shortly after getting home all those months ago and added everything that happened leading to, and on, that fateful May morning. Now I'll be starting on the practical side and my mother's going to teach me everything she knows. Larunda, Purson and Elvi will fill in the rest. And Orobas, of course.

She glances at the middle console, where both of our grimoires are sitting. "I appreciate that you kept mine safe."

"It's the least I could do after reading it," I say with a grin. At least I don't think of it as the Dreaded Notebook anymore.

"Oops, I think she's calling."

"Huh?"

Mum nods at the underside of my wrist, where the burgundy and ginger pony is shining through my skin in all its bright, inky glory. Whenever Orobas wants to chat, her message manifests on my body as a tattoo. I've already noticed another one—a spiky thorn—wrapped around my ankle. Mum says we're bound to share traits and that a few markings aren't a problem, but the tattoos will help us monitor how strong she gets. Our binding works both ways. If I get stronger, so does she, and vice versa.

"Oh, I better take a *nap,* then."

"You do that. We'll be here when you're done." She reaches out for the stereo but pauses for a second. "Chester, I want you to know how proud I am of you."

"But I haven't gotten my HSC results yet."

"You know what I mean."

"I do." I nod and settle back. "Thanks."

She hits the volume button and smiles when the music blasts out of the speakers. "I love this song." It's one of her favorite bands but I can't remember their name.

I check on Gambit and find she's already sprawled and asleep on the backseat. I lean my head against the headrest and close my eyes. Listening to the lyrics about dust, lies and trusting yourself, I plunge my consciousness into my mind until I'm standing in front of the familiar red door. I push it open, step inside and wander into the darkroom.

"Took you long enough," Orobas says with a smile. She's leaning against the counter with the empty trays. "I've been calling you for hours."

"I was busy."

"Ah, yes, the retreat."

"How much do you listen to?"

She laughs. "Don't worry, it's only whatever you choose to share. I'm not prying or anything. Do we still have trust issues, Chess?"

"No, we don't."

"Good, because I want us to become two sides of the same coin."

The thought is both exciting and scary. Exciting because I see how close Dr. Larunda is to her demon, but scary because I'm not ready to share my mind any time soon.

"Don't look so glum."

"I'm not glum," I say as I take in the room. "You can change the surroundings, you know."

"I know." She takes a step, and the darkroom fades away so we're suddenly standing in the middle of a bright meadow with a sunflower patch nearby and a beaming sun in the cerulean sky. "Better?"

"Much better." I get on my tiptoes and stare into the distance. "Is that a long table with a bunch of teapots, cups and saucers?"

"I knew you'd like Wonderland." She smiles. "The rabbit should come along any minute now."

"Is that where this is?"

She nods, proud of herself. "I'll have to tell you the real story I shared with Lewis Carroll one day, but for now... where were we the last time you popped in?"

I shrug because demons seem to be full of interesting stories. "You were telling me about your stint during the Renaissance."

"Ah, yes, such wild times. Let me tell you about this one particular artist I got to know intimately..."

I take a seat on the soft grass while she tells me another of her many flamboyant tales.

Staying in touch with Orobas isn't as hard as I thought it would be. She's interesting and the more we communicate, the thicker our bond becomes and the connection between us feels more like a ribbon than a chain.

Between her and Mum, I'll be an expert in no time.

The parasitic, demonic father who tried to take over my mind, body and soul might be gone but my weirdness will never fade. And for the first time in my life, I'm ready to accept everything about myself.

*A*CKNOWLEDGMENTS:

I love writing and reading stories in every horror subgenre, but I have to admit that demonic possession is one of my favorites. If there's even a hint that some kind of demonic entity is messing with humans, I'm there. And I'm especially interested in exploring the how and why these demonic entities are more likely to target girls and women, rather than boys or men.

I have many feminist theories about this, but that's a story for another day.

Chester, aka Chess, is a character that came to me years ago and demanded her story be told. This is very much her story about overcoming a fate that was assigned to her before she was even born. It's also the story of a mother who is willing to do whatever it takes to keep her child safe, and a daughter who doesn't realize until it's too late. Of course, there's a lot more going on, but family is at the core of this story.

I'd like to thank Tony Anuci for taking a chance on my freaky possession novel with a familial twist, and providing an awesome home.

Chester Bennington passed away while this novel was in the brainstorming stages and he needs a special mention. I named my main character after him. And a big thank you goes to Linkin Park, too. The title of this book is the same as one of their fantastic songs.

And last, but definitely not least, I want to thank my amazing husband for his endless support. No matter what, he always listens to my never-ending ramblings and helps me sort through some of the mental mess.

Of course, THANK YOU, for reading this book.

ABOUT THE AUTHOR:

Yolanda Sfetsos lives in Sydney, Australia with her awesome husband and spends a lot of time daydreaming about dark ideas. Or actually writing them.

When she's not taking notes on her phone or sitting at her desk with her laptop, she loves going for long walks and is sure to be reading something. But if she's not reading, she's definitely buying new books to add to her HUGE TBR pile, or checking out cute Squishmallows. Maybe she's even playing a cozy game or two on her Switch Lite.

www.yolandasfetsos.com